Copyright © 2021 by HJ Tolson

All rights reserved.

No portion of this book may be reproduced in any form without written permission from the publisher or author, except as permitted by U.S. copyright law.

This is a work of fiction, and the views expressed herein are the sole responsibility of the author. Likewise, certain characters, places, and incidents are the product of the author's imagination, and any resemblance to actual persons, living or dead, or actual events or locales, is entirely coincidental.

Cover Art by Mattias (https://baconstrap.carbonmade.com/)

Cover Design by Rebecacovers

hjtolson.com

17.	Crystal Caves	153
18.	The Bright Ones, the Blind Ones	162
19.	Warcraft and Embroidery	171
20.	Ghost Garden	180
21.	Patchwork Army	187
22.	Monster Parade	194
23.	The Tarrasch Rule	203
24.	Blackhole Sun	211
25.	Puppet Show	222
Epilogue		231
Acknowledgements		242
About the author		243
Also by HJ Tolson		244

PROLOGUE

Somewhere in a dank, dark wood two crows sat on a rotting branch and watched as a group of humans crept beneath them. Regret followed the party like a cloud as they pushed through the tangle of vines and bushes. Cursing under their breaths, every one of them wished they were back at the warmth of the inn they had left barely a few hours before.

The leader's name was Tristan and his thoughts were particularly dark. Sweat trickled down his back despite the chill. There was something wrong with the forest and small details which had seemed unimportant at the village now weighed heavily on his mind. Why was the price so high? Why had the town councillor's mug of ale trembled in his hands and why had he seemed so nervous? What had the man said? An easy job, just a typical rogue spell caster causing trouble in an isolated village.

He hadn't mentioned the malady that lay on the land. The last time Tristan had come through Downing it had been a dense grove of wildflowers and oak. Now the trees loomed like ossified giants, their hollowed-out branches twisting against the sky. Mist pooled on the ground, swirling whenever the wind gusted. What still lived had an unhealthy pallor. Lichen grew everywhere. It was more than autumnal rot, he was sure of it.

The oppressive silence was disturbed only by the parties' breath and the crunch of their steps over dry leaf-skeletons. Tristan had half a mind to turn back. The sun was setting behind them and already it felt darker than midnight.

"They should be roosting," the young ranger beside him whispered, pointing under a bush.

Tristan followed the man's shaking finger.

A flock of scrawny chickens huddled under the sparse cover.

"Keep it together, Erik," Tristan said, reaching out to lower Erik's hand. "C'mon, the lot of you."

He stepped forward, pushing aside a moss-laden branch. His hand came away slick with slime. The ground underfoot changed to soft mud and soon his boots squelched with every step. He swore as his foot sank ankle deep into thick sludge. The sooner they were done and back in front of the fire the better.

Up ahead he spotted something shining and he signalled the others to stop. A rabbit lay in a pool of its own blood. Its heart had burst. The sight triggered something in his brain.

"I've seen this before," he said, keeping his voice low. His eyes darted round the grove but they were alone, apart from the crows. "Or something like it. The rabbit, the illness of the forest. Once. In a village far to the north, after a necromancer desecrated it."

Shocked silence greeted this pronouncement. Tristan kissed the bronze sunburst hanging from the chain around his neck and mumbled a prayer to the Bright One.

"Do we go on?" asked Alis. Her face was pale inside the deep hood of her mage's robes.

"We go on. Carefully. Quietly."

Nobody moved.

Tristan looked around at the party, solemn faced men and women, all. "We've faced worse," he said. "The Wildrose lindworm? The mad sorceress of Pendergast? How about that giant salamander that went on the rampage in Berwick?"

"We lost Morris in Prendergast," mumbled Rubin. The young man was shrunk down inside his fighting leathers, gripping the shield buckled to his arm tightly. Erik nodded vehemently, sweat standing out on his brow, while Alis shuffled her feet.

"Aye," said Tristan, bowing his head. "But Paul wasn't with us in Pendergast." The grim-faced paladin dipped his chin in acknowledgement, and Tristan squeezed his shoulder. "We are on our guard. It will be more difficult than we originally thought that's all. Take your potions. I know you are all ready. You know it too. Good. Now let's get this over with, I have a horrible feeling that people are dying while we stand about nattering."

They resumed their tramp through the ailing forest, the two rangers taking up their positions at the rear, bows at the ready. Tristan peered ahead, trying to make shapes out of the fog. By his personal reckoning they should have stumbled across the village of Little Downing some time ago.

"Where are we, Rubin?" Tristan whispered after another ten minutes had passed.

Rubin blinked, trying to find the stars in the gloom. Of course, there weren't any, everything was smothered in mist. Instead the ranger drew out his compass, tapping it for good measure. He shrugged.

"We should be on top of the village. Right now."

The group exchanged glances, then looked around at the ghostly trees. Had the people been transformed into hollow trunks and left to rot in the cursed soil? Tristan shook the thought out of his head.

"Over there," muttered Herold.

A musky breeze picked up the mist, swirling it so shapes began to form. A rotting fence post half sunk in the mud and a bit of fence appeared — it must be the village they sought. The party crept forward, arms at the ready. Just beyond the fence some hovels could be seen, peaking through the darkness, their thatch rotten and wafting a stench that turned Tristan's gut. Crops wilted in their raised beds. Insects crawled on the decaying walls. Fungus spores drifted into the air. It was not natural, but they would put an end to it.

They walked on, hands over their noses.

"There," Rubin whispered.

He didn't need to point. The faint glow emanating from the trees was unmistakable. A low throbbing noise pulsed from the centre of the buildings.

"Are we too late?"

"Shush!" Tristan hissed. "Get ready."

They crept forward, passing into the village.

It stood hollow. Abandoned? At least empty, for now. Tristan focused ahead on the light, thrumming green and unsavoury. He stepped forward, hefting his war axe, shaking his head, his armour creaking into the silence. Sweat thickened on his brow as he forced one foot in front of the other. The others followed, shuffling as quietly as they could, their training kicking in. Now they were close, everyone was focused, ready to act.

Rounding a hovel, Tristan paused, and his mouth fell open.

They had found the necromancer.

They had found the villagers.

A ritual was underway. A stone altar was mounted in the centre of the village square. The necromancer loomed over it, robed in dark velvet, silver dagger flashing crimson in the light. Beneath him lay a pile of corpses. It was too late for most of the villagers, their bodies strung upside down, blood collecting in buckets, dripping from deep gashes in their throats. A few bound peasants lay trussed and docile next to the altar. Tristan couldn't see if they were alive or dead. A single villager lay quietly on the slab.

The necromancer's back was turned to them as he continued his grisly work.

Tristan didn't speak, but gave signals. With hand motions he instructed the party. The rangers and Alis moved to the side, arrows notched and mage's staff gleaming with readiness. The fighters fanned out. All was done silently, and Tristan took pride in his team's efficiency. He breathed in, watching closely, ready to move. The necromancer remained unaware. Good.

The key was speed. The faster they moved the less chance the spell-caster would have to work his unholy magics. Most likely he would try to raise something. Or someone. They wouldn't let that happen. Tristan's knuckles whitened as he gripped his war axe in anticipation.

On the altar the peasant gasped and died.

Thrum.

The throbbing noise vibrated across the square, shaking Tristan's boots.

Something appeared above the altar — an inhuman form shrouded in darkness. Tristan couldn't see its face, if it had a face. A spirit? Some kind of conjuring? Steeling himself, he gestured.

The first arrow flew as Tristan charged forward. It struck the necromancer's arm and the man whirled with a cry. Tristan got a glimpse of an aquiline nose, a dark beard and piercing eyes before a pulse of energy blasted out, blowing them all backwards.

Tristan's body smashed through the rotting timbers of a nearby hovel with the force of a dozen men. He lay on his back wheezing. Dust and debris rained down on him. He gasped, trying to suck in air, but it refused to come. At last he scrambled up, using his war axe to right himself and crawled back through the hole he'd made, tugging on the timbers to pull himself through with a curse. Across the altar he could see Alis, lying crumpled against a building. Unconscious? Richard and Paul were fighting their way up.

Over the altar the floating dark figure moved.

Tristan stumbled as the earth moved in waves beneath his feet. His stomach lurched as the figure turned with insidious slowness. Reality rippled in ink-stained undulations.

The spirit saw him.

It saw them all.

The spirit drew back its cowl and Tristan could not look away. Vaguely human in feature, its eyes were a void — fathomless pits of madness, drawing him in and he was sinking. His limbs grew limp and heavy. His thoughts grew sluggish. Why was he there? The necromancer. People were dying. He needed to help them. He needed to get back to the inn. His brother would be waiting. Vaguely, he was aware of the others struggling. Something was wrong. The necromancer. He strained, urging his body, struggling to free his thoughts. His armour was a cage, crushing him. He could not move.

Thrum.

The world pulsed, the vibration rattling Tristan's bones. He was held in suspended animation. He turned his head to look at the necromancer. The man stood, a single arrow protruded from above his bicep, but he paid it no heed. Tristan watched as the necromancer reached down and grabbed an elderly man, pulling him up by the hair. He yanked back the old man's head and cut his throat with a practised hand. Blood bubbled from the neck wound to dribble over the stone altar.

Thrum.

Tristan watched helplessly. He could move his head, his eyes, but nothing else. Some of the peasants were still conscious. A woman's terrified brown eyes met his and she let out a sob, waiting her turn on the blade edge. Tristan grit his teeth and pushed at his invisible bonds, praying. Across the square he could see Harold with his eyes closed, muttering and Paul straining ineffectually.

A movement caught his eye. Erik was crouched in the shadow of a cottage, eyes wide and staring. Tristan breathed out. The ranger hadn't attacked with the rest of them! The coward might yet save them all. His heart lifted and he met the ranger's eyes. *Do something,* he mouthed. Erik's eyes were full of terror as he looked back at Tristan, helplessly. *Do something, filthy coward!* Erik didn't move.

Thrum.

The vibrations rattled through him.

The necromancer cut another villager's throat and lifted the body to dangle with the rest, his grisly trophies swaying in the breeze. With this last ornament in place the necromancer seemed to reach some sort of apotheosis. A deep smile spread across his face and he drew a glittering white gem from his robe. The necromancer held the crystal high and proud, as if showing it off to the twisting spirit that rotated gently above the altar. Tristan did not look, he did not want to stare into that face again.

Instead he looked at the crystal. It was the size of a child's skull, sparkling in the spell-light and casting spinning, skittering lights of sickly emerald green as the necromancer turned it in his hand. It would have been beautiful in any other place, on any other night. The necromancer set the gem on the plinth at the centre of the altar and stepped away.

Thrum.

The gem shivered. Light pulsed outwards in a shockwave. All around the village square the dead shuddered. Faint glimmering lights appeared, hovering over the deceased villagers. Souls, Tristan realised in horror, souls being stolen from the dead. Wailing, they ripped free and flew into the crystal. The gem's light grew with every soul it absorbed until it was shining like a small sun.

The woman at the base of the altar scrabbled on the ground, searching for something. Tristan watched her pointless attempts to free herself before returning his attention back to the necromancer who turned from his gem with a smile. The woman stilled, feigning unconsciousness and the necromancer's gaze landed instead on the restrained adventurers.

Tristan's breath quickened in fear as the necromancer strode towards Richard. He held Richard's terrified face in one hand. Without changing expression, he plunged his knife into his heart. The body dropped, released from the spell, and Richard's soul hissed as it was sucked into the gem.

The necromancer turned and held out a hand to Paul. He raised it, claw-like, making a twisting motion with his wrist. Paul was pulled forwards as if by invisible strings, his feet dragging, tugged forward as the necromancer reeled him in like a fly. He muttered a spell and the paladin's soul streaked into the gem.

Thrum.

Paul's body flopped forward, released from whatever magic had held him. Tristan closed his eyes, tears leaking from the corners.

Thrum!

Alis' soul joined the others.

Thrum!

The necromancer turned towards Tristan. He prayed to his god, to the Bright One. Surely a boon, after a lifetime of devotion? Was this how it would end? But perhaps his power could not pierce the darkness of this place and he was forsaken. Tristan shut his eyes, praying, forcing himself to take deep, steadying breaths. Opening them again, he saw Erik huddled in the shadows and paralysed with fear.

Move! he mouthed in despair.

It wasn't Erik who moved but the chickens, squawking as they crossed the square. Perhaps the gods had nudged them forwards? A small act in the dark but Erik found his courage as the necromancer looked away. He leapt forward, arrow notched and aimed not for the necromancer but for the enormous, radiant crystal on the plinth. The arrow hit, knocking it askew, hurtling the gem into the face of the spirit.

Reality rippled. Black ribbons oozed outward like a pebble dropped in a pond of darkness and Tristan felt the heaviness falter. He tensed, fighting his invisible bonds, straining his muscles...nearly there. The necromancer spun, lifting his clawed hand and pulling Erik towards him. Tristan pressed forward, one step, two. He broke free, leaping onto the altar and smashing his war axe down onto the glowing gem.

It cracked.

Then shattered.

The light of a thousand stars exploded into the glade. Souls poured out, cascading and frantic like moths in a cage. The necromancer shrieked and leapt on Tristan. The man was surprisingly strong and Tristan fell back as they wrestled, teetering on the brink. He fought frantically, trying to heave the man away, trying to raise his axe for a killing blow but the necromancer pushed the weapon aside, clawing and screaming with inhuman strength.

Somewhere in the gloom Erik shot again, and the necromancer howled. Tristan gave up his axe and pushed a thumb into the necromancer's eye. Roaring in fresh pain the necromancer batted his hand away, then bit at Tristan's throat, tearing his flesh with sharp teeth. Shock shivered Tristan's body. He writhed for a moment and kicked out, feeling the weakness of his limbs. He was going to die choking on his own blood. He was going to die.

The necromancer laughed, spitting blood and flesh, and turned to the shattered remains of his crystal.

Unable to move, Tristan turned his head. His eyes met those of the woman hidden under the altar. Her face was pale, as she watched him die, her eyes feverish. Her hands were busy; she was sawing at her bonds with the fallen iron arrowhead.

"It will be alright," Tristan tried to whisper, but all that came out was sputters of blood.

Thrum.

The vibration started up again. Insistent. Demanding. Rattling the earth. The necromancer stood at the centre of the village, the shattered splinters of the crystal at his feet. The vortex of souls swarmed around him as he pleaded with the spirit. He didn't notice the woman crawling towards him. Tristan watched with the last of his strength. She had the necromancer's dagger in her hand. Good. His body gave a final spasm and he joined the dead.

The woman lunged, rearing up like a cat and cutting through the necromancer's sodden robes. She screamed and slashed, again and again, stabbing till his chest was a mess of scarlet ribbons. He toppled from the altar, his body squelching as it fell, his eyes wide in surprise.

She stood breathing deeply as the necromancer's soul ripped free from his body.

The souls converged, swirling in a tortured vortex, in a widening gyre of light and madness.

Thrum!

The spirit turned slow eyes to the woman. She rose in the air, hovering, held still while the foul wind whipped at curly blood-soaked tresses.

THRUM!

The light imploded, condensing into a pulsating ball of energy no bigger than a fist, powered by a hundred souls. It shuddered, black bright and crackling. Sparks popped and sizzled. Then it exploded outwards. Blinding light tore through the village, flattening houses, felling trees, devastating everything in the vicinity.

Silence.

In the remains of the village there was only quiet.

A lone black rooster flapped its wings and raced away into the trees.

The dead lay still.

All, except for one.

Amidst the pile of desecrated corpses, a body rose.

Chapter One

Awakening

I am dead.

This I know with absolute certainty.

I remember pain and fear, but they seem unimportant, distant and washed away, like an echo of madness. What I feel is anger and it is cold. My emotions feel removed. My last moments had been full of fear and what had it got me? A small voice wants to argue that it helped me survive but I suppress it right away. Cold is better.

Perhaps those memories are just a nightmare. Rolling over, I reach for my blanket, but my hands find only stone. My eyes open to a starry cloudless sky. I am lying on a stone slab.

Someone has killed me.

I am dead. And yet...I am still here.

Focusing on the chill once more, I realise it isn't a coldness of the body, for my body refuses to feel. The body. My body? Whatever this is. It is a coldness of my brain, a thick icy layer of numbness that holds back a bubbling, boiling sea of rage. I can feel it, far away, lapping at the edge of my consciousness.

Sitting up, I look at my hand, seeing exposed bone and sinew. Everything is so thin, the wrists so slender. Everything is delicately joined but as strong as metal. I could crush a skull with these hands, I know it. My fingers flex, eager. Thankfully, I am not bleeding. Perhaps I have no blood, for nothing oozes out as I flex my finger? Curious. When it moves, it doesn't feel like it is my finger. Yet it obeys me.

I look down and see ribs. Bones. Bare bones gleam ivory in the moonlight. I can see the stone of the altar through them. Further down my legs are the same. My body is gaunt but thin and wiry like steel. There is very little flesh involved, only pale, green tinted skin stretched over cartilage. It looks like canvas pulled tight over a frame. I am not quite a skeleton but it is a close thing.

My brain is still intact, I can feel the flesh, the thoughts beating like butterflies against my skull. It is strange but oddly freeing. No more meat to lug around. No more fleshbag. No more pain, no more fear. Although I do feel a little vulnerable. I must find armour! A helmet! Not out of modesty but for protection. And maybe for style.

My skull splits into an ivory toothed grin. I badly desire to look in a mirror. What would I see? I explore the smooth bone of my face with brittle fingertips. There is a dip where my eyes should be and a hole. I push a finger into my eye socket. It is empty. How can I even see? What am I seeing with? Another mystery for the looking glass. I get up, swinging my legs over the stone altar.

Taking a step forward, I am graceful but uncertain, my skeletal limbs testing the ground. Where I tread the soil blackens. Rot spreads outward in a circle—creeping bituminous threads, veining their way through the earth. It does not have much reach. Yet. But it is rather beautiful. I wonder if I can learn to control it?

The deserted ruins of the village of Little Downing loom around me. They are desolate, empty and silent. Two crows watch me from the treetops, but nothing else moves. It is very dark but I can see clearly. Interesting, very interesting.

The cottages and hovels of my neighbours lie around me in rotting pieces. All my eyes find are timbers and bodies strewn about with equal disrespect. Crumpled and broken. Such stillness in death; the remains of my life. The sight grieves me but I have so many questions. What has happened to me? What should I do? Who can I punish for this... abject waste?

Turning on the spot I can find no one in sight. SoI take another step, and then another, stretching over the bodies of my dead friends and relatives. Lying in their heaps, they look like discarded leaves awaiting a fire. The emotions I remember are distant echoes. It would be nice to have my revenge, I suppose.

On whom should I seek my revenge? On whom should I bestow my anger? The world? Perhaps a little ambitious although revenge seems like a suitable pastime for an undead...witch? Is that what I am? I have no idea. I hum a little tune. Hmm. I can still vocalise, that is good. I must find out about undead, I only know a little. Undead necromancers? Evil spell-casters? Am I evil now? I suppose I must be. Was I always evil? Not outwardly, perhaps, maybe. I might have been a tiny bit evil although I kept it well hidden. This would not have happened to a good person, afterall.

Shaking my head to clear the night-moth thoughts I realise I have been staring at Uncle Samuel's exposed brain matter for five minutes. What was I doing? Oh yes. Revenge.

On whom should my revenge fall?

I turn, seeking inspiration.

The necromancer lies sprawled in the dirt. A pity, because he would be a prime candidate. I regard him with distaste. He is tolerably handsome, even in death. If you like that sort of thing. His eyes are wide open, a look of surprise plastered on his face. Stabbed in the back, I note with some satisfaction. Good riddance. Hmm...perhaps I can bring him back from the dead, then kill him again? I don't know if that would be very satisfying though. Can I even bring things back from the dead? I feel like that should be a given but I don't know how.

Either way I kick the necromancer as I walk past, nearly losing my footing on the gore in my enthusiasm. After a moment I go back and grind his head underfoot, just for good measure. It crumples quite satisfactorily. I am so strong!

The back of my neck prickles and I look up.

The wind is moaning through the forest but there is someone there. Who would dare disturb this place? After all I have suffered? I can see them. Fools. My eyes can see further now, and they have not yet seen me—two men creeping along the treeline. They are rangers, toting leather armour and a seemingly endless supply of arrows. I recognise them. I remember watching them slink in the shadows as we fought and died. The cowards survived the slaughter and now they are back. What do they want? I hiss softly.

Turning, I go back to the altar and patiently take a seat, watching as they creep forward, waiting for them to notice me. I am motionless as a corpse, which isn't really surprising. They enter the ruins of Little Downing and begin to talk amongst themselves.

"The councillor said all he needed was the spellcaster's head. So we just find it, collect the reward, and say the job's done."

"We can't just leave them there-"

"Tristan would want us to finish the job. What's the point of suffering for nothing?"

They glare at each other. One of them holds a bow and arrow loosely in his hands but he is not paying attention.

"Do you really want to dig through all that?" says the other. He immediately begins to throw up with a violence that impresses me, further fouling the remains of Mrs Roberts who lies, staring blankly at the sky. Not that she would care. She is long past caring about anything.

I decide to make myself known since the idiots are so self-absorbed.

"Evening," I call, sitting up taller on the altar.

My voice pleases me. A soprano in life now I speak with a rasping contralto; resonant, deep, powerful. Perfect — like dripping honey and venom. How nice. Are they afraid? They should be.

The pair turn in horror, staring at my skeletal form. The one lets out a squeak of terror as I descend from my throne, all icy grace, lightly placing my toes. At least, I hope I tread with icy grace.

"You did not save me," I say, slinking closer. How foolish are they?

"You do not scare me, monster!" one of them cries, despite all evidence to the contrary. His face is damp with sweat and as pale as uncooked dough. And he thinks me unwholesome.

"Who are you to call me a monster?" I hiss, creeping closer. "You made me! You abandoned me! You should have saved us! Whatever I am, is because of you! I saw you quivering in the shadows, you mewling toad. I saw you both. *Run little men, if you wish to live.*"

To my delight one of them flees. The coward trips over his own feet in his desire to be gone, stumbling over tree roots and fallen branches, but the other holds back. Truly, they have worn grooves in the grain of their lives. The brave ranger levels his bow and arrow at me. Anger flares in my brain at the sight of the iron tip.

"Monster!" he cries.

TWANG.

An arrow erupts from my stomach but I feel no pain.

The vitriol rises in me, unbidden, that rising tide of anger unleashed. I do not have time to think, suddenly I am raging forward, my vision swirling red. I let out an animalistic grunt as I sprint across the intervening space, the grass whipping at my heels.

TWANG.

This arrow hits me in the chest, knocking me back. *HSSSSSSSSSSS.* It hurts, why does it hurt? I am dead, so why does it hurt?

I will rip his head off. I will stomp on his skull. No, I will have both their heads and hang them in my cottage. I rush forward, arms outstretched. Nearly there, I can see the sweat beaded in his brow, the shaking of his arms. The colour of his eyes—ice blue and fearful. I reach for his throat, but he fires again.

TWANG.

This time my skull shatters, the iron tip reaching the soft flesh of my brain.

This time, death is merely an inconvenience.

Chapter Two
Hindsight is a Helmet

I awake alone.

Lying still, I gaze up at the stars as they wheel slowly overhead. I imagine I can feel the earth turn beneath my shoulder blades. The stars have shifted slightly. It is a different night and I am in a different part of the forest. This night is fair and a whisper of wind skitters across the wildflowers, caressing my bones.

I am still very much dead. Calm, but yes, dead.

Sitting up I startle a squawking cockerel which races away into the trees, its oily feathers bobbing madly. I glare at it, then my body jolts at the memory of my second death, my mind catching up. The memory is visceral. My abdomen spasms and my hands grope for the arrow that had burst through my belly, through my brain. I search but find nothing. My skull is whole. I am fine, and my skull is whole.

As the noisy cockerel disappears, I am left alone in the quiet glade.

Mist pools in deep hollows under the ancient oaks, reflecting faint silver starlight. It is some time before dawn and there is no sign of my most recent killer. My stomach feels hollow, which is not surprising since I can see through my ribcage from one side to the other. I wiggle my fingers in the empty space, and then retract my hand, staring at it. Is there less flesh than before? I am not sure but I have the horrible suspicion I am more emaciated. Perhaps I cannot die but I can waste away. There are consequences then, even if my death is temporary? I assume I must eat to maintain my new state. I hunger, but for what? For food? For power, for blood? For souls? I need to know what I am. For what do the undead yearn?

Experimentation is required. I must consult my books.

Standing, I find myself in a circle of decay, withered plants and rising fungus. The feeling of hunger intensifies, urging me forward. I walk softly through the forest night, leaving a webbed trail of corruption in my wake. If I move swiftly, the earth barely blackens and is more of a soot-like smudge. If I stand on a spot it becomes noticeable. The pattern, worked over in caliginous black, is marvellous, like a fine glaze on pottery or an onyx snowflake.

I spend twenty minutes meandering through the forest trying to coax the souls from various small night creatures, and then a mushroom. Nothing works so I decide to try eating, just to see what happens.

Wandering over to a cluster of stout speckled mushrooms, pale in the darkness, I bend to pluck one. The mushroom blackens between my fingers, threads of darkness veining through it. It shrivels and dies as I hold it. How vexing. I toss the dust of the mushroom away with more force than strictly necessary.

I try again. This time I am careful, willing myself not to destroy the living flesh. It works! The mushroom is stout and fleshy. I bite down on it and chew. It is a strange experience because I cannot taste—it feels mechanical and slightly weird. I swallow. The masticated mushroom drops straight through my ribcage and onto the ground. I stare at it accusingly.

Not food then.

Stomping on it with my bony heel, I grind the remains into the soil where they blacken and shrivel, turning, like everything else, to dust. I am going to miss eating.

What to do?

I need to find something to consume, the hollow feeling where my gut should be assures me of that. But first things first, I cannot allow myself to die again so easily. I hiss softly at the memory, my skeletal hands going to my head. The bone is whole and smooth, the brain beneath safe. I am not much if an arrow to the face can stop me in my tracks. I must acquire a helmet. Where can I acquire a helmet? Ah, yes.

I walk back to the village, trailing darkness and humming. Perhaps I can blacken the whole world, starting with this forest! What a lovely thought.

I soon reach the outskirts of the village.

Little Downing is not much to look at. The houses were always poor but now it is just a mess. A few of the humble dwellings on the edge remain standing. The rest are kindling, flattened by the blast. The stone altar remains in the town centre, quiet and piled high with the dead. They are waiting for me, unmoving.

Once more I thread my way through them and stand looking at the corpses. Perhaps I can bring some of the villagers back? The quiet, less objectionable ones anyway. I always fancied trying my hand at necromancy, but my previous path forbade it. I turn to the knights who are still lying where they fell, their armour blood splattered and coated in mud and gore. One of them has a rather nice helmet. I pick it up and slide it onto my head.

Instantly I feel better. It is too large, but my precious brain feels happier encased in steel. I strip the man of the rest of his armour and attempt to strap it to myself. None of it fits. It was made to accommodate a large man—a large man with flesh still on him, not the small emaciated skeleton of a short woman. Ug. I take a step forward and rattle around like a bone in a bottle. However it does make me feel safe. Protected. No one will be poking an arrow into my brain anytime soon with this lot on. I take a step forward. I am heavy, waddling even. Oh no.

It's noisy and would be a serious impediment to my speed and dexterity. This I cannot endure. I miss the feeling of the wind on my bones already. In panic stricken hast I unbuckle half the armour, dropping it to the ground. I keep the helmet, the pauldrons, and the cuirass as a happy compromise. No time to fuss, I need information, but at least now I can breathe. Metaphorically speaking. My lungs are somewhere in the corpse pile.

Time to go home.

While the village is mostly destroyed, my own cottage is off in the woods, as befits a witch of my station. Neighbours are overrated. People knew where to find me when they had need of me. My cottage's isolation means it was spared the fate of the rest of the village and for that I am grateful. I am not tired, not in the slightest, but I would like to have my own things around me again.

I suspect I no longer need to sleep. Am I still a witch? I assume not. I feel a moment's pang as I stride through the dark undergrowth, my newly acquired armour clanking gently. Something must be found to pad it.

My cottage is undisturbed, alone at the centre of its shadowy grove.

The moon pokes above the treetops, shining down on the crumbling stone brick, the thatch roof and the somewhat crooked chimney. Opening the little garden gate, I stride up the path, leaving behind me that nebulous trail of black. My garden is well-tended, if a little overgrown. I like it that way. Hives at one end, and all other available space packed up with herbs. Tumbles of flowers line the boundary.

The bees are sleeping and everything is quiet and peaceful. Just as I left it.

I push open the little walnut front door and then I am standing in my kitchen. Home.

Now what?

Normally I would light a fire but I have no need. I am not cold. A faint panic grips me as I realise I can no longer drink tea, but I dismiss it as quickly as it arrives. I am being ridiculous. Maybe souls are as satisfying as a fragrant late-night cup of chamomile complete with a drip of honey. I'm sure they are. They must be or there would be no point to anything.

I look around my kitchen, momentarily at a loss. It is a witch's kitchen, which means cosy, practical and a little cramped. A cauldron and kettle rest on the hearth, bunches of pungent herbs hang from the rafters.

My cat Jenkins stalks in to demand food and affection, probably wondering where I have been. I bend to pet his rumpled head, then freeze, my skeletal fingers hovering just above his head. I straighten. Perhaps it is better if I don't touch Jenkins. I don't want to accidentally wither him like the mushroom. Killing my cat would be a shame, at least not until I know I can raise him again, satisfactorily.

"Go find a mouse," I hiss and the good lad hisses right back at me, annoyed at not having his ears tickled. He does not seem to notice that my body is completely different.

I go to my small bookshelf and rummage amongst my collection, looking for any books that might give me clues or information. Most of them are herbals, and there are a few grimoires. Paging through them I find nothing. There is a small section on the undead but it merely details how to deal with zombie rats and bad spirits. The typical sort of thing a village witch might need to know. There is a short section on draugr and wights but not much. Drat. I must look farther afield.

I set the books aside and look out of the window, pondering where I could find the information. Dawn's pale fingers stroke the horizon, the edge of the night sky flushing primrose. Outside the birds are very busy in the forest, the chorus a pleasant harmony in my... whatever it is I'm listening with. The scent of fresh dew drifts in the open window, along with the smell of burning. I sniff. Nothing should be burning. My hearth is cold.

Leaping up, I scatter my books and rush into the kitchen, grabbing a bucket as I go. I sprint to the well and dip the bucket with feverish haste. Back at the cottage I sluice water over the flames that have just started eating at the corner of my thatch. They smoulder and go out. A plume of smoke drifts gently skyward and I heave a sigh of relief. My cottage is safe, for now. Now. Who would do such a thing?

I turn, slowly, feeling eyes on me. Three men stand at the garden gate.

"Monster! Foul fiend!"

"Scion of evil!"

"Oh," I say, "it's you again."

The ranger who killed me yesterday is back, and he has brought two ruffians with him. One of them is lighting another brand, presumably to toss on my pristine roof.

"I wouldn't do that if I were you," I warn him, "one lick of fire on my thatch and I will rip your throat out with my bare hands."

He stops, his eyes bulging. I bare my teeth in a rictus grin, then remember he cannot enjoy the full impact because my helmet is down. My lovely, lovely protective helmet.

"Who are you, foul creature?" he quavers, his hand trembling madly. "And what do you want with this poor village?"

"What do I want?" I growl. "It is mine. It has always been mine."

There is something familiar about the man. Who is he?

The ranger does not speak, but lifts his bow, and shoots me. His aim is true and the arrow pings harmlessly off the lovely helmet. I take a step towards them, grinning madly. I really want to see if I can snap the ranger's neck. I should have done it last night.

"What are you?" demands the ruffian again. I stalk closer. He is stalling for time, while the ranger strings another bow.

"I do not know." I move closer. The ranger lifts his bow, and aims.

"What is your name?"

"My name-" I hesitate.

The arrow flies, this one hitting the tender exposed bones of my legs. It knocks me back a little but does not do much harm. I see the fear in their eyes and take another step, still pondering. My name had been Maud.

Maud Greenleaf was a suitable name for a healer and a witch who lived in a forest with hives and herbs. Maud Greenleaf is not suitable for whatever it is I am now. I know this instinctually. What is a suitable name? Lilith? Too obvious. Hekate? Taken. "I am a Dark Queen and Stealer of Souls," I say, grandly.

"Maud?" shouts the ruffian. "Maud, is that you? What in the name of all that's holy happened to you?"

I peer closely at the ruffian in the brown trousers and grubby white shirt and recognise him with a flare of anger. Gregory, the blacksmith from the next village over. My ex-lover. The filthy, cheating cad.

"Gregory?" I ask, and I see his eyes widen. "Gregory Smith, why are you trying to burn down my house? Have you not done enough damage already? Was stomping on my heart and twisting it to little pieces not enough?"

"You know this thing?" says the ranger, turning to him accusingly. I sneak a step forward.

Gregory looks at me, taking in the skeletal form, the ill-fitting armour. *Keep talking*, I think. I am nearly close enough.

"Well-" he says, uncertain. "I-"

"I'm not a thing," I say. "I am a *person*. Two nights ago a necromancer came and entranced the whole village, began a summoning, muttering about family. We begged for help, sent word to the Baron. We prayed for aid. And we all died."

"We came," said the ranger.

"You came too late," I say, and then my hands are at his throat.

I was right.

It is easy.

His neck snaps like a piece of dried wood.

Chapter Three
COTTAGEGORE

I look down at the ranger's crumpled body. His head is now attached at a rather uncomfortable angle, his eyes bulging from the pressure. Now if only I had a way to consume his soul. I point my hand at his chest and make the motion I saw the necromancer use. Nothing happens. How aggravating.

I lean closer and bite his neck but the blood doesn't do anything for me. What a pity.

Meanwhile Gregory and the other ruffian are backing away in terror.

"Why did you do that?" the big man stutters. I turn to him with a hiss and he recoils, backing away into the forest.

"Did you miss the part where he shot me?" I growl, taking a step towards him. His friend lets out a mewl of terror. "Did you miss the bit where you set my roof on fire? I have done no harm." I step over the warm body of the man I have just murdered. "I have done no violence. I only desire a quiet life."

At this I lose control and start to laugh, my bones rattling inside the armour, the laughter pouring out of me in waves. It's just too funny. The sound apparently disturbs the two men even further and they stumble backwards, and start to run. Their stumbling terror stokes my good humour as they trip past my gate, flailing to be the first to disappear into the forest.

"Leave me alone!" I scream after their fleeing heels.

I watch as they disappear into the forest, running in the direction of Lowcroft, the next village over. I wait and listen. Will they regroup and come back immediately? Or seek help. I decide they're off for help. Gregory never could leave well enough alone.

I should make a marker, to warn people that this is my territory and mine alone. My eyes brighten at the thought of a craft project. At least, I imagine they do. Oh yes! A mirror.

I close the garden gate and slip inside. Back in the kitchen, I tidy up the tomes from my mad dash to douse the fire, placing them gently back on their shelves. I have one mirror in the cottage, a small hand held one decorated on the back with painted rose buds intertwined with mistletoe. My late mother's. I find it on the dresser in my bedroom and hold it up to my face.

All I can see is my lovely helmet—shiny, undecorated, polished steel. Ug. I remove it and lay it carefully on my bed. Then I hold up the mirror once more.

My face is strange. It is recognisably mine, but half skeleton, the bones showing through in patches. Prodding myself, the skin lies loosely in some places, and as my finger examines the spots, some of the pale green flesh moves. My eye sockets are hollow pits of darkness. Within the darkness burn vivid sparks of blue fire—my new eyes, or what passes for eyes. They gleam as I watch them, sapphire flames in a void of madness, a cold so intense it burns. They are very pretty and I look at them for a long time.

Eventually I tear my eyes away. Dawn is now here in earnest; the first flush has chased away the stars to replace them with a dome of eggshell blue. It will be a sunny day and my first as...whatever it is I am.

I feel no need to rest, but I am nervous to go outside in the sunlight. I would prefer to remain indoors, in the cool dark places but perhaps I am being irrational. Will I burst into flame with the touch of the sun? No, I am not a vampire. If only I knew more about undead.

Poking a cautious arm into a patch of sunlight, I watch anxiously for a few minutes as nothing happens. No curling smoke, no pain, no bursting into flame. Excellent.

That taken care of, I hurry off to gather ingredients for my territorial marker. It should be fairly rudimentary dark magic. I put on my helmet and go back out into the garden, nearly tripping over Jenkins on my way down the stairs. The foolish cat does not seem to notice that I no longer have flesh on my legs and merely squeaks for attention. He will have to wait for his ear scratches.

Blight still flows from me and I walk quickly as I do not want to ruin my dahlias. Out in the garden I gather up the rangers bow and quiver, and stow them in the kitchen. Weapons will come in handy, I'm sure, and I only have my little hunting bow. I make a mental note to sort through the bodies in the town square. I seem to remember one of the knights had a war axe. I would like a war axe, that would be delightful.

In the meantime, I make do with my own ancient wood axe, its handle worn. We are old friends. I have spent many hours chopping firewood with this axe, and I remove the ranger's head from his body without too much trouble. The strength in my skeletal limbs is breath-taking. The grisly token is rather drippy, however, and I am loath to take it into the clean house. I stand in the garden holding the head as it leaks gore into the marigolds and then realise I am being ridiculous. I have already blackened the floor of the cottage with my passage, and it is nothing soap and water won't be able to clean up. A crimson patina on the kitchen table would not be unattractive either.

However, I make a mental note to myself to construct an outdoor crafting table, for the more viscerally inclined projects.

Gathering a few other items, I lay them out on the kitchen table in the buttery morning light. It's a pity I haven't collected any bones yet, but fleshy parts will have to do. I have a feeling there should be plenty of bones lying about before much longer.

I hum as I work.

So. A marker to show this is my territory. Should be easy enough! I arrange the ranger's head as a centrepiece, braiding daisy blossoms into his hair, along with some yew leaves and bits of straggling myrtle. I managed to do this without withering them, to my satisfaction. I am learning to control it.

After a few minutes I stand back thoughtfully, then arrange the bloody strands into a crown. Twigs flay outwards in a fan and I weave them together with some nice green wool that Mistress Robin gave me at the midwinter's festival before last. I should see if her cottage is still standing. It would be a shame to let all that lovely yarn go to waste. Lastly, I scratch BEWARE THE UNDEAD WITCH into a big chunk of firewood, in my best cursive.

All in all, it makes a decent marker, I think, although I'm sure I could do better with more materials. I take it outside, hissing at the golden sunlight which does me no harm whatsoever, and prop it onto the fence post at the end of the garden gate.

Delightful. I am going to need a bigger crafting table.

The sun shines down on my marker, and a crow spirals down out of a nearby tree to admire my grisly project. I leave him to his lunch. The missing bits will only lend an air of organic artistry to the piece.

Back in the cool darkness of my cottage I contemplate my next move. The sun is rising, and normally, after a busy night I would be heading for my pillows. However, I am not the slightest bit tired, nor am I hungry. I am in fact bursting with energy, and this is handy because I suspect Gregory and his unnamed companion will be back at some point. If not them, then the cowardly ranger will no doubt be spreading tales of my existence.

Soon I will have need of more trophies, but I must be smart about it. Part of me wants to lurk in the darkness of the cellar, reading through my books of magic in the hope of discovering more, but this is not a sensible use of my time. I doubt my books hold anything of value and I have already been in the sun, it does not harm me.

I realise my beautiful sapphire eyes have been straining a little in the bright light, so I tie an emerald green ribbon around my eye sockets. Much better. The glare is reduced and now I can work without discomfort.

Starting back to the village, I make sure to take my newly acquired bow and arrow with me. I really need to find better clothing; the armour is uncomfortable and the bow and arrow rattle against it in their sheath. Perhaps if I had a cloak?

Once back at the remains of the village I pick through the corpses for useful items. Another job to add to my growing list—I should probably bury them all before they turn too rank. The smell is already intolerable and my ex-friends and family are already attracting wildlife. Ah, well. I turn away, my shoulder blades itching. I dislike the mess, but it will have to wait.

I fix the fallen knight's war axe to my waist. With helmet, bow and arrows, and the giant axe I feel well prepared. Have I forgotten anything? Oh yes. Picking my way to the altar I collect the shattered remains of the gem the necromancer had been using when he made me. There are quite a few, at least seven or eight finger sized pieces, and quite a few smaller. I stare at them, gleaming in the palm of my hand.

The sunlight refracts into crystals, the light playing across the ivory of my bones. I'm not sure what I can use them for but they have power, and significance, I'm sure of it. They positively vibrate with energy in my hand. My fingers close over them and I curse my lack of pockets. I find a bag and throw them in, looping that around my hip bones also. I will put them somewhere safe when I return to my kitchen.

Next, I look at the surrounding houses for kitchenware and rope. I rig up strings of cutlery and pots, fixing them low across the trails and pathways that lead to my cottage. I don't quite dare encircle the whole village, not yet. I have a feeling people will return before sunset, and strong as I am it still takes time to dig pits. I loop my early warning system into the woods as far I think wise, then return with a spade.

I spend the next several hours digging with fervour. I do not tire and I do not need to stop and eat. Fairly quickly some rather nice holes are assembled. A couple of hours past midday I am satisfied and start lining them with branches and leaves. It is an easy thing to make them blend in with the forest floor. The place is a mess of leaves and debris at the best of times. The pits are not that deep, and some stakes would be fun, but I can always modify them later. When I am at leisure. They are probably deep enough to break a man's legs, if he is stupid enough to fall in. At least I hope so.

Just as I am dragging the last pile of branches into place, I hear a discordant clank in the forest. I straighten. Excellent, my homemade traps are bearing fruit. I grabbed the war axe and stride off, my fingers tingling with excitement.

It is easy to find the interlopers. They are making so much noise it is the work of moments to locate them. A group of squabbling men cluster around one of my brand new pits. There are five of them in total. Two of them seem to have fallen in.

I creep closer, trying to see what has occurred while remaining unobserved. I am light on my feet and they are really not paying attention to their surroundings so it is the matter of minutes to get nearby. Climbing a nearby oak I position myself in a high fork with my bow and arrow. It takes some care to move without clanking, but with my strength it is not difficult and I am soon perched comfortably with a good view.

I spy the oafish Gregory and the cowardly ranger. One of the new ones is moaning, his leg bent under him, half obscured by the branches and leaves. Another stands angrily in the hole while the others try to haul him out, shushing each other and arguing. I listen with some interest as they discuss their plan of action.

After a while it grows dull so I shoot the closest in the back of the head. The arrow goes straight through his neck, exiting the other side of his body in a crimson spray. Easier than shooting deer, really. He tips forward into the pit and falls with a dull smack, his body twisted and limp. The others scream and rush for cover, which I find quite amusing.

I get off another shot at the ranger while they are panicking. That is probably all the good I will get out of the tree so I drop to the ground. I land lightly on all fours, and stalk forward.

"The creature!" one of them shouts, and the three remaining men wheel towards me, eyes wide.

"Now then... er Lady Maud," says Gregory, putting his hands up placatingly. He backs away as I advance. With sinuous grace I rise up onto my legs, smacking the haft of the war axe rhythmically into my free palm. It seems he has learnt from our last encounter. I too am capable of learning from my experiences. This time I don't intend to leave anyone alive.

"The sun doesn't harm it," says one of the men. He wipes a hand across his brow, foolishly removing his helmet. The ranger shoots, and I dodge, the arrow sailing past to land in the soil behind me. The knight rushes forward with a cry and plunges his javelin into my ribcage. It lodges there, trapped between clattering ribs but does no damage.

He tries to pull it out but I grab the shaft with both hands, yanking it with undead strength. The man is pulled forward, landing face first in the leaves with a startled cry. I stomp on his head and it bursts like a ripe pumpkin.

The cowardly ranger shoots another arrow, a whimpering, pathetic thing that falls in an arc and pings off one of my shin bones. I look up at him and grin. He starts to run, and I throw the javelin, pinning him to the forest floor through the stomach. I rip it out slowly, and the body slumps.

Stepping over the bits of splattered brains I smile at Gregory. Too late he realises he should have been running. I smash him bodily into a nearby tree, cracking his spine and leaving a thick smear of blood down the trunk.

Perhaps I will send his widow a card.

Chapter Four
Gentle Crypt-Keeping

The next hour or so I spend creating another pleasant marker. This one is more ambitious, and I use three heads and the remains of the fourth to create a gory maypole hung about with guts and intestines, intertwined with some rather nice satin ribbons I had been saving for a rainy day. I really need some paint but that will have to wait. I add it to my mental list and position the marker in the middle of the forest path that leads to my cottage. It really does seem fair to warn people, but if they persist in bothering me, well then, they deserve to die.

The magpies are most appreciative of my efforts and get to work on their supper straight away. Looting the remaining body parts, I add to my growing pile of discarded weaponry and armour and then tip the remains of the bodies into the closest pit. Just to keep things tidy.

A scream from within the hole reminds me that one of the men is still alive. The original victim! What should I do with him? Killing him is the obvious solution but maybe he can give me some information first. Really, I have enough pets as it is, what with Jenkins and the chickens and the geese. I should make sure the chickens have enough feed, I have been neglecting them in the excitement of the slaughter. Another item for my list.

Pushing aside a branch, I jump into the pit, landing lightly on skeletal feet.

"Congratulations," I say. "You were my pit's first customer!"

The man's scream is truly ear shattering, and he scuttles back on his rear, dragging his broken leg after him. He looks like he must be in a lot of pain, poor thing. I hold out my bony palms, hoping to placate him.

"It's all right," I say, soothingly. I try to keep my voice bright and happy. It's harder to appear harmless when you don't have flesh. Or breasts. "Shhhh!" I say, walking forward, bending to avoid hitting my head on the branches. He looks up at me, whimpering, his eyes almost bulging out of his eye sockets. Should I put him out of his misery? I regard him critically.

"Where are you from?" I ask. "Lowcroft?"

He screams again. Oh, honestly. This is going nowhere.

I kill him as humanely as possible and leave his body cooling with what is left of his friends. I climb out of the pit, making sure to cover it up again after me. The next people who fall in will enjoy it even more, when they find the decomposing bodies. The thought puts a smile on my face.

I will have to go elsewhere for information. It really is quite vexing. I consider my situation as I saunter back towards the village. How much peace will today's adventure have brought me? How long till the men are missed and another group set out to avenge them? Will they just keep coming? How many will I have to slaughter before they leave me alone?

If this is going to continue to escalate then I am going to need a proper plan. Minions, people to do my bidding. Hmm, I don't really like the idea of people. Not having people around is the absolute best thing about being dead. But servants of some sort might be a good idea. Ones that don't talk and do as they are told. Or at least ones that only talk when spoken too. Walls might be a good idea too.

Perhaps I shouldn't have killed all the men, but rather kept some of them to work for me? Taming them would have been a lot of trouble, though, and time consuming. Probably it wouldn't have been much fun. How would I even go about doing that? Oooh, I wonder if I can build a trebuchet! But I am getting ahead of myself. Next job is to tidy up the village square and loot anything useful from my friends and neighbours.

I pop home to feed the chickens and then set off once more.

I always enjoyed walking abroad in the forest, even when I was alive, and now I positively relish the experience. As I arrive back in the ruined village the shadows are beginning to lengthen. Damp is rising under the trees. With it comes that creeping, coiling mist that works its way through the bones and drives the living home to their fires. I no longer have such needs.

Looking around at the bodies of the villagers, most of them still lying where they had fallen, or been pushed by the blast. The crows have been busy here as well. The fleshy, decomposing remains of my life.

I hesitate, not sure how to go about tidying up. In the end I keep it simple. I create two piles—toss and keep. As an afterthought I make a third pile which I mentally label 'crafting supplies'.

Moving quickly, I start to organise the corpses. The strength in my skeletal arms makes it easy, and work proceeds at a satisfying pace. The dead necromancer I put on the 'keep' pile. I have lots of questions for him like 'What in the world is happening to me?' 'What am I?' and 'How do I learn to raise the dead?' Oh and 'Why did he choose this village?' This last is idle curiosity. Once the necromancer has told me everything I wish to know I will kill him again.

After some consideration I move the knight-leader likewise, telling myself he might know something useful. Nothing to do with the broad set of his shoulders, or the cut of his jaw, or the way he looked at me, even as he was moments from death. No, for practical reasons only. I am done with men apart from as carrion fodder.

The rest of the knights I move to the toss pile, once I have denuded them of their armour. The body of the female mage yields a few sparkling gems and a staff that I can feel is imbibed with power. I pocket the gems and set the staff and her cloak and hood to one side. Once I have given it a wash the cloak should fit me nicely. I dislike the red colour but I can dye it a more suitable black. She must have been a fire mage but I know little about them. Fire mages always struck me as a bunch of destructive children tossing fireballs around willy-nilly. My magic had been healing, midwifery and herbs. Lots of herbs.

After some consideration I move my mother onto the 'keep' pile. Then I move her to the toss pile, and then back again. Hmm. Tricky. In the end I set her aside, thinking I can bury her and then dig her up if I need something. All three of my aunts go onto the toss pile, no arguments there, as well as the grandmother who always commented on the length of my hair and the state of my relationships. Uncle Samuel I was quite fond of, but objectively I don't think he would be a useful person to keep around, even as a reanimated corpse, so I chop his head off. I will keep that and discard the rest of him.

The rest of the villagers are easier. I never had many friends, at least, not ones I want to see again anyway. A culling was long overdue. Violet Bennett had a terrible habit of chewing with her mouth open, but she was an excellent seamstress; Philip Ashdown, herbalist and beekeeper—both of them can go on the 'keep' pile. Richard Webb, hunter and fletcher —the man was allergic to water, and my eyes started to tear from the pungency of his armpits, even before he was bloated with the foul stench of death...I waver...keep. A man who makes weapons will be useful and I can stuff his innards with sweet lavender if need be. My sense of smell is just as strong in death as it was in life, perhaps stronger. A mixed blessing, but I find the stink of death less repulsive than I did when I was alive.

By the time I am finished the toss pile is substantially larger than the keep pile but such is life. I sit back on my heels with some satisfaction at a job well done. I have never enjoyed cleaning up but now the town square looks much tidier and I can turn my attention to other matters.

The local graveyard will have to be significantly expanded to accommodate everyone. Of course, I could just make a pit and toss everyone in together but that seems a trifle disrespectful, not to mention how difficult it would be to locate a specific person if I need them. No, I will have to make individual graves with markers. Of course, I am working on the assumption that I will be able to raise the dead. That is really what I need to focus on.

As I stand staring at my handiwork I become aware of a presence in the shadows. I turn with a hiss. Who dares to sneak up on me in my own territory? My fingers tighten on the war-axe. A figure stands illuminated in the pale gleam of the rising moon. It looks like one of the corpses has ambled out of the pile to stand there, desiccated and chewed by the carrion fowl. Actually no, if I look closely this corpse looks like it has been dead for a great deal longer than my neatly stacked villagers.

It is a husk of a being, hung about with clearly rotting pieces of meat. A spirit? A wight? Perhaps a draugr? What is it doing here? Has it wandered free from a lonely barrow? I have heard of such things but never seen one in the flesh.

It takes a timid step forward, its eyes shining with wary sapience, the only part of it that seems truly alive. It is wearing a dusty flat cap and not much else. The remains of a crumbling waistcoat and trousers hang from a frame that is held together with sinew, ropey muscle and some kind of dark magic. What flesh is involved has an unwholesome, greenish cast.

"Master?" the creature says. It shambles closer, peering at me, stumping along. One leg seems to be longer than the other, making its progress ungainly. "Master, is that you?"

"No," I say. A draugr then, since it seems able to talk. A confused one.

"Mistress," it says, to my surprise. It bows, tipping his cap as if it were of the gentry. It is not afraid of me, which is interesting.

"Yes?" I ask, intrigued. "Who are you, then?"

"Roland, Mistress," he says, sniffing. "My name is Roland Halifax, at your service."

This polite response takes me back a little, but then I have never met a draugr, only read of them a little.

"Who are you?" I ask again, stupidly. "Why are you here?"

"I followed my bones, Mistress. Seems you're to be my new Master, Mistress, since my Master is not here."

I puzzle myself through this sentence. Enlightenment dawns, and with it excitement. Perhaps I will have some answers at last.

"You served the necromancer?"

"I served Master Atticus, yes. I do not know what happened to him, but he seems to have gone."

I step around him, examining the draugr's body. He is piecemeal. One hand is small and delicate, yet attached to a thick hairy upper arm with unnaturally stuffed biceps. The other hand could have belonged to a timberman, blistering and calloused, connected to an exposed bone that looked as if it had been formerly a dog's chew thing, all kept in place by intricately woven tendons.

"I have to maintain my body," he says, apologetically, correctly interpreting the look on my face. "I died many years ago, now."

"I see," I say, although in truth I understand very little. His eyes wander to the keep pile and he stiffens.

"Master!" he cries, falling to his knees in front of the necromancer's feet, which are neatly stacked next to his torso. "Master Atticus what happened?"

Roland looks up at me with pleading eyes and starts to sob, great heaving teardrops falling over desiccated cheeks. It makes me feel uncomfortable. I do not want to feel sympathy for the vile man who killed everyone I knew.

"Did something go wrong?" he sobs, clutching at the necromancer's remains.

"That depends on your perspective," I say.

"I told him it was dangerous," he wails. "I told him to be careful." He gestures to the bloating corpse of the necromancer. "This wasn't how it was supposed to be. We planned together for years... I waited. I waited like he told me to but when he didn't come home I thought something must have gone wrong..." he peters off, looking at me guiltily.

"I can see how that could be disappointing," I say. But impatience is getting me nowhere so I try another tack. I pick up a bit of leg and fasten it to the dead man's thigh with a strip of cloth.

"What are you doing?" asks the draugr.

"Maybe I can reassemble him," I say, absently. "And then bring him back from the dead? Would that please you? Can you pass me that wool?"

"Wool?" echoes the Roland creature. He doesn't seem very bright but then I can see some of his brain exposed through a hole in the shabbyhat. I imagine that must be bad for wear and tear.

"Or something to stitch with? And a needle. I can reattach his bits in no time. There in that bag. Bring it to me." He does as I ask. "Do you have saliva?" I say. He nods. "Lick this thread for me. Thank you."

I get to work, my needle flashing in the moonlight. I sew in silence.

It takes some time but at last the necromancer is more or less in one piece. I consider his remains. The body looks fine, improved even, but his face is a mess. In hindsight I shouldn't have smashed it in quite so thoroughly. He will not be able to tell me his secrets looking like that.

I sigh and look through the thread basket, picking out the most garish colours. I will save the good thread for people I actually like. It is a difficult puzzle but at last I am finished. The necromancer's face is recognizable, although not quite as handsome as before. I have patched him up with bits and pieces from the toss pile. He should at least be able to speak. And listen, listening is important.

"Alright," I say to Roland, sitting back on my heels. "There, is that better? Now, how do I bring him back?" I ask casually, as if it is neither here nor there.

"I am sorry, mistress, I do not know how."

I try not to let my disappointment show. This creature might still be useful. Tossing him down the well will accomplish nothing, apart from momentary satisfaction. To pan over the awkward moment, I show him the necromancer's corpse, now with fingers. I have sewn them into place as best I can, using a neat backstitch in lurid green around the base of his digits.

Roland tilts his head.

"I'm not sure if those are his fingers," he said.

"Never mind," I say, slightly annoyed. "I can swap them out later." I bare my teeth at the draugr in what I hope is a friendly expression. "Now if only we could figure out how to raise him. Hmm."

My patience bears fruit. Roland looks down at his late master, and then up at me, with hope in his eyes.

"Master Atticus prepared a place," he says. "A safe place, with all the spells and equipment he would need..."

My eyes flare in excitement but I stay still.

"Oh really?"

"A tower in a ruin to the north. Deep in the forest where no one ever goes. He left instructions for me," said Roland. "And also his grimoire. I think the spell to animate the dead would be there. I am forbidden to touch it, but you...you can read it."

"Well then," I say, springing to my feet. "Show me the way, and we will see what can be done."

The draugr nods, and we set off together through the darkening forest, heading north.

Chapter Five

Tales from the Wild Wood

I follow the undead little man in his faded hat through the forest. It is full night now, and clouds creep over the moon plunging us into deep shadow. We are walking north, and I wrack my brains trying to think of where we might be headed. To the north of Downing Forest is only a great tract of wooded wilderness and some lonely hills and a few bare outcrops. There are no settlements for miles, only the odd wood cutters cabin or abandoned bandit's camp.

"The master had a place," said Roland, his mouth drooping downwards at the corners. "A secure place, at the ruined keep. He planned for this for many long years."

"Well at least his preparation won't go to waste."

The draugr hesitates.

"Yes, ma'am."

We set off through the trees, winding our way through drifts of ferns and night flowering lilies. I can think of only one place the ruin could be located: Dunbarra. An ill-fated fiefdom, long abandoned. No one sensible has gone near Dunbarra Keep in a hundred years.

Now that I think on it, it is the perfect place for a necromancer to hide out unobserved. If this is indeed our location then it explains why Little Downing was chosen as the location for the necromancer's slaughter. Despite being miles away we are likely the closest village.

Dunbarra is rumoured to be haunted by a multitude of restless spirits. The land around is supposed to be cursed. Perhaps it *is* cursed. Perhaps the reach is greater than anyone realised. I have heard it told that the castle was built over a yawning pit, a highway to the realm of the Whisperman himself. Everyone who had ever lived there came to a terrible end. Rivers that pass through it run foul, poisoning those who drink from them. Crops in nearby fields grow sickly and stunted, animals who graze nearby grow disfigured. Children raised near its walls are born weak and prone to illness. Plague swept through the surrounding villages decimating them more than once. Eventually, everyone just moved away.

The last time the castle had been occupied must have been well over a century ago. Since Dunbarra was last abandoned it had been left to nature, slowly falling to ruin, the fields lying fallow. At least that is what everyone had assumed.

And this, I suspect, is the place Roland is leading me to.

My step quickens in anticipation.

The moon rises, casting pale shadows across the land. Somewhere to the west a wolf howls, mournfully, the sound mingling with the swish of the wind through dusky boughs. As we travel further north, the scent of the forest changes from loam and flowers to resin and dust.

Fey lights twinkle in pockets of deep darkness, wisps whisper and call to me as we pass. I do not fear them. How many times had I walked these forests after dark, my heart thumping as I hurried home? And now I stride with ultimate confidence, knowing there is nothing out there more terrible than me. My eyes pierce the gloom and I bare my teeth at the slinking shadow of a wolf. It growls softly and then runs away on its belly. Sensible.

Roland leads me onward, stumping his way over heath and moss. I eye the draugr as we go. His flesh does not look too firmly attached. I hope he does not disintegrate before we reach our destination. That would be most inconvenient. I glance anxiously at my own sparse flesh. Everything is where it should be which brings me comfort. It is unlikely then, that I am a draugr. I am of a superior make. I do not think I need maintenance, but then I am barely a few days old to my second life. Perhaps I am too arrogant. I glanced sideways at my companion. Just how old is he?

"So how did you die?" I ask as we walk together through the increasingly wild wood. "How did you come to work for a necromancer?"

Perhaps if I can get the strange creature talking I will learn something worth knowing. He seems eager enough. Hesitantly at first, but then with more conviction Roland tells me the story of his life, which is, as I suspected, closely intertwined with the necromancer that he calls Master Atticus. His voice wavers and cracks, as dusty as a tomb door but at last I get some answers.

"I was born a long time ago, in a village far to the north," he says. "The second son to a fairly wealthy spice merchant. At the age of nineteen I became the manservant to the Baron of Dunbarra."

Aha! My suspicions are confirmed.

"This must have been very long ago," I comment.

"Yes," says Roland. "Many years. My role was simple and I was happy. I cared for the Baron, dressing him, tending to his clothes and assisting in the running of the household and estates. In turn, my master cared for me."

Roland smiles happily and trips over a stump. Part of his leg comes loose. Fortunately, I had foreseen this eventuality and brought along my sewing kit. I offer to stitch him back together and he accepts. He continues his tale seated on a log as I sew.

"I earned five pounds, six shillings and sixpence a year for my labours," he says, proudly.

"A princely sum," I agree, biting off a thread, and starting a new needle.

"All was wonderful," Roland says, then his face drops. "Until a great tragedy befell." He pauses, his eyes staring into the distance, as if recalling scenes from the distant past.

"What happened?" I prod, stabbing him with the needle more viciously than strictly necessary. He doesn't seem to notice, his mind on his tale.

"A plague," he says, "a plague was the start of it. It took both Baron's children and many more besides. The Master suffered greatly at their deaths but his lady suffered even more. We did not realise how she suffered. Perhaps, if we had realised things would have turned out differently."

"Oh?"

"Once a year the Baron hosted a great entertainment at midwinter. Every year he would throw open the castle gates and invite in every nobleman, merchant and peasant, and every man, woman and child. No expense was spared. The courtyard was filled with jugglers and tumblers, and the scent of roasting chestnuts and the sound of music filled the air. There was food for all! And laughter and warmth. For one day and one night both rich and poor came together to celebrate the turning of the year. For that night, and that night only, the darkness was driven back and all was merry.

"It was a happy time. Or at least, it should have been. The Baron and his lady put on brave faces, despite their loss, determined that the festival should go ahead as planned. None of us knew what would happen. None of us knew. The Lady greeted the festival goers with a bright, brittle smile. If she was quieter than usual, well, it was to be expected.

"She invited everyone in, bade them eat and drink. She held babes in her arms and talked to their mothers. If she held them a little too tight or too long, no one remarked. After all she was the Lady of the castle, and she came with sweets in her pockets. I knew the Master was concerned but still..."

"What happened?" I ask impatiently.

"The loss of her children had driven the Lady mad. She wanted all to suffer as she had suffered. She wanted everyone to share her mortal heartbreak. Unbeknown to all of us the actors and jugglers she had hired were not entertainers but brutal mercenaries. When the midnight hour drew near she withdrew to the parapet and watched, smiling as the entertainers drew their hidden swords and slaughtered every child present. The stones ran red and she laughed and laughed, her bitterness mingling with the screams. The Baron was powerless to prevent their deaths, although he did try.

"An angry mob descended on the castle and razed the Keep to the ground. They butchered the staff and threw the Lady from its highest tower. The fall did not kill her, and they watched as she writhed in pain. The Baron chased them off and tenderly held his dying wife in his arms until she, too, left him for the realm of the dead."

Roland falls silent.

"So many children," Roland says, his eyes glimmering with moisture. "My Mistress. So much death. Such a terrible night."

"There," I say, tying a knot, and patting his leg. "All done. And yes, it is a terrible tale to be sure."

We continue north, Roland walking much easier with his reattached leg. I suspect I will have to get him a new one from the spares pile before too much longer however. The flesh did not feel like it had much wear left in it. I will see if it is worth the effort. We walk on, with only the clump and shuffle of his mismatched legs marking our passage.

I ponder Roland's story as we go. I noticed that he had left out several details. How had Roland himself survived if all the servants were killed? And how did the Baron chase off an angry mob hellbent on revenge? I wonder what had happened to the children. Had the people taken the bodies back to their parish churches or left them where they fell in the burning ruin? Perhaps when I can raise the dead I should raise an army of undead children. That would teach people to keep out of my forest.

After a while Roland picks up the tale.

"Embittered and devastated, the Master fell into a deep melancholy," he says. "I feared he would waste away, for he would neither eat nor drink. Most of the castle had been burned and what rooms had been saved he shut up. He refused to leave his study." A single tear falls out of a decaying eye socket.

"I did my best," Roland continues, "and for many years the two of us lived alone in that great stone ruin, living a half-life, huddled around a solitary fire with the wolves howling outside. Master Atticus never left the room. I did my best to keep him fed and warm, but in truth I suspected that he just wanted to follow his wife and children into the darkness of oblivion. He was just waiting; a bitter husk."

We wind our way through a grove of tall pines, the needles crunching underfoot.

"I assume something happened to change that?"

"Yes," said Roland, his lips twisting. "Late one stormy night, as I was stoking the embers of the dying fire, I heard a terrible hammering at the castle door. We never had guests. Ever. Everyone with sense knew to avoid the place. Alarmed at the lateness of the hour I grabbed my sword and went to answer it. It was a foul night. A great gale was whistling around the chimney tops. I knew nothing holy could be abroad and I had serious reservations about opening that door. I was right. I should not have opened it."

"Who was it?" I asked, intrigued despite myself.

"A woman!" Roland cried bitterly. "A woman! Beautiful but sickly, on the point of collapse, or so she said. With rain plastering her long, raven tresses to her head she begged for sanctuary. What was I to do? Of course, I granted her entry. I thought perhaps, it might give the Baron an interest. A fair maiden in distress—just the thing to jolt him out of his stupor." His lip twisted. "If I could go back to that moment I would push her back into the storm without a second thought, and tell him it was just the sound of a falling branch on the door."

"Oh?" I say. "Who was she?"

"A black-hearted vixen," Roland declares. "A scheming hellion from the darkest pits of the nether dimension; a corrupting influence worthy of-"

"Yes, yes," I say. "I know the type. What happened next?"

"Her name was Morgaine and she was there to rob the house, although I knew it not at the time. Her accomplices waited outside. Once she realised the situation, she quickly changed tack, and bent all her energy to ensnare the Baron with her feminine wiles."

"I gather she succeeded?"

"She did."

Roland's expression was a treat.

"For a while I was pleased," he continues. "My master was imbibed with new life! He left his seat by the fireside, he ate and drank and changed into new clothes for the first time in years. He invited her and her friends to stay, and I turned a blind eye to the disappearance of the silver and barrels of wine in the cellar. As long as the master was happy, so was I. At least he was living."

"I sense this relationship is not going to have a happy ending?" I mutter. We walked up a slope, pausing at the top to admire the view of the forest before continuing down the far side.

"Indeed no," says Roland, pursing the remains of his lips together. "It ended when my Master discovered her, scantily clad and in the arms of the newly hired cook. He murdered them both with a meat cleaver."

"Ah."

"I was concerned that my Master would return to his former malaise but his newfound energy remained with him. It was at this point he became consumed with the idea of raising his family from the dead."

"I see."

"He spent all his time and his not inconsiderable wealth on the task."

"He was unsuccessful?"

Roland looked uncomfortable.

"I was an early experiment," he says. "My Master was able to raise spirits and draugr but nothing more substantial, and never for very long. To raise his family, whole and living, to keep their spirits here forever he needed more power. He needed to transform himself into a lich."

"A lich?" I shudder with excitement. "A lich? Is that what I am?"

Roland looks at me in surprise.

"Why, yes, Mistress."

"And what does it mean to be a lich?"

"You are the most powerful undead possible," says Roland, to my abject satisfaction. "You are immortal, as long as your soul is kept safe."

"My soul?"

"Yes, Mistress, your soul. You will never die permanently unless your soul is destroyed and your soul can only perish by the destruction of its container. If you don't mind my asking, where is your phylactery?"

"My what?"

"Your phylactery? Your soul container? The Master was going to use an enormous gemstone of great clarity. He was very proud of it."

I remember the gem the necromancer had placed on the altar. The one that had absorbed so many souls before the brave knight had shattered it with his war axe, the same axe that now hung at my side.

"My soul is elsewhere?"

"Yes, Mistress?"

"The gem was destroyed," I murmur. "I saw it with my own eyes. So where is my soul?"

"I do not know."

Hmm. A puzzle for another time. At least I have the satisfaction of knowing what I am, and hopefully the necromancer's study will provide further information. We crest the next hill and look down upon an overgrown ruin.

We have arrived at Dunbarra Keep.

Chapter Six

Dunbarra Keep

A tower rises out of a ruined pile in front of us. Decidedly crooked, it veers to one side, propped up by a cluster of fallen stone. It looks like it might once have been part of a fine keep, but the entire structure has long since fallen into disrepair. The outline of the castle is just visible, half reclaimed by the forest. The grounds are overgrown and wild with vines and moss draped over the rough stone. A rocky hill rears up behind it but the trees are on the tower's doorstep, hiding the true proportions of the ruin beneath their hoary branches. If the place is haunted I see no sign of it. Night birds hoot and skitter overhead, and small animals go about their nocturnal business as we pass by. It is humans who have abandoned this place. I think I like it.

I follow Roland as he pushes his way through the undergrowth. He pulls aside a sheet of ivy to reveal a stout oaken door, the freshly sanded wood looking quite out of place. I watch as he inserts a large metal key and the door glides open, revealing only darkness. I follow him in, thankful for my new eyes. *His* eyes do not seem to be as good as mine, although he is clearly familiar with the surroundings.

Roland fumbles for a stub of candle, and lights it. I follow the tiny flame into a small landing area, sparsely furnished, and upwards along a spiralling staircase. The stairs are uneven and crumbling and I take great care to trail Roland's exact steps, as he skips over problematic spots. Various doors lead off the stairwell, but he ignores them heading for the top of the tower. We spill out onto a room that is partially open to the elements. Grey pillars hold aloft the domed arches of the ceiling, and faded velvet curtains billow in the breeze. The floor is black, a scrubbed obsidian that absorbs the weak moonlight. The place smells of forest and dust. Roland moves about the tower hanging guttering torches in silver sconces on every other pillar.

In the centre of the room is a pedestal and on it rests a stupendous suit of armour. I have never seen anything quite like it. I move closer to get a better look. The light glitters off the steel joints as I turn to Roland.

"The Master had it made," he answers my unspoken question. "I helped design it!" I pace around the stand, inspecting it from all sides. The draugr watches me, wringing his hands anxiously. "Do you like it, Mistress?"

"Hmm."

I pick up the massive pauldrons to inspect them. They would be much too heavy to be practical on a human frame but to me they are nothing. They are far, far superior to the ones I have on. I shed my current armour in a clattering pile and place the pair of pauldrons on my bony shoulders. They jut out from either side of my skeletal frame, the spikes protruding heavenward. "Hmmm!"

Roland rushes off to one side and pulls a dusty cloth off an enormous mirror with a flourish. Perhaps he is a handy creature to keep around. I turn, admiring the effect in the looking glass. It is rather pleasing.

"It will do," I say to Roland and he bobs and smiles happily. "Bring me the breast plate." I point imperiously and he rushes over with the enormous piece. I take it in my hands and turn it over. The workmanship is fine but it is much too big, and much too clunky. I wrap my knuckles on the metal and then toss it to the ground with a crash. The pauldrons I will keep. I stride around the room, my long femurs gleaming in the smoky torchlight. It is a shame but I do not think the rest will fit.

"Hmm," I cock my fingers under my chin and turn to Roland. "Have you got anything more... floaty?"

"Floaty?" repeats Roland, perplexed. "No, ma'am, the Master had the armour made specially. From a blacksmith down in Greater Downing."

"A pity," I say. "I will have to visit and get some adjustments made."

The emerald curtains catch my eye. Faded, yes but there is some wear in them. I do not care for modesty, that seems ridiculous but now the idea of clothing is in my head, I cannot get it out. I kick aside the breastplate and stride across the room. I ponder them for a second before ripping the drapes free from their hangings. Standing once more in front of the looking glass I drape the velvet around my hip bones, threading the ends around the base of my exposed ribcage so it makes a long flowing skirt. Not long enough to trip me, but enough to swirl elegantly if I turn suddenly. Nothing that a needle and thread won't be able to sort out, anyway. "Taffeta would be preferable, but it will do."

"Taffeta," says Roland, weakly.

"Or satin, perhaps. I need to visit a haberdashery. Is there a helmet?"

There does not seem to be one included with the suit. Roland points to an alcove on the wall where rests a black cowl and an obsidian crown. *Yes.*

"Bring it to me," I say, and the draugr does as I ask.

The crown is heavy in my hands, pleasantly so. It is also too big, made for a larger skull but with some discreet padding I can make it work. The carved spikes are majestic. I place the crown on my head, and drape the cowl over it. Oh yes. The overall effect is breath-taking. I feel like a queen instead of a wandering skeleton with an impressive stare. Protection and style. I am very pleased.

"This will do," I say, throwing one last glance at the mirror. "For now."

I stalk through the room, my velvet skirts swishing, stoically resisting the urge to break into a grin. But enough of playing dress up.

"Where are the spells?" I demand. "Where did the necromancer keep his books?"

"Through here, Mistress." Roland gestures to a door in an alcove. This one is painted black to match the floor and has a brightly polished silver doorknob.

I twist it open and step through.

Although smaller this room is no less impressive. A cold hearth stands to one side and in front of it an ancient, heavy desk. It is cluttered with parchments and books. A chair stands before it, at an angle, as if its occupant had just stepped away and would return at any moment. As he had fully intended to do.

A large oil painting hangs above the fireplace. I can see it is old, for the paint is cracked and yellowing. A man stands with his wife and two small children, all of them dressed in the formal attire that was in fashion the previous century. The necromancer is recognisable although the face above the fireplace is a much kinder, fatter, and more wholesome version of the man I met above the altar. I turn my back on it.

A podium stands on the opposite side and on it rests a book. As soon as I see it, nothing else matters. I can feel it calling to me. The air tingles, sharp and metallic, like the air before a summer thunderstorm. The cover is wrinkled and stained a dull brown. Tarnished silver chains bind it to the podium, keeping it shut. In the middle, the leather of the book wrinkles in a peculiar pattern. A gemstone? A lump? No, an eyeball. I have seen powerful grimoires before, but never one that exudes its own aura and I am fascinated. It seems the feeling is mutual. A moist, bloodshot eye opens from the wrinkle, swivelling madly about the room before settling on my form. It blinks, then narrows. The book shudders a little and the silver chains rattle.

"Whose eye is that?"

"I do not know, Mistress."

Roland is standing in the doorway, clearly on edge. He seems loath to venture further into the room and I do not blame him. This is not the sort of book mortals should tamper with. I have the feeling it would disintegrate a human, leaving nothing more than a puff of ash.

"Where did your Master get this book?"

"Apologies, Mistress I do not know. He went off on many secret excursions to many distant lands. I assume he discovered it in his travels."

Fair enough. I will discover these secrets on my own. I take a final step forward staring into the eye. It stares back, then winks. I open the cover, taking care not to touch the eye. Close too I can see it is not human. It is too large, and the pupil is slit like a cat. It might once have been golden but now it is faded brown and bloodshot. The grimoire's binding is warm to the touch. As I lift the cover, the eye snaps shut.

I cannot move my hands and I cannot look away. The air around me darkens and a velvet curl of smoke undulates out of the book, streaming through the air till it passes through me with strings of black fire. Black-bright glitter swirls around me, shivering and writhing before sinking into my bones with a tingle. The heavy scent of soot and decay lingers in the air. It is not a bad smell. It is the mustiness of the turning of the year, of the resin of a felled oak, screaming as it falls, ripped from the earth. It is the scent of the muck from which new life will spring. Perhaps. Perhaps I am dreaming and there is nothing but dust.

I blink.

I can move again, and I know I am somehow more than I was. I look down at the grimoire, the binding still warm beneath my hand. I flip the pages. Most of the book is blank. The pages are a thick, heavy vellum. As I turn them, the parchment lets out a gentle scent of rot. Two have writing on them. I inspect them with excitement. Two spells? Each scrawled in crusting brown cursive, the ink fades and blotted.

The first is very simple, merely two sentences:

Soul Thief

Whisper 'Decipula alma'.

"Decipula alma," I say softly under my breath. My body jolts and the book shudders. Darkness lifts from the page and sinks once more. That is all. I hope it is enough. I cannot wait to try it on a living thing. I commit the words to memory and turn the page. The next page is a drawing entitled 'Holding Sigil'. The diagram is drawn in the same fading brown ink. It moves slightly beneath my vision and I have to stare at it sternly to make it hold its place on the page. The sigil is twisted and turned in upon itself like a knot. I stare at it to commit it to memory. There are a few lines next to it, but again very little information.

The title reads:

Creation of Soul Gems.

Whisper "In virtutemortuorum, ego præcipiotibi, captiumanimarumviventium."

Again, the darkness lifts, and is gone. I turn the page. It is blank, as are all the ones after it. The book slams shut and the eye fixates on me, wide and even more bloodshot. I jump backwards, dragging my fingers away, guiltily, as if the thing could bite me but I am unharmed. The words of the spells swim in my brain.

Roland is watching me closely from the doorway. I point my fingers at his desiccated chest, making the gesture I remember the necromancer making. Those memories are burned into my brain.

"*Decipula alma,*" I say, eagerly. Soul thief. Nothing happens.

"Whisper, ma'am," Roland says. He glances guiltily over his shoulder.

"*Decipula alma,*" I whisper.

Light pools along my finger and he gasps, his chest lurching forward, pulled by my spell. My anticipation intensifies, but the magic ends, and Roland settles back on his feet. Nothing has happened. I feel no different. I have not consumed a soul.

I let out a low growl of disappointment.

"Sorry, Mistress," Roland says, apologetically, "but the Master had my soul off me long ago."

"He did? He consumed it? How can you speak without a soul?"

"No," the draugr held up a sparkling glass vial from around his neck. Light shines from it like a small, dim, morning star. He pats it, happily, before tucking it back under his decomposing shirt. "It is not a true phylactery. I am not a lich but it is enough. But I am probably more use to you as a servant anyway."

"Perhaps." I turned away, a little miffed. He is right. Roland *is* more useful as a source of information. Even if he looks like he could fall apart at any moment. I should not be so impulsive.

"You have to start small, ma'am. That was the master's plan. Once he was turned." I poke about amongst the papers and books on the desk. There are one or two that look interesting so I put them into my bag to examine later. There is nothing about how to reanimate the dead. At least nothing that I can see at a glance.

"Is there nothing here for me?" I say, trying to keep the bite of disappointment out of my voice.

"No, no!" he says. "This I know! Let me show you."

"There was nothing in the book about reanimating the dead."

Roland glances as the grimoire, lying still and innocent on its pedestal. The eye seems to know when it is being looked at. It squints at him and he shudders, tearing his gaze away.

"You misunderstand," he says. "Have you learned the spell to consume a soul? Master Atticus said that would be the first."

"Yes?" I say, trying to keep the petulance out of my voice. I am so hungry, it is hard to think rationally.

"Once you have stolen a soul from the living," says Roland. "It is yours. You can consume it, or you can put it in another body. To animate the dead, you are merely controlling its soul. I am unsure of the details. But the Master told me he would awaken hungry and that he would require sustenance."

"I am hungry," I admit.

"He said to start small."

"Then let us heed his wisdom," I say, sweeping down the stairs in a swirl of velvet.

Chapter Seven
Soul Hunt

Dawn is breaking as we head into the forest. I instinctively seek the deep shade where the trees grow thickest, slinking into dappled shadows.

"Where is the nearest town?" I ask.

"A long way," says Roland. "Almost as far to the east as we travelled from Downing." I grind my teeth in frustration. I am so hungry.

"But you need not consume a human soul, Mistress. In fact, I am not sure you would be able."

I whirl at the sound of a faint rustle in the undergrowth. A stag. It stands frozen, watching us with liquid brown eyes.

"Decipula alma," I say, pointing my finger. Nothing happens and it bounds away. Frustration courses through me and I slam my fist into the trunk of a nearby pine. There is a sharp crack. The pine shudders, and then comes toppling down with a roar of shrieking timber. It smashes into various other trees with a succession of crashes and booms and a cacophony of tearing roots. It lands on the forest floor. Birds take to the sky, cawing and calling.

Roland watches as the enormous trunk rolls this way and that before finally settling in the undergrowth.

"Errr... you must speak the spell softly, ma'am," he says. "Or the Whisperer won't hear you."

For a moment Roland's second life hangs in the balance until I convince myself he is merely trying to help. I know I shouldn't wring his neck but I do not know who the Whisperer is and I do not care. I merely know that if I don't get rid of this hollow feeling soon I'm going to get very, very crabby.

A squirrel chitters at us from a branch and I turn to it with a swish of my velvet skirts.

"And perhaps..." Roland withers beneath my stare.

"Yes?" I snap.

"I would recommend starting smaller, Mistress."

"Smaller than a squirrel?"

"Yes, ma'am."

"Would you have me consume the soul of an ant?"

"Perhaps a flower, Mistress."

I momentarily forget my irritation at the wonder of the thought. "Flowers have souls?" I ask, but perhaps I had always known that, working in my forest garden.

"They live, they breathe, they nourish themselves," says Roland. "Perhaps soul is the wrong word. Essence, they have essence, which you can consume as an energy source. Humans have this essence to; it is just more complex. Soul is the word we use to describe something we don't really understand."

It sounds like he is quoting someone, I assume his late Master. I do not care.

"A human soul would be more filling?"

"Aye. In the same way that a tree's soul is more complex than a blade of grass. Or a dragon's to a mouse. Or a leaf of lettuce to a warm stew."

"What about a rose bush and rat's?" I ask. "Which has higher worth?"

"I do not know, mistress," says Roland. "I am sorry. I was never one for philosophy." He scratches at his head.

"Or an owl to a crow?"

He shakes his head but before he can tell me again how he knows nothing, I am face first in the heath, examining a mariposa lily, its tiny yellow flowers speckled with scarlet.

"*Decipula alma,*" I say to it, making sure I keep my voice low. The spell is instantaneous. Small fey light rockets from the petals into my face.

I blink.

I can taste it!

The flower's gentle soul feels like the barest hint of sweetness on the tip of the tongue I no longer possess. It tastes of fleeting sunlight and nights beneath warm summer stars. The petals and stem wither before my eyes, falling to the ground in a tiny ashen pile.

I sigh.

Far from satisfying the hollow feeling in my gut, the fleeting soul has only sharpened the ache of my hunger. Like a starving man offered the scent of warm bread I scramble into the brush, touching every plant I can, repeating the incantation a hundred times, two hundred times. I feast my way through the forest floor on my hands and knees, leaving behind me a thick layer of death and decay. The forest plants wither, their life-lights flickering for a moment before being absorbed into my body.

I pause for a moment to consider that the blight I have been causing with my footsteps, the dark path I leave in my wake might be my body automatically absorbing the small essences of life? Enough to keep me alive at least, if not satiated.

I point to a sturdy pine and whisper: *"Decipula alma."*

The tree quivers but stands firm. Too soon. Oh well. I return to my little plants. Humiliating, but at least I am making progress. Eventually it begins to feel invigorating, giving me some satisfaction. The grass is fresh and light, the mushrooms rich and earthy. The hemlock is a fresh, swelling sting.

I see an ant and steal its tiny soul. It is barely a pinprick taste but it is hot and bitter. The entire anthill on the other hand is a blazing spice, and apparently one whisper will do for the lot. A scurrying beetle tastes like sun baked earth. I laugh in delight. Who needs food when you can consume the world? I will have all their souls. And yet my hunger does not subside, it is a yawning pit inside of me. I must have more.

As I work my way up to trees and scurrying creatures I realise flesh is returning to my body. I point at a young pine and its soul flashes green, the light streaming into my chest. There is a faint thickening of my taut skin. There is slightly less bone showing on my arms. More. MORE. I am so hungry.

From saplings, youthful and springy I move to a nest of sparrows. The souls of the baby birds taste like puffs of cloud. Their mother's soul is a wary crunch, with chicken-like overtones. Unsurprising. I wonder if a chicken's soul will merely taste like chicken? I need to find out. A chipmunk's soul has a distinctly nutty flavour.

I turn once more to a tree, this time a cedar.

"Decipula alma."

The mighty tree withers before my eyes, the decay of a hundred years happening in a moment. The remains of the cedar fall to dust, leaving a delicate patina of soot and rot on the forest floor. The pearl and ombre light of its soul streams into my body. I gasp with delight.

I can taste the age of the tree, feel the patience of the forest lord who spent his days basking in sun and starlight. His soul is mine now.

Looking down I can see my bones have almost entirely skinned over. I hold my fingers up in amazement, turning them over to see the fresh skin. My pallor is now mottled green and pale, an unwholesome white. The obsidian crown sits slightly snugger on my head, and I wonder, how human can I become? How many souls must I consume, and how far can I go? If I consume the souls of a thousand people will my hair grow back? I hope so. Will I be able to walk the streets of Greater Downing without comment? I want to find out.

My hunger recedes somewhat and I decide it is time to be getting home. Jenkins and the chickens will be missing me. All in all, it has been a most satisfactory trip.

I continue to gather souls as we walk home through the sunlit wood but make a beeline for my cottage. Roland trails after me walking over the withered earth that is all I leave behind me.

As we enter the familiar groves of Downing the sun is burning low and red on the horizon. Clouds are gathering and the wind whips at my cowl. I can smell a storm coming. Later tonight, or possibly tomorrow.

I can also smell burning.

I frown. The scent puts me on edge. Nothing should be burning. There is no one here who needs warmth, in this, my personal village of the dead. In the distance, I spot a trail of smoke wafting, upwards, the billows torn to ribbons by the winds. It is coming from the direction of my cottage.

I break into a run, streaking through the ruins and through the woods.

My cottage is ablaze.

The thatch smoulders, huge banks of smoke belching from the windows. I scream with rage. The flame isn't visible, just dense smoke rolling out of the windows. The fire has been started from the inside. There is still time to save my cottage! Rushing forward, I leap the fence, not bothering with the garden gate. Bursting through my back door, I hesitate. Everything is darkness, and even my enchanted blue-flame eyes can't see through the smog. I grope my way through, trusting my memory. At least I no longer need to breathe. In the kitchen I snatch up my broom, then, with my hand on the wall, the heat guides me to the source of the blaze and I can finally see light through the smoke. Whoever started the fire used my bed as the kindling. My entire bedroom is a furnace.

Every moment that passes sees the flames eat away at my memories. I lift the stuffed straw mattress and slam it against the wall with all my strength. For a moment, I wonder if I've made a grave error, as sparks float through the air as the stuffing comes loose. But the heat noticeably lessens and the sparks pitter out. Raising the broom, I bring it down on the overturned mattress, beating the embers.

I am not sure how long passes; rage overcomes me and I beat the fire over and over. That done, I rush to the well, again and again, sloshing great buckets full of water over the thatch. The embers sizzle and go out. Roland helps fill the buckets while I run, handing them to me mutely. All is safe. My cottage is safe. I sit down hard, not out of tiredness but out of relief.

"Thank you," I say to Roland and his eyes widen.

Absentmindedly, I pat out the sparks on my fresh skin. Some of it has burnt away. I did not notice. It doesn't matter, I know what to do now. My velvet skirt has burnt half away, which makes me a little sad.

Then I notice something pinned to my garden gate. I rear up. Something is pinned to my garden gate! I hiss. What is it? Something black, and soft and furry. Something stuck into the wood with my woodcutting axe. I move closer and let out a bitter wail of rage.

It is Jenkins.

Dead.

Someone has killed my cat. It is not enough that someone sneaks to my home and sets it on fire, they have to kill my beloved pet. The rage froths in me and I shake, trying to control the rattle of my bones.

"Roland!" I roar.

"Yes, Mistress?" he twists his hat nervously between two hands. I strap my war axe to my belt.

"Watch the cottage," I say. "Tidy up if you can. Feed the chickens. The grain is in the garden shed. I won't be long. Watch Jenkins for me. Keep him safe, or I will kill you very painfully. Do you understand?"

The draugr glances at the dead cat worriedly but he dips his knees and nods. To his credit the draugr does not ask me where I'm going. In truth *I* do not know where I am going. But I know whoever set fire to my cottage can't be too far away, and I know I am going to kill them. The fire had not been burning for long. I am ready to consume a human soul. If I am unable to consume a human soul…well… I will just have to settle for beating them to a pulp with my axe handle. Perhaps I will pound them into the forest ground and leave them to rot until they grow into a tree and THEN I will consume their soul.

I start to run, making wide looping circuits around the cottage, moving out into the trees. I don't bother to go quietly. The time for stealth has passed. I run, screaming my rage, my impressive voice echoing off the treetops and my bony feet beating an aggressive staccato over the earth. I am coming, and I will make them pay.

The wind howls through the tree tops and whips at my cowl. In the distance I spy a group of people tramping through my trees. There are several—men in armour and a man and a woman in mages' robes.

They are looking around desperately, probably trying to identify the uncanny wailing that issues forth from my undead lungs. I am moving so fast they don't get the chance. I run shrieking out of the trees swinging my axe in wild arcs.

I do not stop to talk; I do not stop to ask them which of them put their hands on my cat or which of them threw a torch on my thatch. I do not stop to ask WHICH OF THEM STOOD IN MY BEDROOM AND TOSSED A BURNING BRAND ON MY MOTHER'S QUILT.

The first strike denudes a warrior of his arms. The second sends a head spinning into the bushes.

The survivors wheel in alarm, trying to gather themselves for a defence. Two arrows ping off my armour, and the sole remaining mage sends a fireball hurtling towards me. Our eyes meet. She looks familiar. Oh yes. Gregory's wife. The harlot. I split her skull in two before she can open her petty, disgusting mouth to screech at me. This has done nothing to improve my mood. Oh yes, I was going to try and consume a human soul. I point to the last of the remaining warriors.

"*Decipula alma,*" I scream.

He blanches, throwing up his arms to protect himself. The fool. Nothing happens because I did not whisper. *I do not feel like whispering.* I settle for screaming in his face and then remove his head from his shoulders with a great walloping whack. It goes flying through the air in an arc, streaming ribbons of bright scarlet and lands in the mud with a satisfying thud.

Now I feel better.

I rotate my shoulder blades and then fix my axe back to my belt. Then I walk over and pick up the stray head. I gather the rest. Hmm, next time I should bring a basket. I attach a couple to my belt by their hair, and carry the others. I turn to tramp back to the cottage, feeling suddenly drained. I will tidy up tomorrow, after I have had a chat with the necromancer.

I want my cat back.

It is time I learn how to raise the dead.

Chapter Eight
The Necromancer

Striding back to my cottage, I hum and swing the freshly severed heads backwards and forwards in time with my song. *Whoosh!* I leave a scattered trail of daisy petals behind me. They flutter down onto the blacked trail like crimson confetti. Since no one is around to see me, I give a little skip. I will teach them to leave me alone. *Whoosh!* I need more though. *Whoosh!* More souls, more knowledge! *More minions.* And I need Jenkins back or I will burn the world down and stack the carcasses as high as the sun and back again.

Alright, perhaps I wouldn't burn the whole world but certainly all of Lowcroft and most of the town of Greater Downing. They can all burn. And it would be a shame if it came to that because then I would not be able to visit the haberdashery in the main street and I am already saddened by the loss of my velvet skirts.

For all our sakes I better be able to bring my cat back, and soon.

Whoosh! I knock loose a particularly fine cluster of dandelions. The spores go floating overhead, snapped up by the brisk wind. I smile at them. Once I can raise the dead there will be no stopping me!

I arrive back at my cottage. Roland is sweeping in the kitchen, his shoulders stooped. He startles as I plonk the fresh heads down on the kitchen table with a squishy thud.

"You are back, Mistress!" he says stupidly.

"I am," I say. Where else would I be? "Thank you, Roland. I have work to do in the kitchen. Perhaps you can carry on cleaning up in the garden? Maybe take a look at the roof?"

He nods, wide eyed, shuffling sideways around the kitchen table to avoid my gruesome trophies and disappears into the garden.

Alone in the kitchen I sigh. Poor Jenkins. Roland has laid him out on a blanket. My beloved cat lies quietly, stiff and cold. Not like him at all. He looks so tiny in death. *Soon,* I promise him.

I turn to glare at the pile of heads. I should use them as mulch for nettles. No! I have a better idea. The blank eyes stare back at me, still open in shock and fear. I will bury the mage and Gregory in the latrine. That should please them both. They can decompose together. Very romantic. But this is not the time for idle daydreaming. I can feel it in my bones. Today is going to be the day I raise the dead.

I should have tried to consume the harlot's soul during the fight rather than letting anger get the best of me. But perhaps the body does not need to be alive for me to consume their soul? Or whole? How long does a soul linger? Only one way to find out.

"*Decipula alma,*" I whisper, gesturing to the mage's head. It is in two pieces, from where I split her skull. Does it matter? Where do soul's live anyway? For a moment nothing happens. Then I feel a jolt. Light pools above the harlot's sticky head and to my delight her soul streams into me in a glittering trickle. It sparkles over my bones and skin like diamond raindrops, before being absorbed inside me.

I gasp in delight.

It is like a meal after starving; a warm, filling stew after a hard day working in frigid fields. I am bathed in contentment. And yet I am not full. More. I must have more. It is the most filling soul I have consumed so far! All those small souls were mere snacks in comparison. I was not built to be a vegetarian after all. It is unnatural. I am almost giddy with delight.

So I know how to consume a human soul! Step one. But how do I reanimate a body? I do not want to practise on Jenkins, he is too precious.

I recall the other spell, the 'Creation of Soul Gems,' and there was that image, the sigil. I trace the sign on my table with my finger.

"*In virtutemortuorum, ego præcipiotibi, captiumanimarumviventium,*" I whisper. What a mouthful. I presume a soul gem is a place to store a soul I do not want to consume, or one that I want to reuse? That makes sense. Do I need a soul gem to reanimate a body? And how do I transfer the soul from the gem to the body I wish to reanimate? I flex my fingers in frustration. I need to ask the necromancer but how can I ask him how to raise the dead without raising him first!

My fists thump down on the table.

I walk out to the garden.

"Roland!"

The little draugr nearly falls off his ladder. He is attempting to repair the fire scorched thatch. He looks down at me with a wrinkled brow. While he has already told me he does not know how to reanimate dead, perhaps there is more knowledge lurking in that rotting head of his than he realises. "What do you know of gemstones, Roland?"

"A little, Mistress."

"Tell me."

Roland sways on his ladder.

"The master kept several casting gems on him at all times, Mistress. Some charged with the sun, others with the moon, others still with the stars."

"He did, did he?" I need to check the necromancer's clothing again.

"Yes, Mistress."

"Can you think of anything else?"

Roland stares at me blankly and I sigh. I am struck with inspiration.

"When your master raises the dead," I say carefully. "Did he use any words? Any phrase you remember?"

"Oh yes, Mistress."

"And what were the words?" I ask, sweetly, patiently, trying to keep the venom from my lips. Roland's brow furrows. I can see his brain matter through the hole in his hat. He really needs a thorough patch job, it is not his fault he is a dimwit.

"*Resurgemus iterum*," he says, after a few moments thought.

"Thank you, Roland." I sweep out of the garden, my eyes bright.

The wind is high as I walk through the forest heading for Little Downing and the trees swish violently in the sky, their branches rushing and rustling. The clouds are heavy with the promise of rain but so far none has fallen.

It's been five days since the massacre, since my resurrection, and already nature is reclaiming the village. Some of my geese are waddling through the ruins, and a few chickens scratch at the small green shoots that have started to poke through the earth between the fallen houses. They are feasting on blood and muck, happy with the nutrients the slaughter provided. The circle of life is in motion. Looking at it for a moment, I consider how beautiful a garden would be in this place. Perhaps, later.

I quickly locate the necromancer's body on the keep pile, which I have stashed in one of the few still standing structures. Rifling through his robes, I find what Roland has told me to be the truth. Neatly tucked in an inseam pocket are a handful of small crystals. They are all different sizes and colours and they tingle with power. Some of them are warm to the touch, others flutter and pulse. One is as cold as the grave. I hold them in my hand and consider, tapping a thin finger against my cheek. Yes, against my cheek, not the bone. Now I have consumed a soul there is flesh again, although it is yet gaunt. More souls will make me more substantial, I have no doubt.

I have never worked with crystals or gemstones before. No, that is a lie. Once I used a crystal to heal my mother and uncle from a severe illness. I purchased the gem from a wandering magic merchant and it cost me dear. My magical path was with potions and simple spells, herbs and nature, this is uncharted territory.

So I have the gems from the necromancer and I also have the fragments of the ritual crystal that were destroyed in my making. The crystal that was supposed to be the necromancer's phylactery. I reach for my pouch and draw out the sharp shards, lying them out in front of me. They are diamond clear and humming with power. Pre-charged, I assume. The necromancer looked like the type to perform ample preparation. I laugh into the wind. He had not prepared for me.

Turning over the various gems and crystal fragments, I can tell they are different, although I am unsure of their capabilities. The shards, I assume are empty: charged and ready to contain fresh souls. The others... I am unsure. Time to experiment!

First I need a test subject.

I turn to a nearby chicken and whisper: "*Decipula alma.*"

The soul of the chicken streams into my body, and the warm, plump body of the hen flops to the ground, dead. Whoops. Fortunately, my flock is fairly numerous. The evil black rooster glares at me from the opposite rooftop and lets out an ear-splitting crow. He does not like me messing with his hens. The soul tastes...like chicken, which is unsurprising.

"Calm yourself," I mutter to the black rooster. We glare at each other. "Fine," I say. My next victim is one of the geese. This time I hold the shard of crystal in my open palm. "*Decipula alma.*"

The goose's soul streams into the shining gem. My fingers fold around it in delight. I can feel it trapped within, fluttering against my fingertips. Good. Now I have one trapped soul and two dead fowl. I pocket the crystal, eagerly. Time to raise the dead. Time to play god! I would never have dared fool with necromancy when I was a human. The risks are too high in a mortal body. Who knew what or who I was summoning, but as a lich I find I care little for such concerns. Death is an adventure, merely a door to transformation. Perhaps I am getting cocky.

I point at the dead goose's body and whisper, "*Resurgemus iterum.*"

It twitches. Then it rises, unnaturally stiff. The undead goose lets out an ear-splitting shriek and then runs head first into a tree. It shakes its head and then waddles off, hissing. I stare at it suspiciously. It does not seem that different from a normal goose. Perhaps I should experiment on a higher life form. I should test this out on a human before I reanimate the necromancer, but whom?

I wander over to the neatly stacked 'keep' pile. After some thought, I haul out my mother, and prop her up against a crumbling wall. She is bloating, as are all the corpses. Bloody foam dribbles from her nose and mouth. I wipe some of it away with one of the neighbour's sleeves. Her curly hair is greying at the temples, and her face looks even older and sadder in death than I remember. All of these bodies will go back to the earth soon, whether I want them to or not.

"*Resurgemus iterum,*" I whisper. My voice is surprisingly hoarse. I did not realise I cared that much. It is lucky I can no longer cry.

My mother's body shudders, and twitches. I wonder if I have overstepped my reach but then she gasps, jolting awake. Fat, dead eyelids flutter open. In her death addled state, she clearly recognises me but then sees the bones; the stretched skin. She lifts a bloated arm then drops it as if she doesn't know what to do.

"Maud!" she exclaims. She blinks, then looks again and starts screaming. "What in the Gods' name happened? I remember? I think? What happened to-"

"Hello, Mother," I start. I hesitate, the words half formed on my lips. But then I realise I'm really not in the mood to talk. I cannot endure this. I pull out a shard of crystal the length of my fingerbone.

"*Decipula alma,*" I whisper.

Her body heaves a massive breath, just as she opens her mouth once more, cutting her off mid sentence. Her chest contracts and her soul leaves her, streaming into the gem. My fingers close around it protectively. I will keep her safe.

However, it does seem that I know enough to raise the necromancer. We are overdue for a chat. I stride past the well and retrieve the man's sorry carcass from the keep pile, dumping it unceremoniously on the stone altar with a damp squish. As I stare down at his once handsome features, and the neat stitching where I sewed him back together, the anger builds in my skull. All of this is his fault. He killed these people. My mother. Everyone. He killed me. I push my rage down beneath the icy calm.

I am just about to mutter the incantation, when a thought occurs to me. It is better to be safe than sorry. Turning to the weapons pile, I pick up a broadsword and turn back to the dead necromancer. It is the work of moments to lop off his arms and legs. He only needs to talk. And to listen. People who listen are underrated.

I toss the broadsword back to the weapons pile, satisfied he won't be getting up to too much mischief without his limbs.

"*Resurgemus iterum,*" I whisper. The words are snatched from my lips by the wind but they serve their purpose. The necromancer wakes with a shudder. Unlike my mother he smiles, and his eyes flashing open, hollow and undead. I hate him so much.

"HA! I've done it!"

His dilapidated torso wriggles on the altar. I watch with grim delight as triumph is replaced with confusion. The smile drops from his face as he realises something is wrong, very wrong and he swears, shoulders thrashing as he attempts to sit up.

"Where is the Whisperer? Who are you? POSTESTATEM AD ME! Am I not a lich? You! *Arrrg*. Roland! What has become of me? WHERE ARE MY LEGS?" As he looks down and bellows, his thrashing intensifies. I take note of the spell the necromancer spoke, wondering its meaning.

"Roland!" screams the necromancer. He whips his head around and I become aware of the little undead man standing in the deep shadows. Perhaps I should credit him with more intelligence after all. Roland is twisting his battered hat in his hands, but he does not speak or move to come closer.

The necromancer's eyes slide to mine as he finally takes note of my presence. I smile. "What is the meaning of this? Who are you?" Realization descends on his stitched together face. "*YOU!* YOU FOUL THIEVING WHORE! THAT POWER IS SUPPOSED TO BE MINE!"

Watching him writhe on the altar pleases me. I step around the stone and stand before him.

"Well," I say, my voice like honey, "seeing as I've raised you, I assume you must do my bidding? That is the way of it is it not?"

"Ha! You know nothing of laws of the dead. Such a waste of potential. Roland! Return my legs to me, at once!"

For a moment, Roland looks between his old master and me, his small undead brain trying to decide.

"Do no such thing, Roland," I say.

"Ye... yes, Mistress." Roland bows his head, caught between embarrassed and shame.

"Roland!" says the necromancer, and there is genuine shock in his voice. *"Why?"*

The draugr bobs his knees in that irritating manner that he has, and rubs his head, as if trying to find the words.

"She sewed my legs on, Master," he says at last, "and sometimes she says 'thank you'."

The necromancer makes a noise like a kettle boiling. His putrid, undead cheeks puff out in his fury.

"GAH! I swear, I'll... I'll..." he stutters and rolls around on the altar. Then his eyes brighten and he stills. I can see that he has hatched some plot he thinks is immensely clever. *"Susurrans in tenebris-"*

Before he can finish his incantation, I pick up his own left hand and jam it into his mouth. His eyes widen and he emits a muffled scream. He gnaws on it, trying to spit it out. I poke the hand in even further.

"I know enough," I say, ignoring the noises. I speak to him as if to a petulant child, raising my voice so he can hear me over his own incoherent mumbling. "So either you behave, or I send you back to the land of the dead! Do you understand me?"

The necromancer stills, his eyes narrowed with disdain.

"Do you understand me?" I repeat. He gives a small nod.

I withdraw the hand.

"*Potestastransferendi ad me!*" He spits out the words before I can shove his hand back in.

There is a gleaming in the air. A subtle light rises from my chest. My breath rasps. Have I made a terrible mistake? The light flutters, yet I feel nothing. The thoughts beat in my skull, strong and wilful. Ha. My soul is my own, no one else's. And it is not here. I laugh and the light dissipates.

"You have no power," I say through a chuckle. "You are no longer alive, and I was the one to summon *you*." It is a gamble. I do not truly know, but how can it be otherwise? I feel this truth in my bones.

"*Vocote, quiscæcusest, exaudiorationemmeam et ego enimdabo vobis Donum vitae meae!*" As he finishes the incantation, a small shadow flutters into being before him and, as quickly as it came, it dispels. I watch with interest, committing the words to memory. What else can I learn from the pathetically angry corpse?

"You have no power," I repeat.

He spits at me.

"*Fine.*"

I turn from him and peer at the weapons pile. I lift the broadsword again. "This is your last chance, or you go back to the dead."

"Never."

I sigh and lift the steel high above me.

"Master, please." Roland squeaks from where he stands, his head hanging in meek reverence. I waver the sword, letting him speak. "She is a lich. She has the power you desired. Master, please. All your planning, it can still be done. Through her."

There is a sneer stuck on the necromancer's face, his eyes glaring at his former servant. "You were always a worm, Roland." Roland's face crumples. "You!" The necromancer draws himself up in an attempt at dignity. "Lich bitch! Whatever you are! Return me to my death. I have had enough of this life. I am ready for eternal darkness, let the Whisperman take me now!"

So dramatic. I smile, hesitating.

"Do it!" he says, lifting his chin. I lower the sword.

"There are worse things than death," I say. "Trust me."

"DO IT!" The rotting head-torso snarls at me. I look about the ruins of Little Downing and spot the well.

"No," I say. I drop the broadsword and grab him by his hair, lifting him off the altar.

"What are you doing? PUT ME DOWN!"

I step lightly to the well and swing his body out over the black hole, holding him suspended in space.

"*There are worse things than death,*" I whisper in his rotting ear. "Why should you get a quiet death when you are responsible for the suffering of so many? Now tell me what I want to know, or spend the rest of your undead life at the bottom of the well with the slime."

"You can't-"

"Tell me what I want to know. Or I drop in five... four... three... two..."

"FINE!" I can hear the panic in his voice, his eyes rolling down as he stares into the gaping void of the well shaft. "What do you want to know, you filthy maggot?"

"I found your tower, your book is rather incomplete."

"Ha! The book would never open for the likes of-"

"But it did open," I say.

"You're lying."

"The fact you're here proves I'm not. How else would I know to raise the dead?"

"You were practicing, obviously. Only a mage in life can become a lich, so you knew the Whisperer's ways."

"I served the Green Lady," I correct him.

"Ah," the head-torso let out a small laugh. "I was done in by a green thumb? By a stinking hedge witch? Ha-ah!"

"Three... two..."

"WAIT!"

"One more insult and I drop you. I'm thoroughly sick of your bad language."

His reply was snarling, gnashing teeth.

"Will you comply?"

"Yes," the necromancer says, through bared teeth. He quietens. "Ask."

"Tell me how it works, raising the dead. Tell me of the gemstones in your robes."

His nostrils flair. "You didn't use them? Tell me you have them safe. Those are rare souls!"

"So they are soul containers?"

"Yes, you stupid whore- NO!"

I loosen my grip on his hair and he slips a few centimetres before stopping.

"To contain a soul you must create a soul gem," he says.

"This I know. I have the words. I saw the sigil. But how does it work?"

"Draw the sigil," he says, "lay the gems at the points where the lines intersect. Speak the incantation and leave them to charge by the light of the rising moon. Or the setting or rising of the sun. Or with the power of darkness at midnight. It is the study of a lifetime, I can't expect a simple minded-"

"How long?"

"That depends on the size and quality of the gem, the type of crystal and the size and quality of the soul. Generally, the longer the better. An hour is good, a day is better."

"What do I use to draw the sigil?"

The dead necromancer wiggles, shrugging his shoulders. "Chalk, blood, paint. Anything with solid lines works."

I ponder this information.

"And raising the dead?" I ask.

"Again," he says mockingly, "you ask me to impart the study of a lifetime as if it were a simple peasant's recipe for a loaf of bread. If you want information you will have to be more specific." I can hear the unvoiced insults hovering like salt on the breeze.

"Do I need a soul to raise a body?"

"No," he spits. I mean, I had surmised as much, with my goose experiment.

"What is the difference?" I ask, as patiently as I can.

"The soulless dead are...empty vessels. Wights. They will do your bidding. To a point. But they are simple and often violent."

"And a draugr is a body with a soul?"

"Yes," the necromancer's lips are pinched thin, presumably as it occurs to him that he is a draugr. That he is the same kind of undead as Roland. The sparse flesh of my lips curve upward.

"How long does a soul linger?" I ask. "After death?"

"It depends," he says. "On the soul, on the connection, on the manner of death. A few days, a week? Longer sometimes. Wraiths and ghosts are made from souls who will not let go."

"I see." I have more questions, many more, but only one more that I need the answer to right now. "One last question," I say. I gesture at the ruined village with my free hand. "Why did you do this? What were you trying to achieve?"

"The village?" the necromancer says, in surprise. "The village was just a means to an end."

"What was that end?"

"Domination," he says, as if it is obvious. "Power. The Kingdom of Einheath under my heel."

"Typical," I say. "Unimaginative." He opens his mouth again. "Blah, blah, blah," I say. The head-torso wriggles, as if making a shrugging gesture but I do not let him speak, gripping him firmly by the hair and swinging him back over the well.

"At least I know where to find you if I have more questions," I say, smiling, brightly.

"What- No! Noooooooo!"

I let go.

The necromancer screams all the way down.

There is a satisfying splash.

"Come, Roland," I say, turning away. "We have work to do."

Chapter Nine
ELDING AND TORA

The muffled rage of the necromancer reverberates up the well shaft as I stride away grinning. He can rot down there for all I care, he deserves it. Roland and I walk back to my cottage, chased by the pitter-patter of falling rain and the distant echoes of his helpless fury. As we enter my cottage garden, lightning forks through the sky. A boom shakes the heavens but we are soon in the kitchen.

"Thank you, Roland," I say, and the undead manservant nods. I tilt my head to listen to the driving rain which is now hammering against the window panes. "Pull the shutters too and carry on cleaning up the cottage if you can, but from the inside. It won't do either of us any good if you disintegrate." I eye his worn and ageing flesh.

"Yes, ma'am," he says, gratefully, and bustles away. I consider how not needing to sleep certainly has its perks, for the both of us. I turn to Jenkins, laying his precious body out on the stout kitchen table. The wound that killed him is still visible so I clean it up and then tenderly stitch it closed with my finest and strongest black silk thread. When I am done the neat stitching blends in perfectly with his soft black fur.

"*Resurgemus iterum,*" I whisper, and just like that, my cat wakes. Instantly every bone in my body relaxes. The undead Jenkins bunts his head against my skeletal knees and I go weak with relief. I lean down to scratch his ears and I manage to tickle him for all of two seconds before he bites my hand. He scampers away and I smile.

Everything is going to be alright.

I fall into one of the kitchen chairs, not tired, but drained. Jenkins rethinks his views on affection and leaps onto my bony knees, settling down to groom himself thoroughly. His rumbling purr is so loud it rattles the dishes on the old wooden dresser. Louder and deeper than it was in life, but quite pleasant. I fear for the local rodent population. Jenkins was a fearsome hunter in life and I doubt those instincts have left him.

He is currently a draugr but perhaps I can make him a lich cat? Then we can be immortal together forever. He could wear his phylactery around his neck like a little bell. On second thoughts, that is a terrible idea he would just leave it in a tree somewhere. But I am curious how liches are made. Would I have to sacrifice mountains of mice? Or other cats? Or just souls in general? Would I have to summon that dark spirit that I saw twisting above the altar on that dreadful night? Was it a spirit or a god? My mind blanches away from this train of thought. I am not ready to contemplate the true depths of evil to which my life is so inexorably tied.

Looking down at my body I notice the bones are showing once more. It seems there is a relationship between soul consumption and raising the dead. It makes sense. One powers the other. I poke at my face. I can tell without looking in my mirror that it will be back to its skull-like visage. I have consumed one human soul and raised one human. The balance has been paid, with a little left over.

This at least is easily put right. I can consume the souls of the toss pile, and those of the people I murdered earlier. But first it is very important that I sit with Jenkins. So we do that for a couple of hours, listening to the storm.

After Jenkins jumps off my knees I busy myself consuming the souls of the remaining humans. They don't need souls to look pretty on my maypoles and markers. Not that anyone is heeding my markers. They certainly didn't.

It would be naïve to suppose that I have earned my solitude. I suspect some vigorous lessons will be in order if I want the local inhabitants to keep out of Downing Forest. I glower at the closest head. Who do I have to kill to get some peace and quiet? This thought nearly makes me grouchy but I am content from the feast. I have also discovered that human souls, like their animal and vegetable counterparts, have unique flavours. Tastes even. I could become quite the connoisseur of soul banquets.

The three fighters are all hardy, with a bitter edge. Their souls are aged, though their bodies were young. I can tell their lives were difficult although not without moments of happiness. The male mage's soul is surprisingly sweet. He wasted much of his life on wine and recreation and was happier for it. I am glad he did. It has been a while since I last had candy.

I hum to myself as I craft the remains into a fetching display. I do not forget my promise and nip out in the rain to deposit what is left of Gregory and his wife into the latrine pit. What had the harlot's name been? Cynthia? Something like that. It is of no import. Goodbye. *Sploosh.*

While I am outside I take a trip to the pits and consume the souls of the gently decomposing incumbents as well. As I suspected it would, my skin returns, and some flesh with it. I could now pass for a starving woman. Which is not, strictly speaking, inaccurate.

Back at the cottage I find an empty notebook and write down every word that I remember the necromancer uttering. I'm sure it will come in handy. Then I look through the papers I had brought with me from the necromancer's tower. They are fairly incomprehensible, with sigils and handwritten notes scrawled everywhere. One seems to be a page about mineral deposits and gemstone types. I squint at it, trying to read the map.

If I want to keep souls, I'm fairly sure I will need to make soul crystals. And to make soul crystals I need crystals and stones. All I have is the remaining shards and a few gems. Before my death I was a green witch, not an aristocrat. My jewellery consists of shells on strings and various colourful seeded bracelets. Gregory once gave me a ring engraved with silver, but I melted it down after he left and sold it to buy healing supplies.

I tap my fingers on the table in a rapid staccato. Where can I find gems? There was some jewellery on my dead friends and neighbours. I get out the collection to refresh my memory. No one who lived in Little Downing was particularly wealthy, they wouldn't live here if they were, but there is a meagre handful of jewellery—a few wedding rings, none of them with diamonds, Mrs Philip's beryl pendant that she inherited from her great-grandmother who was a lady's maid to the late Baron's wife, and some cheap gems. Quartz mostly. Perhaps they will do. If not then perhaps I should visit the local graveyard and dig up some people who no longer need their finery?

The wind howls outside and more lightning cuts across the sky, briefly illuminating the kitchen in vivid white. Rain splatters the glass like twinkling diamonds. A pity they are not diamonds. Diamonds would make fine soul containers. Jenkins hisses at the storm and then climbs inside the dresser to go to sleep. Is he sleeping? The undead do not need to sleep. Perhaps he is just pretending to sleep, but who knows the mind of a cat, dead or alive. Either way he seems to be taking to his new life without much fuss.

Another fork of lighting skeins its way across the dome of the sky outside. I hear the crack of a lightning strike. One of the nearby trees must have been hit. The pouch on my belt quivers and rocks. I jump in surprise and then unstring it, curiosity biting at me. I lay the necromancer's crystals out on the table. They lie still and shining. All except one which is humming. Little white sparks leap off the gem to burn holes on the table.

I remember the gem from earlier, flat and square and metallic grey. Not particularly interesting, or at least so I thought at the time. It is no bigger than my thumbnail but it thrums with power. Whatever could be contained within that the storm affects it so? I cast my eye over the necromancer's notes and identify the gemstone as magnetite, a sort of iron. I tap my fingers on the table thoughtfully, watching it jump and bounce. Then, mind made up I scoop it up and stride outside, slamming the door shut behind me.

I stand in the storm, contemplating my options. Rain slides down my head in rivulets but it does not bother me. I shrug. I doubt that the necromancer is in the mood for answering questions. My lips curve at the memory but I want to see what souls are contained within this most interesting stone. I look around, seeking for a suitable vessel. Most of the forest creatures are hiding from the rain but I spy two crows perched up in the boughs. Their feathers are black as night, and their beaks curved as they tilt their heads, watching me with beady eyes.

"Sorry friends," I whisper. *"Decipula alma."*

Their bodies fall to the ground with twin thuds, landing on the damp earth. I consume their souls, carrion foul but sharp as talons and as fresh as a cold night's flight above the pines. Excellent. I now have two empty bodies.

Holding the vibrating magnetite in my palm, the sparks burn my sparse flesh. I say the words to animate the dead. A shadow streak towards the crows, separating to sink into their feathers. So there were two souls. Huh. The bodies twitch and shudder. One flutters its wings, then they both hop upright, blinking and snapping their beaks. I watch with avid attention. Whose souls have I released into the world? What did the necromancer have in his pockets, carefully saved up for his life as a lich? Had he intended to use them or consume them? I know a moment's unease.

"Ka!" says one of the crows, rustling its feathers. Before I speak it takes flight, shooting upwards and wheeling through the rain to vanish into the storm clouds overhead. The second follows it a moment later. I am left alone on the forest floor feeling rather foolish.

Another lightning bolt skitters across the heavens. I stand and wait, searching the skies for the birds but I cannot see them. It is just me and my pride and the soaking wet forest. I shake my head in disgust, water dripping off my pauldrons in rivulets. I turn to trudge my way back to the cottage.

Thump, thump.

The two crows land on the bough, bending it with their combined weight. Their eyes are unnaturally bright and tiny sheets of lightning skitter over their bodies, racing from beak to talon.

"These will do," says the first, to my shock. Its voice is hollow, inhuman. One of its eyes pops out and lands on the branch. It bounces, before dropping away onto the forest floor, like a squishy gemstone itself.

"You can speak!" I say.

"Ka! I am Elding," it says. Its missing eye is now a gaping hole. It swivels its head to leer at me out of the other.

"I am Tora!" says the other. I notice now that it has a chipped beak. Was it like that before? I cannot remember.

"Ka! You have returned us to bodies, we are grateful," says Elding.

"These bodies have warm feelings towards you," says Tora, tilting its head to one side to survey me beadily. "Why is that?"

"Oh." I am taken aback. Why would the crows like me? "I used to feed them sometimes? Them and the magpies?" My voice goes up in the end like a question mark. I have no idea.

"You will feed us too," says Elding.

"Feed us," echoes Tora. "Ka! Feed us and we will serve you like we served our last master."

"Who was your last master?" I ask. There is something about the pair that is unsettling. They are much, much smaller than me but every instinct tells me they are predators. I must tread carefully.

"We were banished," says Elding, not answering the question.

"Banished," says Tora. Her (I decide she is a she, although I really have no idea) voice is like the echo of an empty chamber, hollow and menacing but higher pitched than Elding's. Like the grate of rusty nails over metal. I suppress a shudder. "Ka! Banished from the Whispers. Banished to the realm of the mortals. We wandered."

"Banished," says Elding, picking up the echo. "Wandered. Lost. Our souls were lost, then captured. Stolen. We were tricked."

"By the necromancer Atticus?" Both crows produce a rattling hiss, deep in their throats.

"Now we are free."

The birds glare at me, and the weight of that gaze is heavy. I do not fully understand the pact that binds us but I know they are not entirely free. I suspect they know it too. I can feel their wills pushing at me, testing the boundaries, the ties that bind. These are no chicken souls.

No simple villagers. They are something else. I wonder what their true forms are.

"Ka! What do you want from us?" asks Tora. Both crows tilt their heads, so far to the side I fear they will fall off their perch. I pause.

"What did you do for...the Whisperer?"

The crows go still as jet statues, holding that position for many moments before speaking. Are they listening? Wary.

"Many things," says Elding, at last.

"Nightmares," says Tora. "Nightmares and messages. Watching, always watching."

"Do you *like* watching?" I ask carefully. I'm not sure I want to know what they mean by nightmares. They don't trust me. Or they are afraid. That is fine, I don't trust them either.

"Ka! Feed us, and we will watch," says Elding. "Watch for you, everything we see, we will tell you and we will see everything."

"Not everything," says Tora, and they both laugh a strange rattling gurgling laugh that does not sound merry at all.

"What do you eat?" I ask. "The crows liked carrion."

"We like carrion too," says Elding, his beak parting in what I assume is mirth. "And other things! Ka! Feed us shinies."

"Shinies?"

"Shiny thoughts," says Tora. She crackles with lightning. "Shiny memories. Feed us."

I stare at them thoughtfully. "You... want to eat my memories?"

"Ka!"

I am tempted to give them the entire contents of my head then and there. A fresh start beckons. I can start again, a glorious blank slate. I open my mouth to say 'take everything', then I shut it. I am being childish. There is treasure, buried there amongst the pain. Who would I be without those memories? Just a vengeful skeleton in armour? No,

I must be careful. I have already lost so much. I will not part with the things that make me *me*. Now, I just have to figure out what those things are.

The crows who are not crows are watching me from the shadowy bough, as if they can sense my internal struggles. Their eyes glint like wet obsidian. They want a memory, but they did not say it had to be significant, only that it be...shiny.

"Here," I say, at last. "You may have this memory." I think of the water reflecting like twinkling diamonds on my cottage window panes as the storm beats at the glass.

The crows spread their wings and take flight. They take the memory with me, stealing it away like a whisper in the night. It is gone, whatever it was. I feel no different.

"Ka! We will watch for you," they caw, wheeling overhead. "We will tell you what we see."

"Thank you," I say. Perhaps they will be useful. It remains to be seen. They disappear into the scudding clouds, just two more shadows abroad on a foul, foul night.

I return to my cottage, slightly confused but it will be handy to have winged spies. Things are going well. As I open the door I pause at the window to admire the effect of the raindrops on the glass, twinkling like diamonds.

"Roland!" I call up the ladder. "Watch the cottage for me, I'm going grave robbing."

It is time to find some gemstones.

Chapter Ten
Grave Robbing

The rain eases up as I walk back to the village, turning from a downpour to fat drops, and then stopping altogether. I walk over to the well to check on my unwelcome guest. Leaning over the cobbled wall, I peer into deep darkness. The water is just visible at the very bottom and the necromancer's bloated, bobbing face scowls up at me, pale and angry.

"Are you sitting comfortably?" I ask. He snarls. It is very lucky that I no longer need to drink water, I would not fancy drinking this. Not one bit. He could foul a kingdom by walking through it so I shudder to imagine what he is doing to the water source.

"Once your body disintegrates," I shout, "does your soul leave forever?" The necromancer gnashes his teeth and screams incoherent obscenities. I guess we will have to wait and find out. I withdraw my head, unable to keep the smile from my lips.

Looking around the rest of the ruin I see glowing red eyes peering out at me from the forest's edge. They whirl in the gloom, menacing and evil. They cannot belong to anything natural, or good. I stalk over, clutching my axe in two hands and then straighten in relief. It is just the wight geese that have wandered off. As I watch, one of the unholy things throws back its head revealing rows upon rows of serrated teeth.

A sound like a thousand tortured souls wailing from the realm of the dead pierces the air, delivered with ten times a goose's normal and already ear-bursting volume. The insanely eerie honk-wails are disturbing enough to raise the hackles on the very little skin I have left. The noise alone might do more than all my pits and traps put together to deter people from entering Downing Forest. It is truly unearthly.

I go to check on the rest of the fowl. The draugr geese patrol the area, trampling anything that gets in their way, just like they did when they were alive. They seem content enough although they have slaughtered the remaining living chickens, leaving only the undead one alone to mind its business. Perhaps they recognise that it is like them? They had an uneasy truce in life. The enormous black rooster is the lone survivor of the barnyard massacre. He regards me balefully from the top of a nearby tree and lets out a mournful cock-a-doodle-do. I can feel his accusing gaze on me as he looks down at the dead bodies of his hens. I raise the chickens so that he doesn't have to feel too lonely and leave the draugr flock scratching blissfully in the dirt. I am going to save a fortune in feed at this rate.

Domestic matters taken care of, I wander over to my toss and keep piles. The smell is becoming unbearable. I have kept the bodies as cool as possible but it is becoming abundantly clear that I will not be able to 'keep' anyone as long as I had hoped. At least not unless I can lay my hands on more crystals, and quickly. If I do not I risk losing all of their souls to the void. How long will they linger? I have no idea. I worry that they will become wraiths, the necromancer implied that violent ends might result in such an outcome.

I'm not sure how I feel about the villagers becoming wraiths. It might not be pleasant.

I have only a few of the crystal shards but I use them to capture the souls of the dead who I most want to keep: the knight Tristan, the fletcher, the seamstress, and one or two relatives. I put the captured souls away safely, wrapped in velvet. The rest will have to wait until I have procured more gems. Hopefully soon.

I briefly ponder walking to Greater Downing and robbing the jeweller that I know works there, before dismissing the idea as too much bother. Where else can I find people buried in their finery? Oh! Perhaps a barrow? I could make a side trip to plunder the personal treasures of some ancient kings and queens. The thought would have appalled me in life but now it excites me. No, no. I must start small. I must stick to my plan to investigate the local graveyard.

Now that the rain has stopped, the clouds are lifting. Pale starlight gleams off the wet puddles. Next thing on the list today: soul crystal creation. I fill a pail with mud and haul it over to the stone altar which will double as a very nice worktable. Mud seems very basic. I'm sure there are better, more permanent ways of marking a sigil but it will do for now. It should hold in the absence of rain, and besides, I have nothing else to hand.

I draw on the altar's flat surface, smearing the earth this way and that as I recall the shape of it. I press my pathetic harvest of gemstones into the points where the lines intersect, as the necromancer instructed and step back.

"In virtutemortuorum, ego præcipiotibi, captiumanimarumviventium," I whisper. The words leave my mouth like shadow breath, twining with insidious slowness over the markings before sinking into the mud. The gems thrum and then lie still.

I look at them, unsure. It feels like something has happened but I do not know if the conditions are right. Will they charge with the dawn? If that does not work...well, I will wait for the moonrise and midnight. I will just leave them and see what happens. There is no point watching a pot boil. I can play around later.

I have spent so much time mucking about in the village that Roland comes out to tell me he has finished fixing up the cottage, and to ask what he should do next. After a little thought I set him digging graves. There is a pleasant clearing to one side of the village that was used as a meadow in the summer. It will do nicely. Normally, villagers would be interred in the Greater Downing church graveyard, or at the smaller parish church in Lowcroft. Little Downing was too small for its own church, and most people made do with small altars in their own homes. The pious made the trek into the town once or twice a week to pay their respects to their chosen gods. I had always preferred to worship privately, and away from the crowds.

However, it just doesn't feel right to me to have everyone buried so far from home. Not to mention the local priests and clerics would likely be suspicious of piles of bodies showing up on their doorsteps. Or rows of neat fresh graves. This way I can watch over them, and also borrow bits of them when I have need without having to walk too far.

Would I even be able to set foot on consecrated ground? I guess I would find out soon enough. I tap a finger against my cheek as my gaze wanders over to Roland who is industriously digging. It *is* nice to have help.

I frown. I don't want to leave my forest and come back to find an angry mob chasing my cat or my birds or my Roland. If I am going to travel to Lowcroft I need to leave it with more protection.

I look up at the sky. Once or twice I thought I saw Elding and Tora wheeling overhead but perhaps they were just ordinary crows. Or perhaps I dreamed the whole thing and I don't actually have my own corvine spies. However I don't sleep so that seems unlikely.

After some thought I dig through the toss pile and find a couple of bodies that are not decomposing *too* badly, an oafish fellow named Alfred and another, slightly old man named Morris. Morris' muscles are as big as his imagination was small. I consume his soul (which tastes like lemons and mediocrity), and raise him up as a wight.

I consume Alfred's soul likewise (as bland as unbuttered bread and stinking of ennui). I pause, then decide, on a whim, to fill Alfred's body with the soul of a goose. My eyes brighten. What will happen? I am not disappointed. It is glorious. The Alfred-goose's eyes snap open, angry and glowing red. He hisses vengefully and then throws back his head to honk into the heavens. I shake my head at the atrocious noise. It is impressive but will he obey me?

"Alfred?" I say. The Alfred-goose grunts and hisses, baring its teeth. I think he has heard me, even if he lacks the capacity to speak. A perfect arrangement. "Sit down, Alfred." The undead goose-man sits. "Get up." He stands. This will do nicely.

"This is Roland," I say, gesturing to Roland who is watching with rather wide eyes. "Protect Roland," I say to both the Alfred-goose and the wight-Morris. The wight grunts and the Alfred-goose honks obligingly. "Protect the village. Do as Roland says. Do not listen to the dead man in the well. Are we clear? Nod if you understand me." They both nod. I resist the urge to rub my hands together in glee.

"Thank you, Mistress," says Roland, and it is my turn to bob my head.

"I'll be back later," I say, and set off through the trees, feeling slightly more confident about leaving.

I break into a run, heading for Lowcroft, sprinting through the wet grasses as the wind chases the last whispers of the storm away. I must hurry. The night is elderly and grave-robbing in broad daylight is probably not the best idea. Someone is bound to object. I make a mental note to acquire a horse. There are none in the village but I'm sure someone in the surrounding area can be persuaded to part with one. If I ask nicely.

Even without a horse my strong legs make short work of the miles and I soon arrive on the outskirts of Lowcroft. The forest gives way to fields and then squat, ugly houses. It is a depressing place. I never visited if I could avoid it in life and now I am reminded why. Little Downing might be poor but we had the forest and all the beauty within. The poverty of Lowcroft is less aesthetically appealing.

I slink past the derelict houses and cottages, keeping to the deep shadows. A scrawny cat hisses at me from a rooftop, and a mangy dog runs yelping when it crosses my trail. The streets are badly maintained and lined with rubbish. None of the houses have window boxes, or even any flowers in the dust patches that seem to double as gardens. Nothing is grown that is not useful, and the wheat is seemingly snatched from the fields before it is ripe. The cows in the fields look thin and sickly, and I suspect that when the sun rises the people who appear will look the same.

But I am not here for the people of Lowcroft, I am here for their dead.

I steal a spade from an unlocked shed and make my way up to the parish church which sits atop a low hill above the village. The building is bare and unlit, there are no worshipers at this time of night. This makes things easy for me: I simply walk in. Looking at the poor state of the burial site I am pleased with my decision to leave my people in Downing. To be fair, the living of Lowcroft likely have more pressing matters to attend to than making their dead look pretty.

I pause, my foot hovering over the threshold that separates village and consecrated ground. Will I burst into flame as I step? Would it matter? No, I will just rise again.

I move forward and wait for the holy fire to purify me. Nothing happens. I am a little disappointed. Am I not evil incarnate? Grrr.

I roam between the ill-tended graves. Like most churches in the area this one is multi-denominational. I see headstones dedicated to the Green Lady, the Bright One, the Wave Walker, the Blind Queen and there, tucked in a far corner, as if to avoid contamination, a grave dedicated to the Whisperer. Perhaps this is why I can walk here, and my evilness is not in question.

The crumbling grave is as good a place as any to start my career as a grave-robber. I scrape a foot over bare soil. Weeds and wildflowers are choking the rest of the cemetery but nothing grows over this one. I bend down and read the inscription: *Here lies Arabella Tenenbaum, murderer most foul*. Well, rest in peace Arabella Tenenbaum, but were you buried in your jewels? A short, robust dig later I discover the answer is no. The corpse is naught but a lonely pile of bones, the vestiges of any earthly raiment long since fed to the worms, and nothing metal to speak of. What a pity.

The body is soulless. I know because I try to consume it. It has long since travelled to the land of the dead, or perhaps it is lost in the void. I fill in the hole, and move to the next grave. The grave of 'Mary Potts, loving wife and mother' yields a poor wedding band with a tiny garnet. 'Agnes Riley, death is sure' was buried with a string of citrines and a rose quartz bracelet. 'Marcus Tomlinson, always in our hearts' was laid to rest with an onyx marriage ring and very nice quartz cuffs.

Scratching through the graves is annoying, especially as half of them contain nothing more than rotting bones in various states of decay. After a frustrating hour or so I recruit 'Mavis Higginbottom, beloved and faithful grandmother' to help me toil. The soulless skeleton makes light work of the labour, despite her great age and seems content to do my bidding. Mavis and I have soon plundered our way through the entire graveyard, filling the graves in behind us and even doing a little light weeding. Maybe I will come back with some petunias in the spring.

As the first flush of dawn stains the eastern sky, we are putting the last of the soil back in place when we are startled by a descending flurry of black feathers.

"*Ka!*" Two crows land with a thud and a boom that should not be possible from two such small, lightweight bodies.

"We watch," says Elding, his voice too loud and too hollow for the peaceful quiet of this place. I glance anxiously at the sleeping village below. The inhabitants are just beginning to stir.

"We bring tidings," says Tora.

"Yes?" I ask, anxiety prickling my spine. "How fares my forest?"

"It fares," said Tora. "It is fair, and it is dying. But that is not why we are here. Ka!"

"Why are you here?" I ask, impatiently.

"Men come," says Elding.

"They are coming now," says Tora.

"Men on horseback are riding the western boundary. They carry shiny steel and their hearts are full of hatred."

"Shiny," says Elding.

Fear grips me.

"Fly," I say, to the crows. "Fly and warn Roland. And tell him I am coming as fast as I can."

I break into a run, clutching the pathetic bag of gems to my chest.

Chapter Eleven
Fresh Meat

Thundering down the hill and through the village of Lowcroft, my bony feet beating a frantic staccato on the main road. Behind me I hear slamming doors and cries of alarm but I pay them no heed. I doubt anyone could stop me even if they tried. Fear chases me down the valley. I rush over the bridge, not stopping to peer into the deep gorge that separates farmland from forest and moments later I am running through the trees as swift as a stag and as vengeful as a hollow wraith.

I am swifter now than when I first woke. The trees flash by, faster, faster. Perhaps the additional souls have made me stronger? Stronger and fleshier. It makes sense, as much as anything about my new life makes sense. But I am grateful. I am running so fast the grass and bushes whip at my legs, I am running so quickly the black blight of my trail is barely visible. Still, it is not enough. I cannot bear the thought of losing anyone else.

At last the trees are familiar. I am nearly home. I do not slow but I do get out my axe, hefting the shaft in readiness. The blood rage rises before my eyes like a red haze. I will drown in it and take them all with me. Perhaps I have been going about this wrong. If my neighbours persist in bothering me and mine, perhaps I need to take steps to ensure there *are* no neighbours. How long will it take me to depopulate every surrounding village? Will they force me to bathe in their blood? Probably it would not take that long, but it is still time away from my crafting which I resent.

I snarl in frustration and keep running.

As I pound through the last grove of trees I lift my war-axe over my head. I can hear shrieks and blood-curdling screams issuing from within the ruins. I see a glint of armour flashing between the boughs. I growl, low and feral, bursting through the undergrowth to emerge in the village square.

I skid to a halt.

A scene of carnage lies before me. The armoured men are in the process of being torn apart by the wights, the goose-man and the incredibly distraught flock of draugr geese. I lower my axe, my mouth falling open. A riderless horse runs neighing past me, its bridle flapping in the bright sunlight. Various blood smeared bodies lie sprawled in the mud. Only two intruders remain upright, and not, it seems for long.

A white-plumed knight sprints across the square, his eyes wild and his arms pinwheeling desperately. Three geese leap on his back and he crashes to the ground with a cry. The knight rolls, attempting to fend them off with his gauntlets. One undead goose is knocked back but it immediately returns attacking with renewed wrath. It throws back its head, revealing a protruding black tongue complete with bitter-sharp serrated teeth. The goose bites down, and receives a mouthful or armour but moments later discovers the tender pink flesh of his face. The knight screams as the flock of geese peck out his eyes, hissing and honking, fighting amongst themselves as they do it. Blood pours down his face and he lets out one last frenzied gasp as they dig through his eye to the meat of his brain.

Only one knight remains alive now. I can see why he is the last. His swordwork is excellent, although he likely has never practised against a flock of undead geese. He stands at the epicentre of a small circle of carnage. The Morris-wight lies in pieces at his feet, as well as various scattered goose parts. He has defended himself well but Alfred is giving him trouble.

It is interesting to watch the man with the soul of a goose fight. The instincts seem to be at war. The resulting creature is at once very bad tempered and harbours an extreme disregard for his own safety. No human would fight thus. As I watch, Alfred tries to bite the knight, hissing as his teeth snap over cold metal. The knight slashes him with his sword, managing to knock Alfred back with his shield. I walk over to get a better view of the fight. Catching sight of me out of the corner of his eye, the knight lets out a startled gasp. His moment of inattention is his undoing.

I smile encouragingly as Alfred rushes him, knocking the knight clear off his feet. He falls with an almighty clatter. The knight scrambles to regain his footing but his armour weighs him down and he is swarmed under by the rest of the flock. It does not take him long to die. His dying screams echo off the treetops.

"Well done, everyone," I murmur, clapping my hands.

"Bravo!" shouts Roland from across the way.

The geese wander back to their regular haunts, their beaks stained red. I reach up to pat Alfred's head and he hisses spitefully and shows me the wound on his arm.

"Can I sew it up for you, dear one?" He honks in my face and I retract my hand. He then ambles off to attack an offending bush, still clutching his arm. Alfred is not the only one sporting a nasty wound. One goose has a wing that has been half hacked off and it is dragging in the mud. I wonder if they will permit me to sew them up? I shake my head. I will come back to tend to them in a moment. At least I don't have to worry about them bleeding out.

I head over to Roland who is waving cheerfully from the freshly created graveyard.

"All finished, Mistress!" he beams, gesturing with his arms. He does not seem particularly perturbed by the pitched battle that had ended moments before. In fact, I suspect he had never stopped digging.

"Excellent," I say, looking around. "Very good. This will do nicely."

"What next ma'am?"

"Place the villagers in the graves," I say, "but do not to fill them in. I will need to make appropriate markers."

He nods and lumbers off to the toss shed.

I walk over to inspect the slain knights. There are five, each one lying where he fell. They are well equipped, and their armour is almost as fine as my own. I lean closer. The heraldry is familiar. A pennant lies in the mud where it was dropped. The standard is a unicorn and a yew tree, white on black, and it is repeated on the knights' shields. These are Baron Downing's men.

This does not bode well.

Why are they here? Their like are seldom seen around the villages, let alone the forest. The Baron prefers to keep to noble society only. Why are his knights suddenly interested in peasant affairs? Am I not to be allowed the intimacy of a private feud with my neighbours without the aristocracy butting in? I have never met or seen the Baron, but I dislike him on principle. Technically I am a subject. I suppose. But any tax collector that comes calling better be prepared to go home in a box. However, I realise I am being impractical. Speculation will get me nowhere. I can raise one of the knights and get the answers directly.

"*Resurgemus iterum*," I whisper, and the nearest knight rises, his body jerking and shaking. He sits up with a clank, and turns to me, one ruined eye streaming goo. He screams. I wonder if death has scrambled his brain. Perhaps it is better to let them rest for a while before calling them back.

"Calm down," I say, "you can go back to being dead in a minute."

The knight screams again. His hair is curling and blond, and his eyes are a fetching blue but his voice is like a cheese grater on my recently fleshed ears. Whisperman help me. "I SAID CALM DOWN." He quiets, solitary eye bulging.

"That's better," I say. "Would you mind telling me why you and your friends are here?"

"Evil!" he shrieks, and then he starts shrieking again. My goodness. "Evil in the forest! We..." his voice trails off at the sight of a draugr goose and he makes a rattling noise in his chest, the whites of his eyes showing. How tiresome. I move in front of him, cutting off his view of the goose.

"Why did you come?" I ask. "Focus. Why are you here? I have done nothing to you. Or to anyone."

"Tales of...people going missing," he blubbers. "The Baron sent us to investigate! A cannibal witch! We were sent to investiga-"

"Decipula alma," I whisper, cutting him off.

His soul streams into my body, and he flops to the ground with a wet splat and a clank. It tastes like figs and discipline with just a hint of despair. Hmm. Maybe they have a point about the cannibal witch. But if the Baron has heard of me... if the Baron is sending men here...this is not good. I need to up my game. I need to expand my plans. When this group does not return it will be fairly obvious what happened. I tap my cheek thoughtfully. I have ideas but I need every soul and every crystal I can gather. There is no time to waste!

I step lightly to the altar. The pathetic haul of soul crystals should be charged by now. At least, I hope they are charged. I lean over and pry the stones from the dried mud. They hum with power as they lie flat on my hand. Excellent! Another crafting project to add to the list: I must make a beautiful box lined with velvet with separate compartments for each gem. Oh! I could have little drawers for the different types of souls. Family in this one, animal souls in this one, useful people in the next and so on.

I sigh.

Like so much else it will have to wait, but at least I know I can make new crystals! Walking to the well to fetch a pail of water, I attach the bucket to the rope and let it go spinning down into the darkness. It lands on the necromancer's head with a dull thud.

"Excuse me!" I yell, grinning down at him. I wave. The necromancer bubbles up at me, his sagging eyes dark with rage. It looks like his lips are disintegrating. This can only be an improvement.

Cranking up the bucket full of water, I carry it to the altar and bend down to scoop up some earth, growling under my breath. Mud seems such a ridiculous tool to work dark magics with. So...mundane. I really would like some paint. Actually! I turn with a skip. There is some blood handy! Much more appropriate! I use the water instead to wash the mud off the altar. Then I walk over to the fresh crafting pile.

"When I'm done, Roland," I yell, "put these on the keep pile, please!"

"Yes, ma'am," he calls.

It is easy to slit a couple of veins on the juiciest of the knights. Their blood is still fresh and flowing. I carry their blood in the pail and use it to paint the sigil anew, using my fingertips to make the marks (making a mental note to acquire or make some paintbrushes). I settle the gems at the intersecting points.

I step back, pleased, and glance up at the sun. It is midmorning. I still have time to do everything I wish to accomplish before the sun sets tonight. First I will test the new soul gems. I quickly discover a minor setback—they *are* charged but they do not seem to have the capacity to contain a human soul. Perhaps it is the size of the gems? Or the fact that they are such poor specimens, the sad rocks of my poverty-stricken neighbours? Or the mud? Or something to do with the time of day? It could be so many things, I must experiment so I understand the variables. I will figure it all out.

They *do* work though as soul containers though. I manage to trap the soul of an ageing oak, and a few flowers, then the souls of the knight's dead horses, of which there are three. Before I forget to do it I also raise a couple more wight-humans to aid in the defence of the village. Then I raise one of the horses as a draugr, to ride later. I chose the all black mare, because I will look nice when I ride her. Her coat is shiny and her eyes gleam a vengeful blue, just like mine. I name her Dark Star. I always wanted a pony.

I leave Star tethered to a fence post and go to fetch my sewing kit.

With a little coaxing the draugr geese and Alfred let me sew them back together. It doesn't take too long and they shamble off looking nicely patched. That stitching should hold for a while. The wight geese do not let me fix them up. No surprises there. I will need to increase the flock size if they cannot be patched. I do like the way they fight, it is a balm to my soul. Wherever it is.

Roland has finished with the graves so I instruct him to start building a defensive wall some distance into the forest. This will take a long time but I think it will be a good investment of time. The wights can assist. To my delight, Roland informs me that he has some building experience and sets to work right away. He seems quite pleased with this task and I am interested to see what he comes up with. I cast my eyes around the village ruin. Despite the dearth of the living it seems to have a surprising amount of activity. It is not unpleasant.

I return to my cottage.

After a little thought I decide that carrying my ever-increasing gems collection around is impractical. I pocket a few and hide the rest in a safe place (in the base of the dusty tea jar). Jenkins comes in from the garden and I scratch his ears a bit. I stand in the kitchen and consider. Things are going well but I can't shake the feeling that I have forgotten something. Try as I might, I can't think what it is.

Chapter Twelve
YOUR GEMS OR YOUR LIFE

The Baron's knights have given me an idea. I have had enough of robbing graves, at least for now. Instead I will try robbing the living. I have a new pony and I want to ride her somewhere. Dressing up would be nice as well. I have had a look at my face in my mirror and feel that I could, at a pinch, pass as human. At night. If you ignore the glowing blue eyes.

Anyway, I ransack the remains of the village for appropriate clothing in shades of black. Not finding everything I want I make a quick trip to the far southern border where I know there is a bandit camp.

I peer at them through the laurel leaves—seven men huddled around a miserable campfire. They are a pathetic bunch, less romantic highwaymen and more desperate beggars fleeing the shackles (and safety) of civilisation. It will be a mercy to put them out of their misery. I do it quickly, leaving the bodies where they fall. I will send Roland to tidy up later. Fresh crafting supplies will come in handy as well. I noticed Roland's ears are looking a little decrepit, he will need an upgrade soon.

Despite the rather poor state of the bandit's equipment, I still manage to put together an outfit I deem suitable. One of them had a good hat, and another a decent quality rapier. I've never used a rapier but how hard can it be? You put the pointy end in people and watch them bleed. Easy.

I set off, riding Star. As I suspected, having a mount is very nice. We canter through the forest chasing the dappled patches of leaf-green shade. My new pony is fast and savage and I love her. I think we are travelling faster than a normal horse can gallop, but I'm not completely sure. I have never ridden a horse before, let alone an undead one.

My cloak flares out behind me dramatically as we go, and I hold one hand to my head, to keep the wide brimmed hat from falling off. My hands are gloved in black, and I have exchanged my armour for black leather, and a wide, puffy-sleeved black shirt. To complete my disguise, I have tied a black band around my eyes. Hopefully the twin sapphire flames of my eyes are dimmed enough not to be visible.

I think I make a more than passable highwayman. Highwaywoman. Dashing, even, like the ones from my racy novels, the ones I used to keep under the bed. I let out a snarl that startles Star. Those books are gone, like most else I kept in my bedroom. Burned away into nothing. Another loss I wish I could carve out of someone's flesh.

Star's hoofbeats thud over moss and peat and in no time at all we reach our destination: the great road on the northernmost boundary. This road links Downing to the rest of the Kingdom in the south, a glorified track that winds its way beneath the boughs to the bridge at Lowcroft, beaten earth hollowed out and worn by the passage of centuries.

Beyond the bridge the land is 'civilised'. Towns and villages are plentiful, and travellers pass through orchards and fields. The pass through Downing Forest is not a popular route. Most travellers prefer the longer but less desolate track that runs alongside the river. The Lowcroft bridge marks one forest boundary, the road another. I consider everything to the side of them to be mine, but I think I will be expanding my borders soon.

I smile. Downing Forest always had a reputation, even before I claimed it for my own. Wolves stalk the snow-covered weald in the winter, and sometimes in the warmer months too. It is easy to get lost here. There are occasionally bandits, and children who go wandering are seldom found alive. And of course, to the far north there is the delight of Dunbarra Keep.

Because of all of this, the travellers who *do* brave the road tended to be wealthy; wealthy, fast and escorted. Or government officials. Sometimes they are all of the above. Either way I am cautiously optimistic that I can catch someone with good taste in jewellery. I don't want to create too much of a stir, so I will resist the urge to kill them all. But really, I just feel like an adventure that doesn't involve blood, at least until later this afternoon.

Beautifully dressed, with my stolen rapier at my side, I await my prey with the nervous eagerness of a girl awaiting her love. I pat Dark Star, as I watch, and the undead mare nickers loud enough to rattle my bones.

We are in luck.

The rattle of wheels heralds the appearance of a carriage. I see it! Large, painted dark blue, and emblazoned with a hummingbird and a bell! I straighten in my saddle. It looks expensive and I can practically smell the perfume coming off the snot-nosed escort riding alongside. He is very fancy in his red-velvet coat and powdered wig. The Baron must be expecting visitors.

I leap off Dark Star and sprint through the trees, light footed and fleet. I run until I find a curve in the road, nip over to a giant pine and give it a push. The mammoth trunk slams across the highway with a crash. The way is definitely blocked. As the carriage rounds the bend in the road I jump on top of it, strike a pose and brandish my rapier skyward.

"Stand and deliver!" I cry, in a gruff voice. I do my best to lower my vocal range to that of a man. It is surprisingly easy since my voice is so much deeper now. Either way, I make an impression. The horses are reigned into a gut-wrenching stop. I wince, the driver really should have more care for the poor beast's mouths.

"Out of the way, cur!" he shouts. I already regret my decision to make this a bloodless excursion.

Meanwhile the fancy escort in his red coat lifts a crossbow and fires at me. I know a moment's unease but then the quarrel goes straight through my middle, puncturing the black leather and silk of my shirt and travelling directly out the other side. Sometimes not possessing internal organs is a real boon, although occasionally I do miss my pituitary gland.

I grin. The escort stares, the colour draining from his face. The driver makes a strangled noise like a drowning goat. No, no! Like a drowning ass!

"*I said stand and deliver!*" I shout, waving my rapier.

"*What is going on out there!*" comes a bad tempered, but decidedly feminine voice from within the carriage. "Why have we stopped?"

"Nothing, madame!" I yell, playfully. "Nothing to worry about!"

The escort is loading another bolt with shaking hands. In two steps I bound over the trunk and knock him off his horse. I land a blow on his head with the butt of my rapier, carefully moderating the amount of force I use but still managing to punch him unconscious. Whoops. I bend to check, but yes, he is still breathing. More importantly, the crossbow is out of action. I slap the escort's horse on the rump. It whinnies and charges off into the trees.

I turn my attention to the driver who is huddled on top of the roof, quivering like a fat, pudgy brown leaf. He does not look like he will be a problem. He does have a nice hat though. I divest him of it without too much trouble. Turning, I advance on the carriage which has suddenly gone very quiet. Presumably the incumbents are peeking through the windows.

Ripping the door off its hinges, I toss it aside revealing a motley, and rather hysterical bunch of nobles, and one dour maidservant. The aristocrats all utter high-pitched shrieks as the sunlight floods the interior. What fun. It is like turning over a soggy log and watching the beetles and slugs panic in the fresh air.

"Henry, are you just going to sit there!" squeals a richly dressed woman. Henry does indeed just sit there. I eye the woman. She is young, and beautifully attired in a lavender travelling gown with hand done silk twist embroidery that makes me quite wild with envy. An eight-piece bodice, smocking on the sleeves...I shake my head. Focus. I am not here for her dress. I waver, contemplating. *No!* Gems, I'm here for gems! I level my rapier at her throat, where hangs a rather nice-looking quartz crystal pendant.

"Your jewellery, madame," I say, with utmost politeness. I try not to let my eyes slip to the lace edging at her neckline. She probably thinks I'm ogling her cleavage which is also very nice but not as interesting as the embroidery. Henry moves to draw a weapon and I swing the rapier across to him. "Uh, uh, uh," I say. "Don't do anything stupid, now Henry, dearest." I wave my rapier to include the whole carriage. "Hand over your valuables and we can all get on with our lives, easy as pie."

The carriage erupts in a fountain of well-bred hysteria and it takes all of my undead self-control not to knock them all senseless and rip the souls from their still warm bodies. Such drama! Clearly these people are not used to having pointy objects thrust at them in close proximity.

I make an example of Lord Henry's face and hand round the coach-man's hat. Reluctantly they place their jewels and purses in it. They are not wearing much, which makes sense as they are travelling but I have high hopes for the strong box that is hidden under the seat. Henry is only too happy to give up the key.

I leap out of the carriage, clutching the box, landing on the road with a thump.

"Thank you," I say, "it has not been a pleasure."

I wave to the coachman and step over the unconscious escort. Hoisting the box over my shoulder, my pockets jingle, so stuffed full of gold are they. I walk into the woods without a backward glance. Behind me I can hear the lady wailing and it takes all my willpower not to turn back and run her through with my rapier, just to get some peace and quiet. Hopefully they will run to the Barony with tales of banditry, rather than dark sorcery. I doubt anyone will believe the escort if he tells them he shot the highwayman clean through the middle. I finger the hole in my silk shirt. Everyone knows the peasantry is superstitious. I should know, I am one myself.

The sounds of noble distress soon fade into the background noise of the forest as I walk back to Dark Star. Leading my mare a way off the road, I tie her to a tree while I inspect my haul. It is decent. Far superior to my pickings from the graveyard at Lowcroft. There are a few nice gems, notably a ruby the size of a sparrow's egg. A few pieces look good but are well made costume fakes. I make to toss those into the undergrowth and then think better of it. The magpies might enjoy them.

I tap my foot on the earth, thinking. The lady is trying to appear wealthier than she actually is. Who is she trying to impress? The

Baron? How salacious! If I have time later I will have to tell my mother. She always did enjoy gossiping about the nobles and she would love to hear about this.

The strong box holds a couple more treasures—a small diamond ring and what I think is a sapphire attached to an ivory brooch. Someone is going to be very angry about this robbery. I wrench the good gems and crystals out of their settings, wrap them in cloth and pocket them. The gold and silver I hide in a hollowed-out oak to fetch later. I can use it to buy ...more gems. Or some satin thread. Or some black lace. Hmmm.

All in all, a good day. These gems should be enough to power more than a few souls. However, they are not a long-term solution. I might get away with highway robbery every now and then but if I become too much of a menace I will attract attention, and my supply of gullible, flashy nobles will dry up. I was lucky today. Not all travellers would have such rich accessories. It will not do.

I could, perhaps, rob some jewellers? Although a career in crime is not quite what I had in mind, not to mention the villages and towns surrounding Downing are all poor, rural communities. I would have to travel quite a distance to get to a place worth robbing. There is an ancient barrow to the east that might be worth a visit, who knows what ancient treasures lie there. Oh! The Baron has a crypt beneath his castle, I'm sure of it. I believe the aristocracy like to be buried with their baubles. But what was the necromancer planning on doing? I can't imagine robbery was part of his grand plan for world domination. I should return to the tower at Dunbarra Keep and see if I can find any clues.

But first, I want to go shopping, and maybe, I should visit the Baron.

Chapter Thirteen
Resting Lich Face

Since I have come this far, I might as well go a little farther. I would like to take a closer look at the Baron's castle and I am so beautifully dressed it seems a shame to waste the outfit.

Dark Star and I detour around the fallen trunk. We ride just out of sight of the road and keep to the deep shade of the forest. I can hear the hysterical nobles attempting to move the tree, but it sounds like there is a lot of talk and not much action. Once we are safely clear, we rejoin the road and canter towards Great Downing. From here it is a relatively short trip.

I bring Dark Star to a halt as the fortified town comes into view between the trees. Suddenly I am nervous. There are so many buildings, so many people. From the rise it looks like an anthill, full of boiling, stupid ants. I look down at my gaunt body. Can I truly pass as a human? It will be fine as long as I am well covered. I just look thin. I will blend in with the other starving peasants just fine. Keeping a low profile, not starting any trouble; that is the key.

I tie Star to a tree because I do not think the general population is quite ready for a pony with glowing eyes. Thinking of this, I make sure my own eyes are properly covered, adjusting the band with my fingers. My rapier I will leave also. I have a small dagger at my side, but it is discreet, the kind people use to cut their meat. The highwayman's hat I switch for the coachman's.

I am ready.

Stroking Dark Star's nose, I whisper that I will be back soon. On the walk through the meadow my shoulder blades twitch. I feel so exposed. The forest ends in an abrupt line and then all the way to the walls is farmland and sad little houses. The town itself is protected by a stout, battlemented wall. The Baron's castle rises in the centre, overlooking the rest like a squat, ugly vulture. It is not an elegant structure, and lacks the romance of Dunbarra Keep, but it certainly looks defensible.

The wind is chilly. Autumn is drawing on and most of the fields lie fallow, awaiting the winter snows. Smoke rises from a hundred chimneys. It hangs over the town like a reeking shadow. Already I can already smell the stench of human misery. Surely it is not healthy to be piled on top of each other like pigs in mud? My unease intensifies as I approach the town gate and join the throng of humanity as it surges through forward. I keep my head down but the guard on duty is half asleep and doesn't even glance my way. There are no cries of alarm, and no one stops me passing beneath the portcullis.

Once inside my senses are assaulted by a cacophony of noises and smells. There are people and animals everywhere: shouting and calling, cooking, shopping, shoving and fighting. I am momentarily overwhelmed, and step back into the shadow of the wall to calm myself. I sort through the sensations one by one. Nothing is a threat, it is just...loud and busy. The only thing that is vaguely ominous is the rotting body swinging from a gibbet on one of the battlements, but I am not here to judge the Baron's choice in wall ornaments.

A little hesitantly I step into the melee.

To one side of the square a blacksmith's forge belches smoke and heat. On the other side there are various stalls selling food and spiced wine. The scents mingle with other, less salubrious smells from drains and gutters. The town has a veneer of energy that disguises a thick layer of muck and deprivation, well hidden beneath the bright bustle. The rats that scurry in the alleys are bone thin. Scrawny beggars cluster around the blacksmith, leaning as close as they can to the warmth of the forge fires. A few underfed prostitutes linger around the gates, many of them looking bruised and ill. Under the castle wall are rows of occupied stocks. Some of the peasants stop to lob rotting fruit and vegetables at the sad criminals contained within, but most are half-hearted about it.

I turn away, looking for the shops I need. There is a list of items I would like to purchase: a trebuchet, some more geese, some paint...My palms tingle. What is that! Sandwiched between a chandlery and a bakers is a haberdashery. I rush over and press my face against the bulbous glass. Within I can see bolts of fabric lining deep shelves, ribbons fluttering from the rafters and rows upon rows of thread and buttons.

I push the door open immediately and go in. A little bell tinkles my arrival. I stand stock still, my eyes greedily taking in the shop's contents. It smells wonderful. The neat bolts of material are piled from floor to ceiling. There is one shelf just of velvet! All different shades of velvet! There is another of linen, another of hessian and another of silk and one of cotton. All of it fresh and new. It is too much.

"Can I help you...er...madame?" the shopkeeper asks. A rotund little woman of middle years, she casts her eye over me and clearly can't decide where to place me. Good. At least she is polite.

"Eight ells of the black velvet," I say, rapidly. "Four of the green, one of the blue and six of the hessian. Oh, and an ell of the silk."

"The silk is dear, ma'am," she says.

"It's not a problem."

Her eyes widen and she scurries off to fetch her scissors. I settle myself into the corner farthest from the candlelight to wait. There are several other customers in the shop and it is impossible not to overhear their conversation. In one corner a pair of ladies are discussing their handsome widowed neighbour. I start to listen but then my ears pick out a familiar name.

"Have you heard the news!" an elderly, well-dressed woman is saying. "There was a massacre at Lowcroft!"

"What?" I speak without realising, but I am perturbed. "A massacre?" Who is daring to murder people so close to my home? Lowcroft is practically on my doorstep.

The old woman swings towards me, her eyes alight. She is obviously revelling in the drama of her tale.

"Some say *dark magic!* I heard it from my darling Betty's best friend's mother who has a nephew who keeps a farm out that way. I don't know what the world's coming to, I really don't."

"Mother!" says a young woman, over by the till. "Stop being such a terrible gossip! You are only going to upset everyone, telling such tales!"

"But it's true," says another customer. "I heard it too."

"*I* heard it was a wight," says the shopkeeper, snipping away, her eyes wide. "A horror!"

"A wight!" gasps the other.

"Yeeeees," says the old woman gleefully. "A skeleton right out of the Whisperman's lands!"

"Oh," I say, tapping a finger against the counter in agitation. Right. I left an unattended wight in the graveyard at Lowcroft. Mavis somebody. The skeleton I raised to help me rob the graves. How unfortunate. "Were there... any survivors?"

"Not many," says the old woman, with relish. "The baron will have to do something. We will all be slaughtered in our beds! The church is mobilising their clerics."

"That's enough, mother," snaps the young woman. "I told you to stop gossiping!"

The younger woman herds her mother out of the shop and they disappear into the square, still squabbling.

Oh dear.

Well, anyone reasonable could see it was an honest mistake. Tap, tap, tap, go my fingers on the counter. Acquiring a trebuchet is probably a little more urgent than I thought. I wonder how Roland is coming along with the walls?

The shopkeeper has finished wrapping my materials in neat bundles. It is more than I had realised. It will be awkward to carry.

"That will be eighteen shillings for the velvet and the hessian," she says, "and ten for the silk."

I pass her the money in one gloved hand. She takes it, looks up at me and the smile falls off her face. I try not to panic. What does she see? I bare my teeth at her in an attempt to look friendly and she lets out a small scream. Drat. Thinking quickly, I slide a gold piece out of my purse and place it on the counter. I adjust the band around my eyes. There. Everything is fine.

"Do you know the hollow oak by the bridge to Lowcroft?" I say, quickly, before she can scream again. Talking is fine. Talking is a human activity and it will soothe her. I hope. "There is a wide, flat stone there?"

"I know it," she squeaks. Good. Her eyes are on the gold. The other customers are looking at us curiously but do not seem disturbed.

"I prefer to shop...remotely," I say. "Now that I have seen your wares I hope we can come to an arrangement?" Her eyes widen, as if she is expecting me to demand the blood of her firstborn. "I will send you payment, and instructions. I will pay extra for delivery?"

She nods, uncertain. I slide another gold piece across the counter to sweeten the deal, and she picks it up before she can help herself.

"I can send someone," she says.

"Good," I say and turn to leave.

"Wait!" the shopkeeper cries, and I stiffen in the doorway. What now? "What shall I know you by?"

"Oh. Hmm. The notes will be signed, the Lady of Downing Forest."

I sweep out of the shop, and back into the stifling crowd.

I am ready to go home now but I have nothing on my list. Time to focus. Moving with haste I find a man who sells chickens and geese, and barter with him for some of each. I pay an outrageous price but I will have delivery, and honestly, I do not care anymore. It is not my gold anyway. Siege weapons I am unlikely to find in the marketplace. Turning I gaze up at the forbidding structure of the castle walls. From this perspective they look very intimidating, for a pile of stone.

"You!" A strident voice interrupts my thoughts. "You! *Yes, you!* You in black! I see you! Skulking in the shadows like a spider. That's an impressive bitch face if ever I saw one!"

I turn in confusion.

Is someone addressing me?

My eyes land on an old woman, who is glaring at me from within the stocks. The wood holds her bent double, and her hands are clamped at either side. She is filthy. Maggots run over her hair, which hangs over her face in grey strings. The boards around her are splattered with rotten eggs and old tomatoes. She twists her stained face and leers up at me.

"Come to laugh, have ye?" she says. She spits. "Get in line. A pox on the whole kingdom, I say."

"What did you do?" I ask, mildly curious. I like her spirit.

"What did *I* do?" she yowls. "I'll tell you what I did! I got old! I got ugly! I live alone and my neighbours have their thieving, foul smelling eyes on my silver teapot! THAT'S RIGHT, I KNOW WHAT THEY'RE AFTER, THE STINKING BASTARDS!" A woman who had come to stand next to me, takes to her heels, darting frightened looks over her shoulder. "That's right, run you manky tart," says the old woman with some satisfaction. "Ignorant fools, the lot of them." She lowers her voice, her eyes meeting mine, suddenly serious. "If you must know I cast a hex on my neighbour's manhood, to make it drop off."

"A witch?" I ask with a slight question. I am intrigued. What magic does she possess?

"Takes one to know one," she says, shaking her head. "The Baron doesn't like witches."

"I know *that*," I say. "But did it?"

"Did it what?"

"Did his...you know," I gesture, embarrassed. "Did it fall off?"

She gives a short, sharp bark of laughter. "It did not. If I had that kind of power, do you think I would be here? Like this? Pah."

"True," I say.

A passing teenager picks up a handful of muck, and lobs it at her. It hits her on the side of the cheek, and falls away, leaving a crimson cut where a rock was mixed in with the earth.

"I know you, Billy Culpepper," she says, her voice suddenly very low. "And I won't be in these stocks forever." The young man goes pale, and runs away. "That's right!" she screams after him. Run, you cur!"

Her eyes, white as milk, snap back to me. "What are you doing here, then? This place ain't safe for the likes of us. Not anymore. The old Baron, he saw the value in having a few wise men and women around. This one. He sees things differently." She points her chin at the gibbet, where the blackened body twists in the wind. "As *she* found out."

"I'll be fine," I say, with a smile. "I'm not a witch."

I turn and walk away, passing through the crowd towards the castle gate.

"I KNOWS ONE WHEN I SEES ONE," bellows the old woman behind me. The sound of her heckling the crowd slowly fades into the distance, and I mentally wish her well. I could have freed her I suppose but then what? I have enough pets and there is shopping to do.

The crowds are already thinning and the chill of evening is settling into my bones. However, as I walk past an alley I see Billy Culpepper teasing a stray dog. I pause. Then I make a quick side trip to consume his soul, leaving his body lying behind a barrel. It tastes like petty cruelty and avarice. No doubt someone will find it later.

I pass through the castle gate. This gate is slightly better guarded, but I am still allowed through without comment. Inside I can see where the money is being spent. Everything is well maintained and flags and pennants flutter from the squat spires. The tramp of armed men training fills the yard. They are all well-fed and well outfitted. The Baron's castle itself is impressive—ugly, but sound. I stare at it for a while, admiring the thick walls, the portcullis gate, the four strong towers and the well defended courtyard. It would not be an easy nut to crack. The whole thing is surrounded by a pea-green moat. It is wasted on the Baron.

There are men patrolling the walls but they do not seem particularly vigilant. I mean, who would they be expecting? The kingdom is at peace, the peasants are nicely ground underfoot. On the other hand, they have barrels of pitch, and an elevated position. And what's that? My fingers twitch in excitement. They have three ballistae lining the walls.

As I take note of the weak spots I hear a clatter and a rattle behind me. I leap aside as a dark blue carriage flies over the drawbridge and into the inner courtyard. It grinds to a halt at the grand entrance and angry nobles spill out before the footmen can emerge to open the doors. I hear the dulcet tones of the lady with the lovely lavender dress. Ah, my friends from the forest have arrived.

I duck away, grinning and head towards the outbuildings that I surmise house the weaponry. I do not want to risk being recognised, after all. I walk along the rows of workshops tucked under the castle walls. A fletcher is at work in one of them and I sidle up to him.

"*Hello,*" I say, trying to appear unintimidating. "I'm looking for the weaponsmith?" The man blinks owlishly at me as I search for the word. "The...engineer?" I am beginning to lose my patience. I have been so patient today. "Who makes these?" I say, gesturing at the ballista. "*Where is the man who makes these?*"

Understanding dawns in the dimwit's eyes.

"Oh, you want Thomlinson," he says. "Um...ma'am," his eyes travel up my body and I see the confusion on his face. "Two doors down."

He carries on with his feathers. I walk along the row, stepping eagerly. Two doors down is an enclosed workshop with a stout wooden door. Rapping my knuckles on it, I wait, tapping my foot. After a few moments a tousle-haired, freckle-faced man of about thirty pulls it open. He looks down at me in confusion.

"Thomlinson?" I ask.

"Yes?" he says, confusion writ plain on his face.

"You know how to operate siege weapons?" I say, pointing, to make sure there are no misunderstandings.

"Yes?" he says. "Who are-"

"You know how to *build* siege weapons?"

"Yes," he says, his eyes narrowing. "Who did you say you are aga-"

"Trebuchets as well as ballistae?"

"Yes?"

"Good!" I say. "I can tick that off my list then."

"I'm sorry, I don't-"

I slit his throat with my dagger before he can finish the sentence, and catch his body before it slumps to the ground. I hope Roland will like him.

Chapter Fourteen
Dark Forest Theory

I contemplate the best way to get my latest acquisition home. I could awaken Thomlinson here in the castle workshop, and we could walk out together? But waking immediately will no doubt cause some rather noisy distress, not to mention the siege engineer now has an inconveniently large and gaping wound in his neck. I should not have been so enthusiastic.

Looking down at the dead man slumped over my arm, I sigh. He is bleeding all over my fancy blouse. Setting him down on the ground I go searching for something to bind the wound. Fortunately, it is the end of the day and there are not many people around. In the next workshop I find some sack cloth, some rope and an unattended wheelbarrow. I steal the lot.

Back with Thomlinson, I wind cloth around his neck and dump him into the barrow. His arms and legs are so long and gangly they stick out. It takes me a few tries to fit everything in nicely without anything popping out. At last I manage it by folding his head forwards to rest between his hunched up knees, and his feet wedged in the corner. Minion thusly contained, I cover him up with more sacking, tucking it in on the corners.

I step back to admire my handiwork. There. No one will even notice just another peasant with a cart. Making sure my own eyes are properly covered and that my hat is in place, I push the wheelbarrow across the castle courtyard and out of the gate. I nod jauntily at one of the guards as I go. He narrows his eyes at me but the sun is dipping towards the horizon and I can tell his mind is on the end of his shift. Or perhaps he is just of a vapid persuasion, but I care not. It is not *my* castle.

I pass through the thinning crowds of shoppers and merchants, past the market square with the gibbet, past the rows of shops and the haberdashery and out to the main gate. I wave at the witch in the stocks, but her eyes are on the muck stained cobbles and she does not see me.

A bell clangs in the distance, and I jump before remembering Greater Downing has a large church of its own. A pity I didn't get a chance to admire the bone garden. However, I am eager to be home and I push my barrow over to join the throng of peasants leaving through the gate. I keep jumping as people jostle me. The crowd makes me very nervous. I snarl at a man who elbows me in the face, and he looks down at me with an expression of abject terror. With some difficulty I manage to control myself, but I am very happy to be going. The shops were nice but now I crave the serenity of my dark forest home.

Striding through the fallow fields, the wheel of the barrow squeaking faintly and scrapes against the dirt. People drift away from the main thoroughfare, disappearing into the sparse comfort of their hovels. Soon I am alone in the gloaming. A weight lifts from my shoulders as I arrive beneath the shady boughs. The tension leaves me at once and Dark Star nickers in greeting. I cheerfully tie Thomlinson's body across her haunches, abandoning the wheelbarrow in the glade and we are soon cantering home through the deepening twilight.

The road is soon dappled by starlight that filters through the canopy. I meet no other travellers and Dark Star's hooves eat up the miles. My mind is full of all the projects I have planned. I twist around and pat Thomlinson's dead shoulder. I am *very* excited by the thought of a trebuchet. When I was a little girl I used to make villages and castles out of mud, and catapults out of twigs and string. Playing with the real sized things will be much more exciting.

Instead of going straight home I made a detour to the Lowcroft bridge, stopping before the large flat rock to see if my purchases have been delivered. To my delight they have been. They must have sent out wagons directly to make it here in time. But then, for the price I paid it is only to be expected. This is an excellent arrangement. I gloat over my packages of material, and the geese who are resting inside a loose wicker cage. Yes, it will do nicely, assuming thieves do not help themselves to my goods. They would only do it once, of course.

I wonder what payment Elding and Tora will require to deliver messages to the merchants at Greater Downing? Hopefully they will be willing because I doubt I could train the draugr geese to do such a thing. Juggling all my new acquisitions, Star and I make our way back to Little Downing, this time moving at a walk so as not to drop anything.

We arrive with the shadows of full night.

Before we reach the ruins our way is blocked by a brand-new drystone wall. It stretches through the glades in either direction, curving away into the dense foliage. Roland has been busy! I am pleased. Dismounting I go closer to take a better look.

The wall is thick, at least five feet wide and as tall as my shoulders. Which if I am being completely honest, isn't very tall. There is definitely room for improvement but I must have patience. A mosaic and some moss would also improve the aesthetic quality. Hmm and maybe some little wallflowers tucked between the slabs. That probably wouldn't lend much to the defensive element, however, so I will bide my time. My eyes glide over the stone. Teeth would make a lovely pattern, and possibly some of the smaller bones. I could make a beautiful entrance gate lined with skulls and daisies. But yes, yes the hard packed limestone wall is solid, and tall enough to make a decent impediment to a man on horseback. Which is the point.

Roland appears, and hobbles over, looking a bit dusty and anxious.

"It's very nice," I say, and he relaxes. "Good job. Where did you get the stone?"

"The ruined houses," he says. "And when we had used all of that I got some of the wights to start a quarry over by the crags."

"Very industrious," I say, approvingly. I turn back to the wall with a critical eye. "Very nice. It's going to take a while to finish to the standard we want though?" He nods. "Perhaps a simpler fence with stakes to complete it? And then you can double back with the stone? Just so we can have it completely encircle the village."

"Good idea, Mistress," he says, bobbing up and down. He peers over my shoulder to look at the body strung over Dark Star's hindquarters.

"I got some things in Greater Downing," I say. I show him my material and then drag Thomlinson off Star's back to show him off. The red-haired corpse dangles limply. "This is Thomlinson."

Roland looks a bit confused.

"*Resurgemus iterum*," I whisper. The body jerks awake. Thomlinson's eyes open in alarm and he utters a small scream. Oh drat, I should have sewed his neck first. Oh well, I'll have to come and do it later. "Hello, Thom," I say, patting him on the shoulder. "Welcome to Downing, I hope you like it here. This is Roland, he'll look after you." Roland blinks up at me. "Thomlinson knows how to build siege weapons," I say brightly, and understanding dawns in Roland's eyes. "That's what he did at the castle. Can you find him a place to work, and get him what he needs? I would like one medium sized trebuchet as quickly as possible."

"What-" says Thomlinson. "What is happening?"

"That's fine, Mistress," says Roland. He takes off his disgusting old hat and scratches at his head. "But I don't know how much use a trebuchet will be in a forest?"

"I don't plan to use it here," I say with a smile.

"I don't understand." says Thomlinson. "I was at the castl-"

I fish out the coachman's hat which had got a bit squashed and hand it to Roland. He takes it in surprise.

"A present," I say. I look out at the wall. "I will make you some more wights, so we can get on even faster. Oh, that reminds me, there are some fresh bodies at the bandit's camp on the southern border. By the dead oak tree that was struck by lightning seven summer's ago?"

"I'm sorry, ma'am," says Roland, he is stroking the fabric of the hat with one shaking hand. "I don't know where that is."

I swear under my breath. Of course he doesn't, he is not from Little Downing. How vexing. I really don't feel like going there now, I want to see Jenkins. Hmm. Leaving Roland to deal with Thom I raise one of the villagers who should know the way. I choose Richard Webb, the fletcher because when he is done he can get to work on some arrows. That will no doubt come in handy.

I sniff, disapprovingly. Richard is... more than pungent, I don't think it will matter how much lavender I stuff into his innards it won't mask that stench. More herbs are necessary. Keeping the bodies tolerable when standing downwind is an ongoing problem that I have mostly ignored so far. I can endure it in the short term, but it doesn't make me happy.

Raising the new geeseI add them to my goose army. Then I return to the altar to check on the gems I had left charging. To my delight I discover the blood painted sigil has resulted in a much stronger soul charge than the mud. Perhaps. Or I left them out longer? Either way I have enough to capture the souls of the rest of the keep pile, which I do so.

If only I had some more blood. No doubt fresh opportunity will present itself at some point, but it's a hard liquid to keep on tap. I search around for something stronger than mud. Something that will last? Tree sap? Maybe. Actually, I have honey in my kitchen, that might be interesting. Hmm...jam charged soul gems. But now I am just being silly.

Richard departs for the bandit camp, Roland and Thomlinson are busy getting acquainted and the wights are working nicely on the boundary wall. All seems to be in order so I make my way back to my cottage.

After putting away my new material and most of the new soul gems, I sit awhile in the kitchen, stroking Jenkin's fur and planning a new dress inspired by the lavender noble lady. Despite the fact that I no longer need to sleep I still get weary. I find a few moments of repose help freshen my mind. It is good to be home.

Idly, I pull over the necromancer's notes I took from Dunbarra Keep, and leaf through them. Thinking about the necromancer reminds me that I really should fish him out of the well. I haven't heard him yelling in a while. I hope he hasn't disintegrated.

I'll look later.

My eyes glance over his map once more. I need to find someone who can read this properly, so I can find these mineral deposits. Perhaps when I am feeling up to another excursion. In a decade or so. Although

I won't be stealing any lavender gowns sitting in my cottage alone, will I?

There are a few words scrawled in the margins. I had spotted them before, but now I am of a mind to try them out. I'm sure they are spells. There is nothing written down to give any indication of what they might do however. Or what I need in order to work them.

There are two: *'Vita mutatur, non tollitur'* and *'Quo vadis'*.

I open my mouth to say the words of the first, and then think better of it. Better to be safe than sorry. I do not want to accidentally ruin my kitchen. Or hurt Jenkins. Who knows what I am saying? Gently I plop the undead cat to the ground. He hisses with displeasure and stalks off, his fur ruffled.

I walk out into the garden, and then for good measure out into the forest. I am equal parts nervous and excited. What will they do? The moon is rising like a pale eye from behind a thick bank of clouds. It looks like rain is coming soon so I should hurry.

Now what were the words?

"Vita mutatur, non tollitur," I whisper.

The leaves above me rustle, stirring gently, but not I think, because of the spell. I look around. Nothing seems to have changed. Maybe I was mistaken and they are just words? Or maybe I need to utilise a crystal somehow? I get one out of my pocket—a rose quartz, charged but empty. Alright, let's try something a little different.

I gesture at a nearby oak. *"Decipula alma."*

The soul of the oak streams into the gem. The grand old tree withers, the rot starting at the base and disintegrating its way upwards. A few handfuls of dust fall to the ground in a soft whoosh. So far so good. And nothing I haven't seen a hundred times before. Now for the spell: *"Vita mutatur, non tollitur."*

I wait, hopeful but not really expecting anything. Just as I give in to disappointment the gem in my hand lights up. Gleaming motes spill *out* of the quartz, the oak's soul dancing through the air, pale and ghostly. They spiral around me, glowing faintly, like tiny moons spinning across the darkness of the forest floor. I am enchanted. What are they doing?

The twinkling lights gather, swaying, fragile things. They stream into the forest, coalescing to occupy the shape and space of the living oak that had existed mere moments before. Slowly the tree is recreated from the speckles of ghost light. Once complete, it dims, but does not lose its glow completely. I look up, staring at the ghost of the ancient tree. I walk around it, reaching out to the trunk with my fingertips. They pass straight through, as though it is an illusion. And yet, this is no mirage, it is a phantasm, the tree's soul, and it radiates peace and contentment.

I sit back on my heels for a while to admire it.

Strange and luminous the spectral branches shake in breezes I cannot feel. I watch as a confused owl tries to land on a shimmering branch. It claws at the air as its talons close on nothing and flies off befuddled to find a safer perch.

The necromancer spoke of wraiths but this is not a wraith. Wraiths are angry things, vengeful and full of fear. This ghost, or whatever it is, is peaceful. Of course, it is a tree, and it died without trauma. My mind buzzes with possibilities.

But there was another spell written on the paper. What was it?

Ah yes. I speak the words aloud in a hushed tone: *"Quo vadis?"*

The air ripples in an ebony shockwave.

Unlike the other spell I know something is happening immediately, and I do not like it. The earth is shaking, juddering outwards in ink-black waves. I've seen that once before. That night. The night I died. I step back in horror. What have I done?

I turn and flee, running as fast as I can, rushing away from the black stains that vibrate through the very fabric of my reality, sending panic skittering through my bones. I must get away. Faster, I must go faster. Maybe I can outrun it.

Thrum.

Terror grips me. I rush through the dark woods as swift as a deer. The vibrations make me sick, they rattle through me, a spinning whirl of memories and anguish threatens to overwhelm me. Feelings rise up unbidden, feelings long suppressed, that ice cold dam breached in a chilly instant. Fear grabs me by the throat, crushing my windpipe. I can't breathe. No! I don't need to breathe, I am dead, I don't need to despair, I don't need it. I am better than fear. Then why I am so scared?

THRUM

I can't see, it is dark, where am I going? Everything is falling apart. My bones rattle. A fallen tree looms out of the darkness, I leap over it, stumbling as my heels sink into mud. I roll, and carry on running, dashing under branches, the twigs twisting and grabbing at my hair. Wait? I don't have hair. I don't need to run. I am in control. I am dead. Why am I dead? That noise! I remember that noise. I must go faster, I don't know where I am going but away, I must get away. What have I done? I cannot get away.

THRUM

A rip opens in the fabric of reality, directly in front of me. I stumble to a halt. It looks like a slit, like a narrowed, unblinking eye. It is looking at me, seeing me as I see it. It is aware. Through its pupil I can see...sand? Falling snow? A dark starless sky hangs above a bleak desert of nothingness. No. I don't want to go. I scrabble to get away. A bitter wind tugs at me, grasping at me with clinging fingers. It smells of...dust and of decay. It is pulling me in.

The world tilts.

I am falling.

I am falling.

The void sucks me in and seals with a pop.

Chapter Fifteen
WHISPERS IN THE DARK

I am standing in a desert. My feet sink into fine, shifting sand. It moves with a dull hiss, grains tumbling over each other in dry waterfalls. Like waterfalls but there is no water here. Water would mean life and this place is utterly lifeless. I look up into a black void. It is not the comforting darkness of a moonless night but the bleak oblivion of an empty vacuum. Of nothingness. No stars, no birds, no moon.

It is bone-numbingly cold.

Where am I? All I know is that I do not want to be here. It is not safe. I take a step forward, uncertain, and my footsteps smell of dust and death. They smell like the dry, unliving hollow of a forgotten tomb. The sand skitters with me. I bend down, scooping some up to examine. The grains are tiny skulls, each one perfect and grinning. I let them fall through my fingers, streaming away into the air.

I walk and the wind is a sibilant hiss in my ears. Almost, I can hear words. They caress my body but I do not want to listen. I must walk and find a way to escape. Through that unchanging landscape of rolling, unending desertI walk for a long time. How do I get home? I don't even know where I am? I turn, looking back the way I have come but there is nothing to mark my passage. The wind has already buried my footsteps.

I want to go home. How can I leave this unliving, featureless blight? Perhaps if I repeat the spell that brought me here? Maybe it will open another doorway?

"Quo vadis?" I whisper.

"Quo vadis? Quo vadis? Quo vadis?" whispers the wind. No doorway appears, no rip in reality. I carry on walking. I trip over something, half buried in the sand. I bend down, brushing away the grains. It is a cat's skull, as big as my fist. There are twin emeralds pushed into its eye sockets. I pick it up to examine and it is a comforting weight in my hands. I look into the twinkling eyes and take it with me as I walk.

"Quo vadis?" hisses the wind.

I do not listen. I am trying very hard not to think about whispers, or about the dark monster of a god to whose existence I am bound. Perhaps it is only fitting. I deserve this. I always was a monster pretending to be a woman. Looking down at the cat's skull I find strength.

I walk.

A rabbit rushes across the desert. It is running very fast, and does not leave tracks. It stops when it sees me, in a spray of sand.

"Do you even know where this is?" the rabbit asks. *"Why did you leave me?"*

It turns its fluffy head and I can see one side of its face is eaten away. I can see its jawbone and teeth exposed through the ragged, rotting flesh.

I blink, and it is gone.

"Why did you leave me?" the wind whispers, and I start to run. *"Where are you going? How have you lived? Are you listening?"* The wind picks up, an insistent hum, rustling through the sand and making it ripple. *"Quo vadis? Where are you going?"*

The whispers hiss and rustle around me, and the sand stings my legs. In the distance I see something bright is flying towards me and I slow. As it comes closer I see a giant lunar moth. It leaves a trail of shimmering gold dust, and smoke. Its wings are on fire. I hold out my fingers and it lands, surprisingly heavily on the tips. As its soft feet touch my flesh it bursts into flames, sizzling away into soot and burning me to the bone. I howl in pain and squeeze the scorched fingers tight to my body, trying to ease the hurt. The ashes float away, mingling with the whispers.

What is this place?

"What is this place?" whispers the wind. Can it hear my thoughts? *"Where are you going? Why are you afraid?"*

I start to run.

"Why are you running?"

It is hard to move in the sand, and the whispers push against me. It is like striding through deep water, through sticking mud. My limbs are so heavy, my bones feel like they are lined with ore. It is a struggle to lift them but somehow I do. The whispers chase me, surrounding me in a vortex, sibilant and uncanny. The layered effect is both terrible and awe inspiring. *I'm afraid. I want my mother, I want my mother, but I am grown and she is rotting in the ground without her soul, unable to speak, why did I do such a thing? Why? Where am I going? So fragile. Perhaps it is better. Better to embrace the void.*

That is not my voice. I squeeze the cat's skull and come to a stop.

"Where are you going?"

"I am going home," my voice is tiny and defiant in that vast place.

There is a hushed silence.

The wind drops. I know a moment's peace and then the sand starts to vibrate. Staggering I stagger fight to keep my balance. The wind quickens to a gale, ripping at my clothing, snatching at me with stinging fingers. With a rushing roar, a figure crash lands into the sand, as if fallen from a mighty height. The shockwaves of its coming leave circles in the desert, knocking me backwards.

I tumble over and over in the wind and lie sprawled in the sand. As I look up, the figure rises off one knee. Robed in black, its face is cowled and cast in shadow. I cannot see its features and for this I am grateful. Darkness flairs from its back—like wings, extending upwards and outwards, disappearing into the ether. If I look carefully into that darkness a pattern emerges. I can see my face, mirrored many times over: my face now, my naked skull, the face I once had, and the face I might have yet. All of them shifting constantly. I do not look too long.

The creature is carrying a heavy silver hammer over one shoulder and it is encrusted with black. Old blood? Or rust? The whispers flock to it, encircling the weapon, writhing across the silver finish in an ink-black sequence my eyes struggle to comprehend.

The figure leans forward, lifting the great hammer.

"Come back when you are ready to listen."

"Yes, Whisperer," I say, as softly as I dare.

I look up into the silver metal of the falling hammer. It fills my vision. Pain ripples through me. I hear my bones crunch and splinter.

I die. Again.

I awaken.

My mind roils, crashing from anger to despair to relief and back again. Looking up, I can see stars gleaming through dark branches. I have never realised how much I love the stars. There they are twinkling down on me like little sparks of hope. The night sky is so nice. Emotions war in my brain. My insides feel hollow. My head is pressed into the dirt. I lift my fingers to brush my face. There is only bone. Bones. I am a skeleton again.

The wind rustles in the trees and I stiffen. But it is just the wind, and I relax once more. I lie in the muck for a while, appreciating the lack of sand and the lack of whispers. I do not want to go there again. I need to be more careful. I should not dabble with things I do not understand but how else will I learn? Perhaps I should try to be nicer to the necromancer but the thought sickens me.

Muttering the filthiest curse I know anger swells to fill the empty space between my ribs. I turn my head. A black rooster is staring at me. I sit up with a shriek.

"NOOOOOOOOO!"

The sound echoes off the treetops.

In the distance birds take flight. "Roland! ROLAND! NOOOOOOO!"

The undead little man runs over to me looking concerned. I am lying right in the middle of the ruin of Little Downing, I can see the altar and the draugr flocks milling about, both goose and chicken. Beyond them I spy the comforting presence of the new wall and the dark boughs of the deep wood.

"What is it ma'am? Are you alright? You've been gone for a long time? Did you die?"

"No, Roland," I say with icy calm. "I am not alright. And yes, I died."

I point an accusing finger at the rooster. "I think I found my phylactery. I think my phylactery is the damn chicken."

Roland turns to look at the bird, and his jaw drops.

"What?" he says.

"My soul!" I say, hysterically, "is in the rooster!"

"How do you know, Mistress?" he says. He walks over to the rooster, peering at it with interest. The evil bird looks at him haughtily. As he reaches a hand out to grab it, it pecks one of his fingers off with a vicious bite. "Ah," he says, nursing the stump.

"I know because I keep waking up next to it. And they were there, that night, the damn chickens! Ug! I mean, I'm not sure, how would I even know? I don't want to kill it to test the theory. If I'm right does it mean my lifespan is going to be the same as the stupid bird? Do I only have a few years to live? I thought I would have centuries! When the rooster dies will I die? Finally, I mean? I don't want to die. The stupid thing would probably kill itself jumping over a puddle."

We both stare at the giant black rooster. It spits out Roland's finger and saunters off, waving his glossy, black plumage.

"I... I don't know, Mistress," says Roland, twisting his new hat between his hands. His eyes narrow thoughtfully. "Perhaps not though. To kill a lich the soul container must be destroyed? A dead bird is still...not destroyed? The Master planned to put his soul in the gem. A gem is not alive so perhaps your soul would be fine until the actual body is destroyed?"

"If I fed him to someone," I say, speculatively, "perhaps they would become my new phylactery? Maybe I should eat him myself." I glare at the retreating back of the stupid bird.

"I wouldn't advise that, ma'am," says Roland. "You are a lich, your soul is supposed to be severed. Eating him might have unfortunate consequences."

"I can't eat anyway," I say, bitterly. Right now, I am so hungry I could eat the world. I *want* to eat the world.

I get to my feet and look down at my body in disgust. I am naked in my bones again. Apparently when I come back to life my clothing does not come with me, which is fair enough. Not that any of this is reasonable. It is most unreasonable and someone is going to suffer for it. I grab a charged soul gem and stalk to the well. I peer down at the disintegrating necromancer. His eyes gleam up at me. He is still alive, or rather he is still undead, but only just.

"Decipula alma," I whisper.

His soul stays where it is.

Of course. I am a skeleton again, I cannot consume a human soul until I have fed on smaller souls. I let out a ferocious snarl that startles the geese and my minions both.

Striding back to my cottage, I mutter under my breath. Fortunately, I was wearing my highwayman outfit when I went on my little...trip. My armour is where I left it in the kitchen.

Strapping on my helmet and my pauldrons, I stop only to pet Jenkins, all the while cursing under my breath. Dear Jenkins. His green eyes are as brighter in death than they were in life.

I look down at the necromancer's notes and curse again as my eyes fall on the spells in the margin. I snarl, softly. My eye scans the map idly, as I tighten a leather strap. Then I lean in closer. A deposit of limestone is marked in brown ink. Turning my head, I can see the outline corresponds to a position that looks a lot like the forest crags where Roland has the wight minions mining. There are no buildings marked on the map, only natural features. I turn the map this way and that. I trace one skeletal finger down a line of blue. That must be the river that flows under the Lowcroft Bridge.

I tap my fingers on the table. If I am correct then it means the crystal deposit is much closer to the Little Downing than I first thought. I scour the parchment, my bony chin barely an inch from the parchment, tracing the lines, eagerly. I am right, I am sure of it! If I am reading it correctly that means the large crystal deposit is directly under or next to Dunbarra Keep.

I grab my war axe and head for the door. I can feed myself as I go, and perhaps by the time I get there I will have burned off some of my rage.

Chapter Sixteen
The Long Way Down

Striding through the forest, I glut myself on the souls of the weak, leaving a wide trail of decay and devastation. Everything falls to my hunger and the savagery of my rage; moss, lichen, flowers, bushes, the small forest creatures, saplings and then birds. I spare none of them. Not the moon-touched lilies in their perfect elegance, nor the gleaming fireflies, and not the sleeping owl and her nestlings. I consume each and everyone. I do not savour the tastes. I do not linger. In this world at least, I am not weak. I am in control and I want to keep it that way. So everything must die.

As the sun peeks through the trees, I finally swallow the soul of a vast forest elm.

I pause as the worst of my hunger abates, stopping to get my bearings. The dawn light filters through long trees that cast shadows in green and gold. It is morning. I rotate in a slow circle. The blight of my passage is clearly visible and for a moment I am ashamed. Blacked earth stretches back into the trees, stretching as far as I can see. I turn my back on the withered forest.

Without Roland to guide me I am not completely sure of the way to Dunbarra Keep but I know I am close. The rise and fall of the surrounding hills is familiar, as are the sights and smells. It must be nearby, buried in the natural growth of the forest. I pick the direction I think most likely and a short while later, I stumble across a moss-covered flagstone, half buried in the loam. From there it is easy to identify the rest of the ruins and soon I am looking up at the ivy-choked tower. I have arrived.

Shaking the last grains of sand from my mind, I search for the door that I remember is obscured at the base. I find it and step through into the dark interior. It shuts behind me with a creak. I look around at the sparsely furnished landing. This time I am alone, and I fully intend to indulge my curiosity.

I vaguely imagine there must be some sort of dungeon or basement level that leads to a cave system where I will find the mineral deposits marked on the maps. In order to find it, it is imperative that I open every door I can. Including the little ones in the chests and cupboards. I am interested in the necromancer's domestic arrangements. Sadly, I find nothing more exciting than cobwebs and dust. One heavy dresser yields spiders and rusted cutlery, but that is as exciting as it gets.

Most of the rooms on the ground floor are empty tombs. The ruin of the castle is a rotting shell. One room contains a bookshelf with a grimy portrait of a woman in it. I clean it off a little and recognise the haughty visage of the necromancer's wife from the painting in his study. The books on the shelves have long since rotted to pieces, the remains falling apart when I try to lift them. In other rooms I find decaying drapes, and more heavy furniture, some of it covered in dust-clogged sheets. The weave on these coverings is so fragile that they disintegrate when I accidentally brush against them. It is fairly obvious that the necromancer lived in the tower rooms only. I find no stairs leading down.

I give up and roam the rest of the tower.

Halfway up I find another furnished room. This one is small and unremarkable, almost a cupboard. The ceiling is low and a narrow, rickety bed takes up most of one wall. On the mantle are more paintings—not fine and grand, like the others but small doodles. The kind a servant might have. They depict several people. One of them is a short man, smiling and dressed in old fashioned servants' attire. His face is very pink and he wears a fine velvet hat. Is it Roland? It is hard to tell but I think it might be. I peer at it for a while trying to decide.

Stalking my way up to the tower room, I am annoyed not to have found any sign of the location of the crystal deposits. However, while I am here, I might as well look in on the grimoire.

The evil, wrinkled eye swivels towards me as I enter the room. Once more I can feel its presence, weighing heavy on the air. Tendrils of darkness drift from the book, hanging in the air around it like ink stains. I walk to the podium and flip aside the tarnished silver chains that bind it in place. The eye snaps shut and I pull the covers apart. Once again, I am surrounded by the scent of rotting things, pungent and rich as the thick vellum pages fly open. They are still mostly blank, but I can see there is more writing than the last time. Does the book write itself? If not the book then who? I lean in to look.

Last time there were two spells written inside in that stained, brown ink. Now everything I have learned is catalogued in order. In addition to *'Soul Thief'* and *'Soul Gem Creation'* there are *'Reanimate Dead'*, *'Summon Ghost'* and lastly and most ominously *'Whispers'*.

How does it know what I have learnt? I assume we are connected in some way. Running one bony finger across the vellum I can feel that the page is warm. It feels like skin although it is paper dry. The book shudders at my touch and I snatch my hand away. The grimoire snaps shut with a thud, and the eye opens wide, glaring at me balefully from the wrinkles of the cover.

Consideringly, I look at the chains binding it. Really its location so far from my home is most inconvenient. I seize the book in both hands and try to wrench it free. It refuses to budge despite the not inconsiderable pressure I apply. I let go. Perhaps that is for the best. The grimoire might be more secure hidden away here than kept back at my cottage where I seem to have so many unwelcome guests.

I refasten the silver chain, and the eye narrows, watching as I back away. It occurs to me that the book might not be entirely defenceless either. The chains do not look as though they are designed to keep it from being stolen. They are restraining the book itself. Regardless, I should consider laying some traps around the tower and perhaps boosting the defences here. If my new life so far has been any guide, sooner or later people will show up. It is amazing how no one can let me just be.

Hmm. Perhaps I could disguise the door to this room? I could build a dresser into the front to conceal it? I would really hate anything to happen to the book. As a temporary solution I drag one of the heavy cupboards up the stairs and position it across the entranceway. It is not subtle but it would be hard to move, and does disguise the fact that there is a door there. I blow some dust into the corners and then resume my search for the crystals.

Half an hour later, I am growing more than a little frustrated.

I'm not sure what I expected, but perhaps a cave under the castle, accessible only from the interior? What do mineral deposits even look like? I had assumed they would be hidden—valuable gems would not just be lying about, after all, but this is ridiculous. I go outside to explore. I assumed the entrance would be located within but maybe it isn't. Could it be in the cliff walls? Really, I have no idea what to look for. Geology has never been a particular area of interest to me. At least until now.

Grumpily, I wander through the overgrown grounds, stomp my way through the undergrowth and poke about. To be fair, anything could be hidden in here. Large parts of the castle are open to the elements. Walls have fallen in and there is a massive oak growing in what I assume was once the great hall. After another hour of search I can quite adamantly say there is nothing cave-like, at all.

I look down at my map and growl. The crystals are here, I'm sure of it. I hold it out, lining up the outline of the surrounding hills. Yes, I should be standing right on top of it! I kick an inoffensive foundation stone. It cracks open, falling into pieces.

This is a waste of time.

I should just go home and plan my next robbery. I stalk off glaring at the horrible tower and then pause thinking of the cupboard hiding the grimoire. One last look then, and this time I will check for secret doors.

My hunch pays off. All of the furniture in the basement rooms is just furniture, it moves aside when I push it. Not so the bookcase in the room with the portrait. *This* bookcase is attached to something else and conceals a hidden doorway. At last! I pull it open with a bit of effort and it swings open to reveal a narrow, black staircase leading down.

This is more like it! I step into the deeper darkness, pulling the heavy door closed behind me. It shuts with a gentle click. I have a moment's panic before I remember that if I can't find the handle I can just smash my way out.

I descend.

The passage is very narrow, barely wide enough to accommodate the width of my shoulders. If I am not careful my pauldrons scrape on the wall, so I have to twist sideways. The arched ceiling is only just tall enough for me to pass. The stairs are rough, cut into natural stone and left unfinished. The air is stale and unmoving.

I walk downwards for a very long time.

At last the stairs twist to the left and then open out into a cave. Or what I think is a cave— there is evidence of human toolmarks on the walls. Unlit torches line the walls but they are as thick with cobwebs and dust as everywhere else. There are two doors, both lined with iron bars. To stop things getting in or to stop them getting out?

In between the doors is a rotting wooden throne, and seated in state upon it is a skeleton. The skeleton has a ruby and gold pendant around its neck. The ruby is the size of a duck egg. I watch the skeleton carefully. It occurs to me that the necromancer might not have left his treasures undefended, but the skeleton does not move. For good measure I try to consume its soul, but whatever happened to its soul it is no longer here. These bones are just bones. Hollow and empty. The skeleton's hands are extended, palm out. On each hand lies a key. One is made of crystal and one is made of obsidian.

I hesitate and then reach for the ruby necklace. The enormous gem is as red as blood and hums with power. It is charged but empty. Curious. I thought perhaps it might contain the soul of the throned skeleton but it does not have the vibrating heaviness that I have come to associate with a filled soul container. I tuck it into my pouch with the meagre supply of charged gems I had brought with me. Then I consider the keys.

The crystal key hopefully leads me to what I am seeking, that much is plain. Curiosity prickles me, however. I pick up the obsidian key, from the left-hand palm and turn to the corresponding door.

The key clicks in the lock, and I pull it open.

A blast of cold air greets me. I stare into darkness.

Whatever is there, the space is so large even my undead vision cannot penetrate it. There is a sensation of vastness. I move into the space, shutting the door behind me. I pause as I hear something. Something skittering. It stops as soon as I stop. I take a step forward, and I hear *tap, tap, tap, tap* like little legs on stone. Walking forward, something sticky and soft falls on my face. A cobweb. I tear it aside with my fingers.

I am standing on an obsidian floor which stretches away for a great distance. The ceiling is high and vaulted. Rows of black slabs lie in orderly rows, giving me a sense of the vastness of the place. Sarcophagi. This is a crypt. Or an underground cathedral? Whatever it is, this place is a monument to the dead. I suspect I have finally found the children of Dunbarra Keep.

Once more I hear that faint skittering. I turn my head in time to see an enormous spider leaping for my head, its pincers clicking. I am reflected in all eight of its eyes.

I punch it in the face.

The spider crumples to the ground with a wet crunch. I move to examine it. Like all spiders, it looks smaller in death than it did in life but it is still the size of a large dog. I have never seen such a massive arachnid in my life. Is it natural or the result of some magic or experiment? Its legs are long, awkward and spindly, and it has a shining black orb on its back.

I consume its soul which tastes surprisingly bland. Perhaps a little like the crab I had once, long ago when a travelling merchant visited the village from the sea? Then, because its body is too interesting to leave behind, I raise it as a wight. I don't think a giant spider will be that useful in a fight, but then I am much stronger than the average human. Perhaps it can spin? Spider silk has some distinct crafting possibilities.

With the wight-spider clicking along behind me like a large, rather ugly puppy, I stroll between the tombs. Some of them have carvings of people on them. Since they are carved in black against dark space it is hard to make out the features. I lean over to inspect one. It is a sculpture of a small boy, his eyes shut and his face immortalised in stone. There are plaques with information, each letter beautifully etched into the rock. This is a labour of love, and it puts my simple efforts at Downing to shame. I must try harder.

At the end of the vast chamber is a black altar. On it sits a silver candle, and a skull. Above it on the wall a blank mask. The air stirs as I look at it and I hurry away. I do not want to look at the altar. I can explore later, for now I need crystals, which are presumably in the next chamber. I have learned my lesson about rushing in without thought, so I let whatever is sleeping in this place rest a little longer.

I leave without reading the inscriptions and return to the cave entranceway, locking the door firmly behind me. Returning the key to the skeleton on its throne, I gently pick up the crystal one. Taking great care, I open the door on the right. The key feels very fragile, and cool to the touch—smooth like glass, but the lock clicks open without any trouble.

Another stairwell, leading down. I follow its twisting spirals around and down and down. The spider wight trundles along behind me, seemingly unphased by the adventure. After a few moments we emerge into a natural cave.

This cave is large. I have never seen anything like it. Stalactites cling to the roof, and bulbous columns of rock thrust up through the uneven floor. Water drips from the ceiling, but it is surprisingly warm. A large pool of water is collected to one side, on the other I see a passage leading onwards.

There is another throne here, resting between two mighty rock columns. This throne is made of gleaming transparent crystal and like its rotting wooden twin in the antechamber, it is occupied. This is not a skeleton however, but a ghost. I nearly miss her as she is almost as transparent as the throne on which she sits. Her features phase in and out of existence. Her skirt is full and flowing, and of an indeterminate colour. Her hair is neatly coiffured and hung about with ribbons. Over the ghost's shoulders is an ermine wrap, and she nurses a goblet in one hand. Around her neck is a ruby pendant. My fingers close over its twin

I recognise her from her portrait: this is the necromancer's wife.

Only her eyes move, watching me as I walk towards her. I have to go near her if I want to follow the path. As I get closer I see bones scattered at her feet. They look human. Some of them are very small. There is no flesh on any of them, they must be very old.

"They took my babies," says the ghost. Her tone is flat, even.

"Oh?" I say, awkwardly. Talking to the living was never my strong point, and I feel like a conversation with a traumatised dead woman is unlikely to be pleasant. I get out my war axe for good measure.

"They took them," she whispers. Her eyes are staring. Can she even see me? Or is she too wrapped up in her personal grief to comprehend anything more than a disturbance? I suspect the latter.

I take a step forward and the ghost blinks, her eyes snapping to mine, clear and alert. She stands up, her hair popping loose from its bindings. It drifts in a breeze I cannot feel.

"They took my baby," she screams.

Her jaw opens wide, impossibly wide. She rushes at me, fingers extended like claws. All I can see is teeth and rage-filled eyes. I block her with the axe but she goes straight through it. She goes straight through *me*.

I feel a rush of cold and slash wildly.

It is like fighting mist. Her fingers leave matching lines of pain across both sides of my face. I don't have much skin but she scrapes me to the bone. It hurts. I back away warily as she circles around. Her fine dress is ragged now, the ends fluttering in that unearthly breeze.

"WHERE ARE THEY?" she screams. Her voice echoes back a dozen times and the cave starts to shake. This is not a ghost, I realise, this is a wraith. How can I fight what I cannot touch? Then I come to my senses.

I do not need to touch her. I can command the dead.

"Decipula alma," I whisper.

The echo bounces around the cave, magnified over and over, a rolling, building susurrus.

The wraith explodes into motes of gleaming light and her soul disappears into the enormous ruby with an ear-splitting scream. I tuck her away safely and carry on walking.

Chapter Seventeen
CRYSTAL CAVES

The path takes me past the crystal throne, the scattered bones, and along a winding way that twists through the cave. The wight-spider pitter-patters behind me, its spindly legs beating a raindrop staccato on the rocky floor.

At the far end of the cave I come to another door. This one is low and round, and so is the matching crystal doorknob. It is warm to the touch.

"Stay here," I say to the spider. It sits, folds its legs in on itself and starts to spin. Leaving it in peace I push open the door and step through.

Beyond is a tunnel, almost completely spherical, that looks as if it has been hacked into the rock. It angles down, following a gentle curve to the left. As I walk I wonder how deep underground I am now? I have travelled a long way. The temperature has also risen, which is strange. The air is hot and sticky, oppressively so. I would have expected it to be cold underground, but then I know nothing about caves. I will have to buy some books on the subject of minerals if cave crawling is going to become a serious hobby, which I suspect it might. It is tremendously enjoyable.

Up ahead I notice a pale light. At first, I think I am imagining it, it is so subtle, but as I draw closer it intensifies to an unmistakable glow. Hurrying along, I wonder what I will find at the end of it? A sea of ghosts? An ancient lantern, somehow still burning untended? Or an underground forest full of fireflies? But no, it is something better. I step out into a cave and stare up in dazed bewilderment.

I have found my crystals.

The cave is not large, perhaps only thirty feet across but the walls are jagged and ice-white. I tread further in, my mouth agape as I look around. The rock crystal formations are spectacular. A fragile luminescence emanates from the crystals' bases, bathing the walls pale blue. The rocks sparkle, white, glass-clear and milky blue. The crystals themselves capture and refract the light, throwing it back in all its prismatic glory. It is like walking through a star field. No wonder the necromancer chose this location to be the centre of his lichdom. It was well chosen. Or perhaps lichdom was inevitable? Such a natural wonder must call out to whatever magical strands bind our world together, begging to be used.

I wander deeper into the heart of the earth, enchanted by the visions around me. I smooth my finger over a nearby crystal. It is hard and smooth like glass. I tap it sharply and it lets out a sound as clear as a bell. The other crystals sing out in answer and for one magical moment I am standing at the epicentre of a vibrating orchestra.

The cave opens out into another, and then another. The cave system is laid out in a row of varying cavity sizes. They are interconnected as if I am following a fault in the earth, or some gleaming fissure. Perhaps that is simply what it is? I drift through, feasting my eyes on the beauty until I come to another door.

This door is stout and thick. The grain is rough. It looks rather weather and stained, out of place in the beauty of its surroundings.

This doorknob is not just warm to the touch, it is hot. I open it and am blasted with scorching air, my cloak rippling out behind me. The heat in this cavern is excruciating and the air tastes slightly of sulphur. It would undoubtedly be problematic if I was in a fragile human body but I am not. I pay it no heed because my mind is full of the sight before me. My mind is full of crystals.

They are enormous.

There are towering spurs and spires of gypsum taller than my cottage. On one side there are jagged, human length prisms, on another circular starbursts the size of wagon wheels radiating outward in spirals. Rosettes, pillars and stars, the crystals come in many forms, and each is larger than the last.

I walk forward and my reflection walks with me.

I gaze in wonderment at the closest crystal. It is mirror clear and shaped like an exploded star—an underground sun, hovering in an eternal moment, the rays forever immobilised and immortalised in glass.

My legs feel a little weak.

This is beyond my wildest ambition. The cave contains the largest crystals I have ever seen in my life, no, in my dreams. One is close to forty feet in length, and as clear as a mountain stream. I stare at it in bemusement. This is a crystal fit to trap the soul of a god, if such a thing were possible.

I tap my jaw speculatively, but these are thoughts for another time. I have no need of crystals this size. I do not yet hunt gods and monsters. The thought is a little bit too exhilarating so I put it away, far away, at the back of my mind to turn over when I am still and all the immediate threats have been dealt with. It is also extremely hot in this cave and while I am not bothered by the intense heat I can smell it cooking what little flesh I have left on me.

Retreating to the earlier chambers I harvest what I need. With my unnatural strength the beautiful crystals are easy to acquire, snapping off at the base with ease. I soon fill the large bag I brought for exactly this purpose, with crystals of a variety of shapes and sizes. With these caves at my disposal I feel like I could conquer the whole kingdom. Although that would cut into my knitting time. Hmm.

I trace my way back through the cave system, collecting my pet spider as I go. The temperature cools as I rise, past the crystal throne and the dark, gleaming pool, and out into the antechamber with its skeletal guardian. I lock the door behind me and deposit the key on the outstretched palm. It is as good a place as any to keep it.

That done, I start the long ascent up the rough-hewn staircase to the surface, enjoying the cool air on my bones as I go. I let the wight-spider scuttle through into the tower, and then close that door as well. I make sure the bookcase is well and truly concealing it before turning away.

I look down at the spider. I could do worse than finding some of its family and bringing them up as well to guard the interior. On my next trip I will do that.

"Stay here," I say. "In the tower. Protect it from intruders."

I have no way of knowing if the wight-spider understands but basic commands seem to work on the geese. The spider jumps on top of the bookcase and starts to spin, looking like a very large, very ugly gargoyle. I think it will do well as a guard dog. Satisfied I heave up my giant bag of crystals and exit the tower.

I am looking forward to getting back home.

It was morning when I arrived at Dunbarra Keep and now, as I set off through the singing woods, it is early afternoon. My underground adventure did not take as long as I thought. It is a warm day, probably the last of the good autumn weather, and the small creatures are busy in the trees. Birds are twittering and my head is full of plans as I walk. The bag full of crystals jiggles at my side and I take a little skip, jumping over a fallen log.

Once these are all charged I'm going to take some time to sew a new velvet skirt for myself. One that will go beautifully with the armour, with deep pockets, and split skirts so I can kick things properly if needed. One that will swirl as I kill things. I have not yet decided on black or the deep emerald velvet. Or blue to match my eyes but that might be a bit much. And embroidery, there needs to be embroidery but what kind? I could do little skulls on the hem, perhaps in silver thread. Hmm, no, that would be garish. It should be in a colour to match the skirt so only the truly discerning can appreciate the detail before they die.

Two crows land on a branch in front of me, startling me.

Little crackles of lightning ripple backward and forward from their beaks, across their bodies to their talons and then back again.

"*Ka*," says Elding, and he looks at me with one beady, black eye.

"Greetings," says Tora, tilting her broken beak. "We bring tidings."

"Oh no," I say. My hands curl into fists and anxiety rising like a flood. "Is everything alright at home? What is wrong this time? Is someone there?"

"There are peasants," says Elding.

"Peasants," echoes Tora. "Not at your nest, no, but peasants at the old stone altar. By the rushing water. By the bridge. They have left things. *Ka*."

"What sort of things?" I say confused. "What do you mean peasants?"

"Humans," says Elding, as if I am stupid. Maybe I am. "The lowly humans. Lowlier than most. Waiting."

"Peasants with shinies," says Tora. She tilts her head, bright eyes blinking. "We hunger."

The sentence floats ominously in the space between us. How often will I have to feed them my memories? But I cannot deny that they are useful.

"You would like another memory?" I ask, just to be sure and they nod.

"You smell of the old place," says Elding, conversationally. "The old place, old nest. Not safe. Give it to us. We will eat it. You can forget. Happy mind."

"No," I say. "I need to remember it. So I don't go there again, by mistake."

Both crows dance on the branch, cackling a little, the lightning twinkling between their talons.

"Wise," says Tora, rustling her feathers and settling a little. She opens her beak in that panting laugh that grates on my nerves. "Perhaps you will survive the nesting season."

I think quickly. What memories can I spare?

"Here," I say, "you can have this. Actually, wait! Can you deliver a note for me first?"

Tora nods, her eyes bright and curious. Hastily I search in my bag and find a scrap of paper. I scribble a note on it and hand it to her. She grabs it in one wicked talon.

"Leave it on my kitchen table," I say. "Thank you. Here is the memory."

I think of my favourite book, feeling a little smug. I will enjoy reading it again without knowing any of the twists and turns. The crows seem satisfied with this gift and take off without a word, disappearing into the skies.

LICHES GET STITCHES

Shaking my head, I set off once more, adjusting the angle of my approach so that I will pass by Lowcroft Bridge. I am curious. What do a bunch of peasants want with me? Retribution of the destruction of Lowcroft? I am not really in the mood for slaughter, I want to get home to my sewing.

It does not take me long to reach the old road. Water gushes along the gorge, in the river far below and I turn towards the bridge, scanning the forest ahead anxiously. I get out my war axe and stalk forward, parallel to the road, but keeping to the undergrowth.

Shortly before the old altar stone comes into view at the roadside, I spy the peasants. There is a group of them, maybe four or five, huddled in a badly hidden cluster on the opposite side of the forest road. They probably think they are well concealed but my eyes are very sharp. Is it some sort of trap? If it is, I will soon teach them not to attack innocent liches on their way home.

Something does not add up however. Why would peasants try to attack me? And these are poor specimens even for peasants. Two of them are barefoot, their clothing hanging off them in tatters. They all have the gaunt, hungry appearance of people who have not seen a hot meal for some time. One of them looks rather sickly, like he should be home in bed. Why are they here?

I step out next to the stone and I hear the peasants gasp, clutching at each other in fear. One of them points, rudely. They stay where they are, and don't show any sign of moving, so after glaring fitfully in their direction for a minute or so I turn to look at the items laid out on the stone.

They appear to be...gifts? I look at them with great suspicion. There is a roll of hessian, and some coarse cotton thread, some bread and some rather stunted root vegetables. On the other side there is a bunch of wildflowers tied with an old ribbon. Those are very nice, and would look darling on my kitchen table. There is also a tatty wicker basket with a note tied to the handle.

As I move closer to pluck the note, the basket makes a cooing noise. I freeze, my fingers outstretched. There is a baby. There is a baby in the wicker basket.

I stare at it.

It is very pink, with a red, screwed up face. Its eyes look at me, sleepy and unfocused. It is wrapped against the cold, in a ragged blanket. I poke it. The infant is very squishy. I sniff it carefully. It smells like milk and wasted potential.

I turn to the note which reads:

"To the Lady of Downing Forest,
I beseech you take our blood that you might know we mean ye no harm. Take these offerings of peace and protection."

Ug. I pick the infant up out of the basket. It wriggles like a giant, pink grub. Scowling I turn towards the bushes and yell angrily: "*Come and get your brat!* What kind of a mother leaves her baby on a stone as a sacrifice! I can't do anything with this! The parts are barely developed and its soul would be no more than a morsel at best. I'd rather eat a ferret!"

None of the peasants move. There is a tense silence, and the baby starts to cry.

I brandish the squalling child.

"I said come and get it right now! Don't make me repeat myself, I don't like it."

There is a hasty conference and then a pink-faced young woman comes rushing out of the trees. She is dressed in an ancient brown dress and a filthy apron that looks like it hasn't been cleaned in weeks. Her limbs are very thin.

I dangle the baby at her and she grabs it, clutching it to her chest.

"Sorry, ma'am," she says, curtsying frantically. "I'm sorry the offerings were not to your liking."

She backs away, her eyes skittering over my body, wide with fear. Suddenly I feel very self-conscious about my exposed femurs. Bizarrely I don't feel naked when I am just bone, but as soon as there is skin and flesh involved I start to feel unseemly. I will make sewing a new velvet skirt a top priority.

"The flowers are nice," I say, grandly. "You should keep the food, it does not look like you can spare it. Some paint wouldn't come amiss. But no babies. No children. Understand?"

"Yes, my lady," she says, bowing her head, her ears pink. I hope she doesn't drop her offspring.

"Hang on," I say, and fish the gold necklace out of my bag. I toss it to her and she catches it in surprise. "For the paint," I say. "And perhaps you could find me a couple of pigs. Use the rest to buy food or whatever."

Her eyes widen so much I feel like they might pop out of her head. She curtsies again, clutching the child and the necklace, and retreats back into the bushes, her cheeks pale as ash.

"Hmmf," I say. An interesting development.

I turn to the flat stone and sweep up the hessian, the flowers and the thread, stuffing them into my bag, leaving behind the rest.

"No babies!" I yell into the forest.

Then I set out for home, my bag bulging with crystals and presents.

Chapter Eighteen

The Bright Ones, The Blind Ones

I wander happily along the forest road, heading home towards Downing. It is a pleasant afternoon, and I enjoy the feel of the last rays of sunshine lightly caressing my bones. I plan the skirt I am going to make in my head. It will be gorgeous, better than anything I had in life. I will use the hessian sack cloth to make a template before cutting up the expensive fabric, to make sure it fits perfectly. I should make an adjustable waist to allow for my ever shrinking and expanding body. I could add a belt? That would be handy for things I don't want to keep in my pockets. Of course, there will be many pockets, I can't stand garments without adequate pockets.

Perhaps a deep, emerald green velvet, rather than the black. To match the forest. It should only take a couple of hours to sew, if I can decide on the number of flares. I want to go for maximum swish so I will probably need to add quite a lot. Yes, a full circle skirt, slit in places to allow ease of movement, and reaching down to my ankles. That will do nicely.

Velvet is quite heavy though. In the spring I think I would like a floatier material. Taffeta, definitely, if I can find some. Tulle has possibilities? Hmm... that might be going too far. But velvet is more than adequate for autumn and winter. Not that I mind the cold, but for the look of the thing.

My eyes wander the tree line, admiring the shapes and thinking about embroidery. An oak leaf? Too jolly. Perhaps some mistletoe? It is rather pretty. Now, if everyone would just leave me alone for a bit I could make some real progress. Head full of these pleasant thoughts, I round the bend in the road.

There are people on the road.

Not peasants this time, but trouble of a sort I have not faced so far. These are not fighters or mercenaries, or the Baron's knights. The clerics have finally come for me. Standing conferring are two sun paladins and an acolyte of the Blind Queen. Behind them are a handful of foot soldiers. They have really brought out the circus today.

Both paladins are resplendent in burnished steel, and seated on perfect white chargers. The plumes of their helmets and their surcoats are spotless. The sunburst symbol of the Bright One is emblazoned on their silver shields, and I can smell the virtue like a stench in the crisp evening air.

An acolyte of the Blind Queen sits between them, perched on a donkey led by a plainly dressed servant. She wears robes of brown and cream, simple, but beautifully cut. A silver bell hangs around her neck, gleaming against the pale skin of her neck. On her brow rests a black iron crown worked in the shape of twisted thorns. It looks painful, cutting into the flesh of her forehead. A black silk blindfold covers her eyes. She has recreated herself in the image of her goddess. If she is devout she will have given her eyes to the Blind Queen in return for...strange abilities. I suspect this is one such.

This is going to be interesting.

Surreptitiously, I put down my bag in the centre of a bush and shift my weight. They have already seen me. It is too late for me to slink away into the forest. Even if I did, I suspect they would have ways to track me down.

Better to deal with this here and now.

"There it is!" shouts one of the sun paladins, pointing at me with his sword. His voice is boisterous and full of life. His eyes are sparkling green, and his cheeks flushed with excitement. I hate him instantly. The other one is quieter, but no less shiny.

The acolyte urges her donkey forwards, the bell tinkling as she moves.

"Scion of evil," she intones, deep and melancholy. "Cast aside your earthly sins. Give up your body to the sleeping thorns! The bell of the blind one tolls for thy lost soul."

"I'm just on my way home," I say, tightening the grip on my axe.

"*Solemfero!*" bellows the first sun paladin. Not in a listening mood then.

I leap to the side as twin suns wreath his hands in golden light. The miniature balls of flame rotate around his palms, blazing a burning orbit. He hurls them at me, and they come hissing through the air, scorching trails of fire. I dodge the first but the second catches me on the thigh, sizzling the sparse flesh. It hurts.

I hiss in anger. Two can play at this.

"*Decipula alma,*" I whisper, gesturing with my hand.

The two paladins throw up their shields, in a well-rehearsed motion.

"*Ægisfortissimavirtus!*"

My spell rebounds off the magically reinforced shields, doing no damage whatsoever. Their souls remain untouched.

Uh-oh.

They urge their chargers into a gallop, thundering down the road. Swords brandished above their heads, flames ripple up and down the blades in cascades of brilliant white. I hold my ground, then dive, rolling nimbly to one side. I slash at the underbelly of the nearest horse with my axe as I pass below. It screams and rears, throwing its rider. The paladin lands with a heavy thump on the road. I can't stop to see what he does because the foot-soldiers are charging towards me.

"Decipula alma," I whisper, my breath hoarse.

One of the footmen stumbles and falls, but the rest do not falter. I duck under a spear thrust, bending myself almost double before sweeping my axe in a wide, savage circle. I catch several of them at the waist, cleaving them in two. Bloody torsos thump to the ground, followed by their legs.

Fireballs come hurtling towards me. I twist aside, narrowly avoiding them all. The air moves, hot and noxious. The fiery blade of the grounded paladin passes within a hair's breadth of my head. I regain my balance and kick him in the chest. My feet clank against his breastplate and the paladin flies backwards, crashing into the remaining footmen. They tumble to the ground in a heap.

The thunder of hooves alerts me to the return of the first. Turning, I squeeze my axe with tense fingers and whisper: *"Decipula alma."*

"Ægisfortissimavirtus," he shouts.

Our spells clash and dissolve against each other.

I hear the tinkling of a silver bell and my skin crawls. The acolyte! Where is she? I whip my head around but not in time to avoid the glittering chains of light that wrap around my body, binding my arms tight against my side. I hiss as the incandescent links burn into the sparse remains of my flesh.

I push with all my might but I cannot break free. My axe is still gripped in my hand but I cannot move it. The marrow freezes in my bones. For the first time in a very long time I have to contemplate the possibility that I might be outmatched. I do not like the sensation and let out a low, rumbling growl, thrashing this way and that.

The sun paladin lifts his sword, and I throw myself sideways. The blade whistles a deadly hymn inches from my neck.

I land face first in the dirt.

"*Resurgemus iterum*," I whisper, wrenching my head up. Three of the dead foot soldiers lurch into life and attack their fellows. The two that are in pieces go for their legs, stumping along without their own limbs, biting and ripping. The mounted paladin is momentarily distracted as a wight-torso attacks his horse.

"*Decipula alma,*" I whisper, trying not to bite into the dirt.

This time, I get him.

I grin as his soul streams into me, bright and filling. His body slumps in the saddle and his charger whinnies. It panics, bolting for the treeline.

"*Resurgemus iterum!*" I whisper urgently, but the distance is too great. His body is lost to me as the horse disappears between the trees. The last foot soldier dies with a scream, taking the final surviving wight with him.

I turn my head to regard my remaining adversaries.

Only one unhorsed paladin and the acolyte are left, but I am still bound by she-devil's chains of light.

"If you think that you can kill me," I shout, to stall them as I struggle to stand, "then you are ill-informed." I kick out, trying to balance, rolling to my knees.

The acolyte is no longer smiling. She urges her donkey forward, through the pile of freshly fallen bodies, her lips a flat, sour line. The sun paladin stalks with her, small balls of light rotating ominously around his hands and sword.

"Lost soul," she says in a way that I can tell she really enjoys the sound of her own voice. She is annoyingly serene but I can see the paladin is losing his cool. "It is you who are mistaken."

I test the chains but they are as strong as steel. I shuffle to my feet with a groan.

"Tell that to your friend," I say, tilting my chin towards the forest and the acolyte's lips press together in pinched displeasure.

"We expect to kill you over and over," she says. The paladin stalks closer, the restless orbs spinning. I back away, trying not to fall. "Each time we will get closer to your soul. And once we have found it, we will destroy it. And you will be dust."

I feel the prickle of icy fingers squeezing my spine. They know what I am.

The acolyte's bell rings, an ominous shiver of sound hanging in the air. I don't know who to watch, the paladin or the acolyte. I pick the acolyte as the greater threat.

"*Fortis est veritas,*" she says, just as I whisper, "*Decipula alma.*"

Our spells cross.

She is jolted forward, falling over the neck of her donkey with a gasp, but her soul does not leave her body. I am also pushed forward, and fall to my knees with a snarl. The vitality is being leached from my body. She is stealing my energy! I look down at my chest. I am so thin. I have to get out of these chains. I strain, but they do not budge.

"Finish it," she says, dismissively to the sun paladin.

"*Solemfero,*" he growls, striding towards me with deadly intent. He is haloed in light which does little to disguise the blood and gore that splatters his armour. No longer so shiny.

I throw dignity to the wind and roll, aiming myself towards my bag that I left concealed in the bushes. The bag that contains my meagre supply of soul gems, and the red ruby containing the wraith. With every roll the light chains dig into the sparse remaining flesh, scorching my skin but I am nearly there.

The silver bell rings, and once more I am made less. Skeletal, as bone dry and helpless as when I wake after each death. I do not want to die. Who knows what the acolyte witch and the paladin will do to Downing in my absence?

I cannot die. I refuse.

I hear the hiss of the sun paladin's flaming sword. I squirm away desperately but the blade catches me—not on the neck but on the leg, as he slices through the tendon and bone with a grunt. My bones crack and I howl in agony. A red mist rises before my eyes, but I fight to keep my mind calm. I scrabble for my gems, gulping the souls within.

If I don't escape, the next blow will sever my leg clean off. Or my head.

"Decipula alma. Decipula alma. Decipula alma," I whisper, but always the paladin counters. The souls lend me their vitality. I clench my fists, pushing at the magical binding. The chains splinter and break, dissolving into the approaching twilight like evil little fireflies.

Exploding free, I grapple the surprised paladin, headbutting him viciously. He reels backwards from the force of my assault, unable to defend himself.

I take his head off with a clean strike from my axe. It bounces into the bushes with a metallic clank and lies still. The plume of his helmet is no longer pure and white, but stained rust brown and crimson.

I regard it in satisfaction before turning to the acolyte. Blood drips slowly down the haft of my axe and onto my fingers. With my free hand I stoop and pick up the sun paladin's sword. The flames have gone out. My leg hurts so much, I can tell it is badly damaged. I ignore it as best I can, flexing my freed limbs, a weapon in each hand.

The acolyte's sightless face turns towards me. She has not yet lost her composure, despite the sea of death surrounding her. I watch her lips, and she watches mine.

How does she see? I do not know but I can feel her attention.

The silver bell rings and her lips curve upward. I panic. I have no shield against her magic. I can only try to fight. I throw the sword at her, and miss. Once more she steals my vitality and I rush her, trying to smash her with my axe.

The acolyte mutters an incantation and a whip-chain of light snakes out from her hand to crack across my torso. I falter, my injured leg dropping to the ground, severed at the hip. I fall, clutching at the loose limb, and she cracks her whip again. One of my ribs snaps. The pain is excruciating and I let out a hollow moan.

I grope towards my bag.

The acolyte slips off her donkey with the smug grace of a princess who does not want her slippers to drag in the mud. Her cheeks are dripping crimson. Is she weeping blood from her eye sockets?

I crawl through the grass at the edge of the road, dragging my twisted broken leg with me. I can nearly reach what I need. The acolyte peers down at me with haughty grace. Then she stomps down on my wrist and I scream. I hear it snap, a cold thing now, limp and unmoving. She kicks away my war axe with her foot. Agony shudders through me.

It does not matter, I have the red ruby safely in my other hand.

The acolyte looks down at me with a snarl, blood streaming down the sides of her face.

"Vita mutatur, non tollitur," I whisper.

The trapped wraith is released into the world with a vengeful howl. The impassioned spirit flies at the acolyte ripping at her face, bits and pieces of flesh stripped away in bloody chunks. She wails in agony, trying to ward her off with shaking arms, stumbling back on the wet ground. Her bell is wrenched from her throat. It rolls away in the dirt.

I struggle to my feet, gripping my own thighbone to push myself up. I hop forward on my good leg, gritting my teeth against the pulsing pain. It is worse the second time. I am close enough.

Lifting my bone over my head I scream and bring it down on the acolyte's bloodied skull with a dull impact that sends her sagging down. Her arms twitch one last time as the spectre rips into her back with wild abandon. I fall and catch myself, wincing but the acolyte is at my mercy.

I consume her soul.

It tastes delicious.

Chapter Nineteen
Warcraft and Embroidery

The wraith finishes mauling the acolyte's body and drops it into the dirt. She turns to me with an ear-splitting wail, but I am ready. Brandishing the ruby high, I whisper the words to trap her inside. She screams as her soul flies, buffeted by the winds of my magic. I am grateful for her wrath, it has served me well today, and perhaps it will again in the future. The ruby pulses hot in my hand.

Collapsing onto my coccyx, I sag in relief.

That was a near thing. Too close to be comfortable. I lie back in the dirt and look at the cloud-filled sky. It is just visible, peeking through cobwebs of branches. The forest around me is eerily silent, trapped in that quiet hush that sometimes falls across the land before day drifts into night. A single orange oak leaf leaves its family and floats softly downwards to rest on my ribcage. It will be winter soon.

I sit up.

I have decisions to make. The bodies of the clerics' party are strewn around me. The road looks like the site of a massacre. Which... I suppose it was, but massacre makes it sound like it was easy. I will send someone to clean up. I really don't want to draw this kind of attention to my location, and this happened too close to my village. Although, as I look down at the blooded corpse of the Blind Queen's acolyte I realise it might be too late for that. Her blindfold has been knocked loose and the gapping hollow of her right eye stares sightlessly into nothing. These were not lackeys; these are expensive humans. Their disappearance will have consequences.

What am I going to do? I can stay in my cottage, build up my defences and fight off all intruders. However, it pains me to be reactive. A defensive strategy will always have me on the back foot, waiting to see what happens, at the whims of my enemies.

I could go to ground. It would be easy enough to disappear into the wilderness. Nothing in nature can harm me, not the bitter snows of winter nor wolves or bears. I am the apex predator. But the life of an uncivilised troglodyte sounds excruciatingly dull. I am to all intents, immortal. This plan would have me gnawing on a tree trunk in less than a week. And why *should* I do that? I have done nothing wrong. My existence is not a burden. I am not, by myself, inherently evil no matter what the clerics believe. I refuse to accept it.

I have power, yes, I have ability. How do I use that to get what I want? Which is to live simply in my cottage with my cat and my crafts. So how do I make them leave me alone? As I sit in the dirt, with my dead enemies strewn around me and my body in pieces, I begin to formulate the beginnings of a plan. In truth, it is already set in motion. Now the daydreams must become reality.

First things first.

My leg is detached and my wrist is shattered. Will I heal if I consume souls? I hope so. From my seat in the dirt I consume the souls of the foot soldiers. The answer appears to be disappointing no. My skin and flesh thicken noticeably, but the wrist remains broken, and the leg does not grow back. Interestingly, the severed limb grows its own new skin, as if it is still part of me.

I need to reattach it. I will get nowhere hopping on one leg. Rummaging in my bag I pull out the thread the peasants gifted me. Black cotton. Serviceable but sturdy. It will do nicely but I don't have a needle. Hmm.

My eye falls on the acolyte's corpse. I'm sure she would appreciate being useful. I crawl, wincing and grunting over to her side, dragging my severed leg with me. Humming softly under my breath I snap one of *her* legs off. Haha! After all, it is only fitting. Removing the skin and flesh from her bone with my axe does not take long, although it is awkward with one broken wrist. I chop the knobbly ends off the tibia, so that just the ivory, straight tube remains.

Perfect. The bone is, of course, nice and fresh. Full of oils, it is beautifully flexible. The acolyte will make a lovely set of needles. Actually, now that I think of it, I can use some of her sinew as well. The black thread is prettier but not as robust. I will use both. Splitting her tibia into pieces, I pocket the excess for another day. One piece I set aside for a splint.

Finding a suitable stone by the roadside I grate the bone strip vigorously, rotating it carefully and rounding it into a slender point. Lastly, I use the tip of my dagger to make a hole, being careful not to damage the bone. There. I am the proud owner of a serviceable needle. Limited edition 'acolyte collection'.

Grinning, I sew the splint to my wrist, pushing the broken bits back into place and holding them there with stitching. Instantly it feels better. It does not heal, but the fingers move without pain, and the wrist feels mobile again.

I start attaching my severed leg to my torso. It is not a particularly pleasant experience, but it does not hurt anything like as much as it would if I was human. It is very hard to get the stitching neat at the rear but I do my best. Not the finest job I have ever done, but serviceable.

Cautiously I get to my feet.

I am held together with thread, but my leg seems to function normally. Whatever black art powers my body decrees that I am whole. I take a step, and then one more. The road is firm beneath my foot. Interesting. Something else to experiment with, when I have the time.

A soft, mournful bray draws my attention. The acolyte's donkey. It is the only creature left alive, and it stands amongst the corpses gently trembling, its eyes liquid brown. The poor thing doesn't know what has happened to its stuck-up mistress. I briefly contemplate leaving it alive, but no, I want to take it home. It would be afraid of all the dead things.

Better if it belongs.

I use my last charged soul gem to take the donkey's little soul, and then raise it as a draugr. It can be a friend for Dark Star. I will have Roland start work on a stable for the pair of them. The acolyte and the paladin will have to wait. They might be worth keeping so I don't consume them straight away.

I pick up the acolyte's thorn crown from where it has rolled in the mud and retrieve her blood-stained silver bell. I am curious about her magic. I have no interest in the Bright One, but the Blind Queen is an interesting figure on the pantheon, and one that I know precious little about.

That done, I retrieve my bag full of crystals and fasten it to my new donkey's back, along with one of the footmen's bodies. I want to charge the new crystals as quickly as possible and so far, blood seems to be the most effective paint.

Together, we tramp home through the chill shadows of evening. This has been a particularly long day. Soggy leaves squelch and crunch underfoot and I am pleased when I see Roland's wall, looming between the trees.

It is coming along very nicely. I briefly stop to admire his progress and to ask him to collect the rest of the bodies from the road.

"Clerics, ma'am?" he says, his brow wrinkled in alarm.

"Yes," I say. "Two sun paladins and an acolyte of the Blind Queen. A few others."

I can see the worry in his eyes and I turn away. I find myself not wanting him to know how close I came to dying.

"I have a plan," I say, as I stride away into the village.

"So did the Master," I hear him mumble behind me. I hiss like a kettle on the brink of the boil. It is not the same. I will not underestimate my foes.

I introduce the little donkey to Dark Star. The large black mare leans down and snuffles at his head, showing an unnecessary amount of teeth as she does so. However, the donkey seems as mellow in death as he was in life, and stands there patiently as he is inspected. I leave the two to get acquainted and lug my heavy bag of crystals over to the altar. Once there, I harvest all the freshly charged gems and repaint the sigil in the foot soldier's blood.

Laying out the new crystals takes some time. There are so many I have to send Roland to fetch me a second body. Running out of space on the altar I end up painting sigils wherever I can find a flat surface. I leave my bountiful haul charging under the bright of the rising moon.

Chores done, I start back to my cottage, stopping off at the well to fetch some water for the wild flowers. The bucket comes up gunky and foul smelling. Ah yes. The necromancer. I peer down into the darkness. At this point he seems to be just floating chunks. How fitting.

Tempting as it would be to leave him, I summon his soul and trap it in a freshly charged soul gem. I will think about where I can put him later. Maybe in a chicken? I would enjoy that, but then perhaps I have enough evil fowl running around as it is. I cast a baleful glance at the enormous black rooster which is currently camped out on top of the altar. It glares at me and crows. Has it grown in size or was it always that large?

I kind of want to see what happens if I put the necromancer in an animal's body. Would he be able to talk? Elding and Tora can, but I don't think they were human when they started. However, I'm not feeling playful so I decide to postpone the experiment till I am in a better mood. The fight with the clerics shook me more than I care to admit.

Perhaps inspecting the newly built trebuchet will cheer me up. I can see it sticking up in the distance. I also have not checked in on the engineer and I would like to see how my impulse buy is settling into his new life. What was his name again? Thomas? Thomlinson! That was it.

The freshly dead ginger haired man has set up shop on the western boundary of the new wall. He and the fletcher seem to be sharing a rough workshop and the area hums with activity. Various piles of wood and tools lie scattered about in orderly chaos.

The trebuchet itself is breath-taking. Or it would be if I had breath. I turn towards Thomlinson in excitement. He appears to be on his hands and knees fiddling with something under the main body of the platform.

"Is it ready?" I ask eagerly, and he jumps, banging his head.

"Nearly," he says, sliding out and clambering to his feet. He looks at me sideways. Of course, he didn't see me properly before. Having a lich instead of a Baron would be a bit of an adjustment. I instantly feel self-conscious about my exposed bones and roughly sewn joints. I'm not sure why I feel so flustered, but then I always was a sucker for men with freckles. It was one of my weaknesses but it's not like liches have sex drives anyway. Probably. At least I don't think I do. I'm just excited about the trebuchet.

The trebuchet is a beast. It is seventeen feet high if it is an inch, and I can smell the pleasing scent of freshly cut spruce and fresh oil coming off the frame. The throwing arm is long and slender. The whole thing is balanced with deadly symmetry. It looks marvellous, better than I had imagined. I jump up and down on the spot, tapping my feet in excitement before I remember to be dignified.

"I'm just testing it," says Thomlinson. He looks a little bemused by my enthusiasm, but then he's probably not used to being dead yet either. "It er... doesn't work very well in the forest. The trees get in the way."

"Oh, I don't intend to use it here," I say at once. "Make sure the wheels are sturdy, it will need to travel."

"Yes... my lady," he replies. His eyes flicker back to the trebuchet and his voice grows impassioned as he talks me through its working. "It should be able to hurl three hundred pounds of rock three hundred yards or further," he finishes. "In the open at least." He frowns up at his creation and scratches his head. Then he turns towards me, his eyes bright. "Would you like a demonstration?"

I clap my hands together and he hurries off, grinning.

Together, he and one of the other draugr workers load an enormous rock into the sling. Casting anxious glances at me, Thomlinson oils the channel with a heavy horse hair brush and then steps back.

"Ready?" he asks, and I nod, excitement skittering along my bones.

Thomlinson pulls on a rope. A sturdy peg pops out of the frame and the beam begins to rotate with a heavy mechanical clicking noise.

The sling slides along the oiled channel with a swish, gaining momentum before it shoots up and out with thrilling violence. The rock goes soaring through the air, disappearing high above the treetops. There is a sharp crack followed by a boom.

I race through the forest, with Thomlinson at my heels, eager to inspect the damage. The rock has flown much further than I expected. After a brief search I find a hefty pine lying on its side, the rock in pieces next to it. The mark of the impact shows in an exploded radius of splintered wood.

"Excellent," I say, a grin spreading across my face.

Thomlinson beams in satisfaction. I congratulate him on his incredibly attractive building skills and leave him to work on the wheels. I head on back to my cottage, clutching my flowers and still smiling broadly.

Jenkins arrives out of the garden to have his ears scratched and I pet him absentmindedly, rooting around in the cupboard for a stout clay jar to hold my flowers. Something cream catches my eye, and I turn with a frown.

There is a piece of parchment on my kitchen table.

Who would come in and leave a note? Has someone been in my cottage? Who would dare come in without my permission and why would they leave me a letter? I move through the rooms, clutching my war axe, but I am alone. Nothing is disturbed. Strange.

Returning to the kitchen I unfold the note with great suspicion. It is addressed to me. In my own handwriting. Huh.

It reads:

Dear Maud,

Please read 'Captain Ferrell and the Robber Baron's Daughter', at your leisure. I think you will enjoy it very much.

Love Maud.

What a peculiar thing.

I do not recall owning such a book. Something to do with the crows I assume. Not being able to remember is very vexing. I walk over to the bookshelf and look through the sparse contents. I don't own many books, they are too expensive. Next to my spell books, there are some recipes and one or two well-thumbed works of fiction. One spine of faded brown leather I don't recognise: '*Captain Ferrell and the Robber Baron's Daughter*' by HR D'arcy. I flip it open, not sure what to expect. It seems to be just a regular story book. I scan the first page, and my eyes widen. Then I shut it firmly.

Yes, I will enjoy reading that.

I will treat myself later. For now, I want to make a start on my skirt and have a good think. I get out the hessian and the velvet. I have always thought best with busy hands.

I spend a pleasant few hours stitching and make a good start on the embroidery. Picking out a dark green silk thread that is almost an exact match for the velvet, I make a little pattern of skulls and mistletoe leaves around the hem.

By the time midnight rolls around I have a beautiful new skirt and a workable plan to depose the Baron. I bite off the thread with my teeth and tie a knot.

It is all coming together.

Chapter Twenty
Ghost Garden

Five minutes later I am doubting myself once more. I stare down at the drawings I have scratched on the parchment, at the creations I have planned. One thing I *do* know is that I am going to need a lot more thread. This can be arranged.

Writing out a letter to the haberdasher in Greater Downing, I ask her to deliver the thread to the stone altar at Lowcroft Bridge. I sign it the 'Lady of Downing Forest'. I frown, thinking hard. Then I add a postscript asking her who the Mayor of Greater Downing is and where they live. For later.

Letter done, I roll up the piece of parchment into a tube and tie it closed with a length of black satin ribbon. Hmm. I don't have a wax seal and it looks a little plain. After some thought I gussy it up with a sprig of hemlock and one perfect dried thistle, tucking the plants between the paper and the satin. I pause, to admire the effect. Better, but it needs something more. For *gravitas*. I cast my eye around the kitchen, searching for inspiration.

I know! When Jenkins was alive he had a habit of hoarding mice and other body parts in the kitchen cupboard, and I assume they will still be there. I stoop to open the cupboard door and my resting cat looks up at me accusingly.

"Excuse me," I say.

He starts to wash himself rather pointedly. I grin and peer into the corners, looking for his pile of little dead trophies. Ah yes. In death he has continued the habit. The size of his prey has increased dramatically, however. A wolf's head stares back at me, its glassy eyes dull. I'm glad he left the rest of the carcass outside.

"What a clever boy," I say approvingly. He ignores me. I grab two delicate mouse skulls. They are dry and smooth in my hands, like brittle shells. "Jenkins," I say, "can I have these?"

Jenkins doesn't object so I take them back to the kitchen table, leaving him to his ministrations. Back at the table I loop the ribbon through the skulls, letting them dangle together like little ivory bells. Perfect. I find a gold coin and leave it next to the letter. The crows can deliver it next time they are around.

I glance once more at the list I have made, and the little drawings in the margins. My plan is not fancy, and involves a great deal of violence. The Baron needs to be persuaded that it is not in his best interests to send his knights here, and that he should dissuade the clerics from sticking their noses where they don't belong. That much is clear, but how to do it?

I could send him a strongly worded letter, but I suspect mouse skulls and my finest ribbon won't be enough. I could visit him in the night to have a chat. My eyes brighten at the thought of midnight shenanigans. I could sneak through the castle looking dashing. My fingers clutch the edge of the table in excitement and I accidentally gouge a chunk out of the table top at the thought of thieving the lavender dress from under the nose of the noble lady! She probably has so many she wouldn't even notice it gone.

Then I slump in despair as soggy reality washes away my daydreams. If I go to talk to the Baron I have to be prepared to kill him. I am strong but I am not invulnerable. The man is likely well defended. So when I talk to him... that's it. I need to approach from a position of strength. I can't give him an inch. Visiting him and then leaving him alive would just lead to more trouble. My hand clenches into a fist.

Killing him is the obvious solution. There are very few political situations that can't be improved with a little blunt force trauma. At least in the short term. But if I kill the Baron, who do I replace him with? *I* don't want to be a ruler. I don't want to have to deal with politics, or people, or paperwork. I shudder at the thought. It might be fun for an afternoon but no more than that. What I *need* is a ruler who is sympathetic. Someone who understands the importance of privacy. Someone with a respect for bones and an appreciation for aesthetics.

If the Baron can't be persuaded that Downing Forest is off limits then I guess I will have to make a new Baron. One who knows which side his bread is buttered.

I rap my knuckles against the wood.

Would the nobility notice that they are being ruled by a draugr? I have seen the amount of powder and funny wigs involved. Maybe they wouldn't notice. According to my mother, who admittedly was not an expert, the aristocracy spend all their time carousing or high on narcotics. This seems unlikely however. A puppet Baron *might* be worth a try, at least until I can find someone more...pliable.

Worrying about it gives me a headache, and all the tranquillity I got from making my skirt goes tumbling away like leaves in the wind. I stand up, shoving aside the chair to pace the kitchen. I wear tracks around the table and finally, in danger of wearing a groove into the flagstones I wander out to the garden. Perhaps this will ease my mind.

It does not.

I've been so busy the last few days, I haven't really had a chance to take a good look at my garden. Things are different now. I know this.

Mostly I am pleased with the changes but... my garden is dying. My bees have already died. Everything is rotting. The blackened blight of my passage had at first been limited to the space between door and gate, and the stones of my kitchen. Now it has spread. While the darkness is beautiful I cannot help but mourn the loss of my dahlias, of my herbs and my bees. My garden has never been so silent before. I don't like it.

I wander over to my hives. They are empty and still in the moonlight. The tiny carcasses of the bees lie everywhere, their little bodies shrivelled and blackened, the jolly yellow stripes no more, their gossamer wings still. A breeze rises a little, and they move, shifting in the air in a subtle mockery of life.

Next to my hives is my small forest altar, worked into the bark of an ancient oak. The walnut carving of the Green Lady stands forlorn, her hare ears poking through the tangle of vines that make up her hair. Now the vines are withered, crumbled like the strewn dead flowers that are left over from the last time I prayed.

I step forward and a late autumn rose snaps under my foot. Its stem is black and cracked, the petals festering grey, the last of its colour crumbling into dust as I pluck it. I let the remains drop from my skeletal fingers to drift away. Perhaps I was always a husk, waiting to die, poisoning everything with my touch. Perhaps this is why being a lich feels right. This is just... fitting. My natural state.

Standing in the centre of the blight I have created the heart I no longer possess beats hollow. What am I but a creature of destruction and death after all? This is my kingdom of decay. It was not meant for me to nurture the living and I should accept that. Not for me the buzz of bees in a hive or the heat of a honey drink before a roaring fire in the evening. Not for me children, or the warm embrace of loving arms on a cold night.

No.

My chest is a dusty tomb and I will make the most of this frigid cage that is my existence. I would cry but I no longer have tear ducts. Instead I fall to my knees in the blackened earth and sit, as still as the goddess' statue, letting the despair take me.

I do not know how long I stay like this but the stars wheel overhead as I mourn.

As I clamber to my feet, a shadow lifts from the moon. A glimmer catches my eye, twinkling between the dense foliage of the surrounding forest, just a little beyond the garden wall. My bones heavy, I walk forward through the trees to see what it is. Ah yes. The ghost oak I summoned a couple of nights ago.

I stare up at the beauty of those spectral branches and something eases in my brain. As I step backwards, my feet crunch in the gently decomposing debris of the forest floor.

I should be preparing, should be making sure I am ready for the attacks that I know will come, but suddenly I have something much more important to do. What point does my wretched existence have if my garden is taken from me? The idea catches fire in my brain and I run, sprinting through the trees, streaking past a grove of startled deer too fast for them to react, too fast for the blight to take.

I grab a large bag of charged soul gems from the cottage cupboard and dash back into my garden. I hope the tiny little souls of my bees still cling to their bodies. My fists clench in fear and anticipation.

"Decipula alma," I whisper. For a moment nothing happens and I bite back my sorrow. But a moment later gleaming sparks float from the bees to trap themselves in the soul crystal. I have them! *"Resurgemus iterum!"*

Delight pools in my eyes, sharp like pain, as first one, then another, then the whole swarm rises in the air. I sit back on my heels, speechless. Just like that I have a swarm of draugr bees. Their buzz is low, and melodic, far from the wild hum of living but still, music to my undead ears. It vibrates through the garden, shivering up my bones in a slightly ominous rumble. What will my undead bees harvest? I look around wildly at the withered garden, and the decomposing flowers.

I reanimate a withering dahlia, watching as the sagging plants perk up, straightening and standing tall, the deep pink of its blossoms transforming to velvet black. The stem is no longer green, transforming into a brittle latticework of whites and greys, as delicate as my finger bones. It is so beautiful I have to stop and stare for a while.

In a rampage of happiness, I rush through my garden coaxing to life the corpses of my lavender, sage, sorrel and my mint. I catch the fragile, battered body of a butterfly and bring it back. Its wings are a delicate, lace-like skeleton that beat eerie-soft in the moonlight. The lemon tree comes back dark and twisted but with gleaming bone-white veins of leaves.

I intersperse the draugr plants with ghosts. Spectral roses and dandelions, thistles and myrtle stand amongst their skeletal counterparts. The draugr plants are particularly interesting. Their souls sing faintly in the night, the ghosts of their old bodies clinging to the corpses of the new, phasing in and out of reality. Spectral petals gleam in the dark, hovering over, through and around blackened stems.

The garden lets off a soft light. It is not constant, now darkness, now glitter, but it is a living death, as elusive as the wind.

The soft hum of the draugr bees soothes my soul.

As if summoned by the thought the enormous black rooster and his brood of undead hens arrives, clearly approving of the changes I have wrought. Jenkins comes to see what is happening, stepping with gentle paws through the ghost flowers. He swats absentmindedly at a nearby corpse hen with his paw, and then comes to curl at my side. I boop him on the nose.

For a long moment everything is as it should be.

Chapter Twenty-One
Patchwork Army

I assemble my wights and draugr in front of me in the ruined square. The black rooster glares down at them all, clearly unimpressed. I pace back and forward, trying to make up my own mind. The world's finest undead army they are not, but they are not without potential. The geese I dismiss immediately. There are no improvements to be made there. The human wights and draugr on the other hand... I don't have time to sew modifications but I can outfit them better, from the supplies I have been collecting.

The reconstituted bandits and fighters are happy enough with their weapons and armour but the villagers are useless.

"Mistress Maud," says Duncan, the blacksmith's apprentice. I raised him because I thought his big muscles would be more useful spent in the defence of my forest than rotting in a pile. "I do not know how to use a bow and arrow."

"You can practise while you wait," I say, slightly annoyed. Of course, he doesn't know how to use a bow and arrow. Why would he? He spent his life hammering bits of metal. Undead strength is useful but doesn't create skill where previously there was none. I might have to rethink this. Wights probably make better soldiers. They do not think and if I tell them to attack they will. They won't worry about how. They won't worry about dying. On the other hand, they would be easier to defeat by a skilled swordsman. Or a cleric. Ug, the clerics.

Flesh and blood is easy enough to deal with, but gods and spells... I am at a disadvantage, at least until I have had time to properly educate myself. So I must move quickly to secure my position, before the churches get too involved. Once the fiefdom is under my control I can give instructions, by proxy, that there is no need for clerics. If everyone leaves me alone, I am content to leave them alone. Assuming they don't get in my way, of course. What is needed is mutual respect and politeness.

Blah, blah, blah.

"Carry on with your chores," I say to the waiting villagers, and they disperse back to the jobs Roland has given them. He casts me a worried look from the top of his wall. It is like being watched over by an extremely ugly nursemaid. I know he is anxious but he really has no need to be. I turn my back on him and march into my crafting shed where I have laid out my supplies on a freshly constructed stone table. Hopefully it will be easier to wash than the wooden one in my cottage.

There are plenty of leftovers lying about and it is time to use them up. My cold storage is piled high with bits. I tap one long bony finger against my cheek as I consider. Then I crack my knuckles and get out the sketches I have made, laying them out on the table. On the other side I place my basket with a selection of threads and ribbons. Then I nip out to the cold storage shed and bring in a selection of body parts. They are in varying states of decomposition and there is not a whole body among them. A clean-up is really overdue.

Humming to myself I take a seat and thread my needle, starting with a serviceable cotton. Lopping off some likely looking limbs with my axe, I match the thread to the skin tone. Too late I realise I am working with two mismatched right feet. Ah well. This is just an experiment after all, and my stitching is very nice. Deftly, I join the feet together, finishing them off with some daisy stitches in deepest blue. I knot the thread before I get too carried away.

Sadly, I don't think too many people will stop to admire the needlework and I don't want to spend too much time on things that will likely just get hacked to pieces. Or set on fire. The resulting project is a little ungainly, but should be serviceable.

I kiss the top of it, for luck and sit back.

"Resurgemus iterum," I recite, moving my hand in a slow, lazy circle. My creation does not need a soul to fulfil its purpose. And apparently wights do not need to be...whole.

The feet jolt upright, the toes twitching.

As I suspected, the two right legs are a little awkward but seem to have no problem moving. They take one step, then two. It takes them a moment to figure out they need to work in concert. Once they do, they are surprisingly fast. The feet scamper off the table and rush across the floor before smashing into the stone wall of the repurposed cottage. It falls to the ground, a little dazed. Then the little monster-thing rebounds, hops, and limps its way at speed in the opposite direction. This time it knocks itself over on the table legs.

Oh, dear. I should have made one with eyes.

I set the mismatched pair of feet free in the forest and sit back down to try again.

This time I select four men's hands. I stitch them together at the wrists so that the palms are down and the fingers spread out around the stumps like a flower. It takes me a while to find a head with a small enough neck to fit. When I do I sew it to the severed stumps. It is old Mr Philpot who lived in the cottage by the tannery.

"Helloooo Mr Philpot," I say to him as I work. "Aren't you happy to be a useful member of the community in your old age?"

The decomposing head does not reply, which is probably for the best. I tut. A crow or some other vermin has eaten his eye but he really only needs one to see where the hands are going. At least I hope he only needs one. We shall see.

I whisper the words to reanimate him and sit back to see what happens. The fingers twitch as they are suffused with new life. Mr Philpot's remaining eye flies open, glaring wildly, the whites showing all the way around. Yay! This project is a success! I observe happily as the Mr Philpot-Hand-Monster scuttles about the room. It screams a little as it goes, but this only lends to the cuteness. Hopefully he will strike fear into the hearts of my enemies. Or at least bite their ankles.

"Come here," I say, and it scampers over, the fingers flexing like an anxious tarantula on the stone floor. The little monster glowers up at me. "Sit." I say, and the fingers relax, the stumpy neck thumping to the ground. "Fetch me the blue ribbon."

It hesitates for a moment, and then starts to climb its way up the table leg. It darts over to the ribbon basket and pauses once more. I can see it is trying very hard to think. Then it dives headfirst into the ribbons, remerging with a green one between its teeth. It rushes over to me, and spits it out, beaming proudly. I wonder if Mr Philpots was colour-blind. It seems likely.

"Well done," I say. Good enough though. It can obey simple instructions. "Go and wait in the long barn until I need you. Off you go."

It plops to the stone and scuttles off, the fingers tip-tapping over the floor.

Now that I have proof of concept I set in to work in earnest. I just need to remember that the little monsters need eyes to see and presumably ears to hear my commands. I'm not sure about the ears, maybe the magic is enough? Just in case I will make sure they all have ears. There are plenty lying about. Mouths seem superfluous as they do not need to eat to sustain themselves. Psychological warfare is a consideration, however, and lips can be decorative.

I lay out the body parts and rub my hands together. Time for some serious creativity! I have a wide variety of monsters I would like to make, and lots of ideas to try out. All of them are patchwork, but in a way I think it makes them more attractive, and not just because of my stitching.

I start off with little ones that scuttle and creep, and then move up to medium sized ones. I make a rather beautiful one with concentric circles of shell-like ears and fingers but have to remind myself it will likely be near-useless in battle, no matter how pretty it is. I stitch far into the night and through the next day. Elding and Tora arrive to watch for a while. They help themselves to some eyeballs until I shoo them away. Roland comes to check on me. I assure him I am fine and show him the little monsters. He is gratifyingly impressed and returns to his chores.

When night descends once more I go for a walk to stretch my legs. I am not physically tired, never that, but my mind needs a break. I check on the progress of the trebuchet and am pleased. The wheels are looking grand and Thomlinson has started work on a second. I don't think more than one will be necessary but it never hurts to be prepared. The draugr knights are attempting to train the villagers with varying degrees of success. That is fine, they will have the geese and the little monsters to support them.

Tora ghosts by on night-dark wings to bring me a letter that has been left on the stone altar at Lowcroft Bridge. I unfold it. It is from the proprietor of the haberdashery in Greater Downing and includes the information I requested about the mayor. I draft two letters in response, one to the proprietor, and one to the mayor himself. What they choose to do with the information is up to them.

Keep your people inside tomorrow night, if they want to live. Come to the castle at dawn.

Love, the Lady of Downing Forest. X

Will the mayor heed my warning? Do I have a reputation? Based on the presence of the peasants at the altar, I think yes. But will it have spread to such an austere personage as the mayor of Greater Downing? We shall see.

Tora flies away to deliver them, and I return to my stitching.

It occurs to me as I sit down that I don't need to be constrained by human size, and I make some truly inspired monsters. Big ones. I stitch together bunches of arms, and bouquets of legs. I find if I attach too many heads to a single monster it gets a bit befuddled. I do make one with lots of eyes, all of them glittering with malice and it is beautiful.

Next I construct a monster the size of a horse, made from the parts of at least twenty people. It is a fascinating puzzle and I have to remind myself not to get carried away. Interestingly, the larger monsters are slower to move. Like the ones with more than one head they tend to be slightly confused. I think they will be able to do some damage, however, but it will be no good if they are destroyed quickly, and their size makes them a target.

With this in mind I force myself to return to the little and medium sized ones. I promise myself that I will experiment in the future. Eventually I will build the perfect monster but right now I must focus on the present.

By the time night falls once more I have a shed full of exquisite monsters all ready to go. I get to my feet and stick my needle into my pincushion.

I fasten my helmet and buckle my pauldrons.
Time to restock my inventory.

Chapter Twenty-Two

Monster Parade

There is one last job I need to take care of before we set off. I frown down at the sun paladin's body. The acolyte's soul I consumed in the passion of battle, and one sun paladin's corpse escaped into the forest with the panicking horse. I have been unable to locate it. The last, however, I recovered, albeit in two pieces.

I have sewn his head neatly back onto the stump of his neck using a cheerful thread—dyed sunshine yellow with a concoction I made of onion skins, cold tea, rhubarb and tansy petals. It amuses me to see the embroidery but I hope I don't come to regret my black humour. How far will his god's protection go? Will he retain the skills of his life? I badly want to know. Having a minion who can perform magic might be the difference between defeat and victory if more clerics are involved.

I frown down at the paladin's slumped body, at the vivid white sunburst emblazoned on his shield. The armour is now dented, and his once spotless surcoat is splotched and bloodstained, which is honestly an improvement. A bit of ruggedness never hurt anyone but perhaps I can scorch it a little so that the sunburst looks a bit less...cheerful.

I open my mouth to bring him back and then shut it again. No point being anxious. There is only one way to find out what will happen and it is better to know now. I killed him once I can do it again.

"Resurgemus iterum," I whisper.

The body shudders, the armour clanking. The sun paladin's eye's snap open. He blinks, gasping, his chest heaving for breath that will not come. Hazel eyes focus on me, and a ragged scream rips from his throat.

"Monster!" he howls. His body twitches and spasms, then his hands fly to his throat as memory returns. He gropes at the stitching. "You killed me!"

"Yes?" I ask. "Hello."

"I'm dead!"

He seems intelligent. I watch with interest as his hands scrabble at his side. Is he looking for his sword? I have hidden it on the other side of the room, at least until I can see how he responds to his new life. I can tell he is fighting harder against my control than the villagers ever had, harder than anyone else I have raised. Intriguing. He gets to his feet, clanking, and growls in frustration, clutching one hand to the side of his head. Standing up he is fully half a head taller than me, and I have to tilt my chin to meet his eyes. For a moment I think he is going to attack, but then he sinks down again with a moan of agony.

"I don't understand," he says.

"You died," I explain, "and then I brought you back to serve me."

I am impatient, but death can be disorientating. Twisting the fingers of my right hand in the folds of my skirts, my left hand tightens on my war axe. I think I know what will happen if he invokes the Bright One, but it is a hunch only, an educated guess. I want confirmation.

"Summon your god," I taunt. He looks up in surprise. "Do it."

His eyes brighten. Perhaps he had forgotten his spells in the confusion of his rebirth, but I can see the memories flooding back. It seems to bring him strength.

"Solemfero," he shouts, leaping up.

Bright light covers him and I step back, shading my eyes.

"Yes!" he says, laughing, "do not forsake me Bright One!"

He advances, the golden glow snaking around his armour, lighting up the interior of the cottage and throwing my crafting table into eerie relief. Twin orbs of blistering light rotate in his hand as he steps forward menacingly.

The paladin falters, his eyes suddenly clouding over. His magic stutters. The orbs start to shake in his hands and as I watch, corruption seeps into the edge of the light. Is his armour corroding? Or had it already started to rust? Suddenly there is no doubt. Black ichor trickles from the joints and his hazel eyes are washed by darkness. He screams, clawing at his face as the sclera turns solid, inky black. The radiant light turns to darkness. The suns are no longer suns, but void black balls wreathing his hands in ebony.

"Whisperer take me," he cries, falling to his knees. His eyes do not change back. I look down at him, a little sadly.

"He already has."

I sheathe my war-axe. I have my confirmation.

Walking over, I reach down and pat him on one dejected shoulder. He does not move, but his shoulders shake slightly.

"What is your name?"

"What?"

"What is your name?"

"Sir Timothy Arkwright," he says, his eyes downcast.

"Don't worry, Sir Timothy Arkwright," I say, awkwardly. "You will be useful."

This does not seem to console him. I walk to the door, and turn back. "Come on."

Without meeting my eyes he gets up and follows. All the fight has gone out of him and inside my ribcage contracts. I don't really understand why. It is certainly easier for me to compel him to obedience but his helplessness makes me uneasy.

He is before me as I am before the Whisperer, and I dislike the reminder. I dislike it intensely.

I walk out into the forest, my face set.

With my new void knight in tow, I stop by my cottage to collect my war kit of charged soul gems, and thread. I sling them into an old leather foraging bag and then turn to leave. Briefly, one skeletal foot hovering over the threshold I contemplate stopping to make myself a more stylish bag. One that matches the elegance of my skirts? But no, time is of the essence. After I have dealt with the Baron there will be ample time for crafts. I will sew a new bag, and new clothes for everyone. Roland can get a new suit, Timothy can have a nice new surcoat in black and Thom... I will think of something I can make for Thom.

I stomp my way back through the trees. The Baron is waiting. Or rather, I hope he isn't waiting, but I am so looking forward to having a chat. I'm sure it will be a civilised conversation. Grinning, I adjust my pauldrons, and check for the millionth time that I have everything. I do. There is nothing left to do but go.

Elding arrives on ghost wings to bring me news. Several hours earlier I had sent him off to watch the church at Great Downing.

"No clerics, *Ka*," Elding says, tilting his head and fastening his sole beady black eye on me.

"Good," I say. "No one at all?"

"Not at the church," he says. "A priest, idle peasants. No clerics. No god touched. No shinies."

"Thank you," I say, and send him back, just in case. I send Tora ahead to scout the town. I want eyes on that castle. It is time to go.

The sun is just setting and the forest is golden. Autumn-stained mists rise between the trees as my little monsters scuttle and chitter through the leaves. I leave Roland in charge of the village, with a handful of wights and a couple of draugr, just in case. Then, doing my best to contain my excitement, I assemble the rest of my patchwork army and herd them off through the gloaming, heading for the forest road.

It is slow going.

The trebuchet, pulled by Dark Star and the little draugr donkey is quite mobile, but it is heavy and awkward, and it keeps getting stuck on the treetops. I have to keep a careful eye on the geese, especially the wights. They keep getting bored and wandering off into the forest to harass the local wildlife. By the time we reach the forest road I am feeling quite flustered.

The trebuchet, at least, trundles easier once we hit the road. In the end I pair up the monsters—a human draugr in charge of a group of wight geese, another herding a group of little monsters, and for a while we make better time. The biggest problem is everything moves at different speeds, and the wights are basically brainless. The giant torso snake in particular is very slow.

I had built it at the end of my marathon sewing session after I realised I had a lot of dismembered chests left over. Originally it was intended to be a centipede but I ran out of feet and hands. Instead, I stitched rows and rows of ribs, joining them horizontally. The resulting monster is a delightfully snakey thing that undulates along the ground, pushing and slithering.

Its tail, purely for aesthetics, is made of a tapering trail of leg bones (I could only spare three). The head belonged to the late Mrs Roberts and looks a bit ridiculous. A monster of this size needs a proportional head. A grizzly bear or a moose perhaps. Alas, I didn't have anything larger available, although I was able to find a pair of antlers which made her look slightly more imposing. The torso monster is degrading quite rapidly as slithering over rocks and ground is not kind to the already decomposing flesh. On the other hand when it gets down to bare ribs it seems to move more easily so I let it be.

Slowly, my monstrous army parades through the rapidly darkening woods and along the moonlit road to Greater Downing. We don't meet anyone along the way, and a few slow hours later we arrive in sight of the town.

I bid my little army to still themselves and wait in the trees.

With the void knight at my side, I walk down the deserted road towards the gates. It is approaching midnight now, and the houses and fields lie quiet and empty, soaked in the grey of the scudding clouds. I draw the elegance of my skirts around me, and hold my shoulders back before rapping sharply on the gate.

A tiny peephole shoots open.

"Yes?" barks a sleepy looking watchman. He looked down at me, his jaw dropping open. His eyes widen and he lets out a rather breathy whine. I can imagine my eyes would be rather startling if you are not used to their sapphire fire. I assume he is looking at my glowing eyes, and not the gaunt flesh or the bone of my exposed scalp.

"Greetings," I say formally. I have a little speech prepared. Unfortunately, before I have the chance to give it, he starts to shout for his fellow guards. I do not want him to cause any alarm so I wrench the iron lattice off the great gate and shove my hand through the narrow hole. It is decent workmanship, and takes more than a little effort. I am able to grab him by the throat, a move that seems to take him by surprise. My slender arm only just fits, but it is enough.

"Excuse me," I say, pointedly, pulling him towards me so that his head bangs on the wood of the opposite side of the gate. He gasps, turning purple. If I stand on the very tips of my toes I can glare at him. It is annoying having to look up at people as I intimidate them. "I'm here to talk to the Baron. Will you please open the gate?" He gurgles something. "I'm going to put you down now. Don't do anything stupid. Just. Open. The. Gate."

I open my hand and let him drop, fully expecting stupidly to reign supreme.

It does.

The instant his feet hit the ground he is screaming for his colleagues. I am forced to consume his soul, and the souls of his compatriots as they come running, just to keep the peace. I used a lot of soul energy to create my little monsters so I am slightly disappointed to discover that the gate is only guarded by three men. They do take the edge off my hunger, however, at least for the moment.

I raise one of them as a wight and instruct him to unlock the gate, which he does. The heavy gate swings open with a soft creak.

I beckon to my little army and watch with pride as the creatures spill out of the forest, undulating and scurrying down the hill to join me. Moonlight reflects off a myriad glinting eyeballs, off ivory bones and teeth and off gently decomposing flesh. The trebuchet comes last, a tall, rather menacing shadow bringing up the rear. I can see the Mr Philpot-monster dancing this way and that along the beam as it trundles.

"Quietly now," I say to the monsters, as they reach me. They pick up their feet, (or whatever it is they are walking with) as softly as they can. I appreciate the effort as I can see it is taxing. The undead geese in particular have trouble being quiet. It is likely that demonic honks will issue forth at any moment, with or without my blessing, so I hurry them forward, beneath the portcullis and into the town proper.

I walk through the midnight streets of Greater Downing, surrounded by my minions and monsters. The town is much more to my liking at midnight. The shops are shut and boarded and there is not a living soul to be seen. The streets are swathed in purple shadows, with only a few fitfully burning torches at irregular interludes. I doubt many people would be abroad at such a chill hour anyway, but perhaps the mayor has common sense after all.

Only once do I see a curtain twitch in an upstairs room. A pale face briefly looks down at my undead parade and then the curtain is hurriedly pulled back. Wise.

The scurrying of the little monsters is a soft susurrus across the cobble stones. Tora coasts overhead on soft wings. The trebuchet has been oiled within an inch of its life but a quiet rumble marks its passage. Hopefully the townspeople will assume a cart in the night. I don't particularly want to kill the humans so I hope we can pass without most of them noticing. It is the Baron who needs to be persuaded of his proper place in the universe. I look up at his banner hanging from one of the run down buildings with distaste. Those will have to go. My cottage needs new drapes anyway.

We make our way through the town square. It is devoid of life and even the stocks are empty, their reflection glinting in puddles of fouled rainwater. The rotting body of the witch still hangs from her noose, twisting briefly in the wind. It is a pathetic thing, barely even recognisably human. I pause, looking at it.

It could have been me, if I had had the misfortune to live in Greater Downing. Or if I had been less canny.

I send a little monster with a knife in its mouth to cut her down. The corpse lands on the cobbles with a wet thud. It is the work of moments to reanimate what is left of the witch's body. Her soul has clung on. She rises into new life with a spite and energy that makes me think she was close to becoming a wraith. She has no mouth left with which to speak but I can feel the hatred radiating off her in waves. I am sure she will enjoy "speaking" with the Baron almost as much as I will. I invite her to join us.

My sinister procession passes through the town without further incident and we are soon making our way up the winding path to the castle. The castle gate is blocked by a lowered portcullis. I send one of the monsters to knock on the watch door and a sleepy guard answers. Like his fellows at the town gate he is unreasonable, so I eat his soul, and ask his wight to raise the gate, which he does.

At this point stealth becomes untenable as the portcullis is sorely in need of grease. The iron gate clanks and creaks as it inches its way upwards. Shouts sound from beyond the wall, and lights flare from the castle battlements.

They know I am here.

I grin, and gesture the trebuchet forwards.

Chapter Twenty-Three
THE TARRASCH RULE

The trebuchet wheels through the gatehouse followed by the squealing, screaming horde of monsters big and small. I give up trying to keep them quiet. Wights are not really cut out for stealth and the castle knows we are here anyway. The castle ramparts are boiling like a poked hornets' nest. I bid my army to stay back for now. Perhaps they won't be needed. Perhaps the Baron and I will have a polite conversation and then we can all go home. Ha, ha, ha.

A wide expanse of parade ground stands between us and the moat, and beyond that the inner curtain wall and the keep. The main castle itself is round, chubby stone with fortified towers at each corner. The grounds are lit by various smoking torches and braziers, which throw the walls into lurid orange relief. I send a wight to snuff out the surrounding torches so we are bathed in shadow and instruct Thomlinson to begin preparations on the trebuchet.

Tora flutters down and lands on my arm, her talons digging into my sparse flesh.

"Do you see the Baron?" I ask, and the crow shakes her head.

"Sleeping," she says. "Ka!"

"Not for long," I say, looking up at the battlements. Cries echo up from the stony courtyard and I can hear doors banging. Men rush along the parapets, yelling and pointing. They seem as excited to see us as we are to be here.

"I smell one," Tora says, flexing her talons into my arm. I feel a claw scrape against one of my bones, and lightning sizzles there briefly, illuminating the veins and sinew. "Burning."

"A cleric, or a fire mage?"

Tora's beak parts in that laughing, taunting manner, or is she tasting the air? The crow shrugs.

"One god-touched," she says, "smells like ash."

"A sun paladin," I say, throwing a glance at my black knight. Timothy stands beside me, stoic and collected, his eyes pits of darkness. He does not react to our conversation but I know he is listening. "Just one?" Tora nods affirmation.

That doesn't sound too bad, although I suppose it depends on the rank of the cleric.

"Stay here," I say to everyone. I walk across the parade ground and over to within shouting distance of the castle gatehouse. Tora drifts after me, ghosting on dark wings. I think she is enjoying herself, but then the chance of carrion tonight is fairly high. One way or another.

The drawbridge is shut tight, and the moat gleams evilly, the wind scudding little ripples of orange light across the surface. I make sure to stop short of arrow range. I feel naked and small, standing alone in front of those great walls, and I have to remind myself how glorious my skirts look with my pauldrons.

"Hello!" I shout, cupping my hands. "I'm here to speak to the Baron!"

I wait, but this pronouncement only seems to stir the castle's defenders into a fresh frenzy. Red, angry faces are just visible between the ramparts as the men shout and swear at each other. Some of them stand, aiming crossbows and a flurry of arrows hiss through the air, peppering the lawn in front of me like a pincushion, but I am safely out of range. Unfortunately, they are also out of range of my soul magic. A pity, but I had anticipated this.

"Hello?" I shout again.

No one attempts to talk but I can see the scoundrels are heating something up behind the walls. Just as I am about to turn on my heel, Tora lands once more, this time on my shoulder. She caws loudly in my ear, looking up.

A man and a woman walk out of the tower and stand at the centre of the ramparts, looking down at me. The man I can safely assume is Baron Alderton, the lord and master of Greater Downing and the fiefdom of Downing. I have never actually seen him before but his armour is ceremonial and gaudy, and his belly substantial. He looks uneasy, as I grin up at him.

The woman is a sun paladin, there can be no doubt. She gleams gently in the night, a soft star bathing all near her in the gold of her glow. Like the others before her, her armour is blindingly shiny. Her hair is long and loose, tumbling over her shoulders in an untamed glory of sun-kissed blonde. She might as well be holding a pennant with 'look at my enormous ego' embroidered on it. That stuff is a hazard in a real fight. I can tell she is not used to things getting dirty. While her body is suffused with light, her eyes are as hard as agates. No soft gold there.

"Scion of evil," she cries. "Who are you and what ill wind blows you to our shores?"

"Since you asked," I shout. "I am the Lady of Downing Forest, and I'm thoroughly sick of people invading my home. I'm here to make it stop."

"Begone foul beast!" screeches the Baron, as if I haven't spoken. He clutches the stones and leers down at me with anxious energy.

"I would very much like to be gone," I say. "I had much rather be at home with my sewing but no, I had to lug my tired old bones halfway across the countryside to make a point."

"What are you suggesting?" asks the paladin. At least *her* ears seem to be functional.

"A truce," I say. "Downing Forest is mine. I don't care about anything else. Stay out of my forest and I will stay away from thee and thine."

The Baron makes a noise like a tea kettle coming to the boil.

"We cannot suffer a lich to live," says the sun paladin. She lays one hand warningly on the Baron's arm and the sunshine of her hair floats around her in a self-righteous halo. "The gods will not allow it."

There is a pause.

"Then I believe we are at an impasse," I say, and turn on my heel.

"That's right," screeches the Baron at my back, "begone foul beast! We will hunt you down, have no fear."

"I did not say I was *leaving*," I say with dignity. I don't know if they heard me, and it doesn't really matter. Ah well. I was never great at talking to people. I make my way back to my army that is restlessly quiet in the shadows.

The Baron and the sun paladin are still watching me from the ramparts. The paladin leans down to speak to the Baron. He glares at her and then lets himself be ushered into the relative safety of the tower interior. The sun paladin turns to the armed men who are waiting on the rampart. Her voice is loud and clear, I can hear her instructions as far away as I am.

"Kill it," she says. She glances my way once more, before she too, disappears from sight. The paladin does not think her magic will be needed. Perhaps I will scalp her and use her hair as a wig. I lift one rather self-conscious hand to my helmet, to the bald patches of flesh on my skull that I know lie beneath. No, that would be weird. I just need to consume enough souls that my own hair grows back. Perhaps tonight will be the night.

Time to set my plan into action.

I look over at Thomlinson.

"Ready?" I ask, and the good-looking ginger nods, a little anxiously. He has oiled the channel to a sheen and the pouch sits waiting. The counterweight is tense and ready. Excellent! All it needs is the payload. There are probably siege engines that would be better suited to attacking this castle, in fact I'm sure there are. Thom tells me there are many varieties.

Now, I am a simple woman, or rather I was a simple woman when I was alive. A witch has no interest in sieges and or military manoeuvres. As a witch my sphere of influence was small and I had what I needed. Violence does not excite me. Alright, that is a complete lie, but the truth is I have no fancy plan. I am going to load my little monsters into the trebuchet and shoot them over the walls. They can murder everyone and then I can go home. This is my plan.

Sometimes simple things are best. Perhaps if I do this again I can try a different engine but it will take a lot to persuade me that trebuchets are not the best thing ever. I crack my knuckles and turn to my little monsters.

"Alright," I say brightly. The undead things chitter and slither in the darkness. "Six or seven of you! Into the sling. Not you big ones, just the small and medium ones. That's right! In you get! That's enough. Alright, now listen closely. Once you land, kill the ones in armour and anyone else who attacks you. Leave the others alone. Open all the doors you can find. See if you can open the drawbridge and let the rest of us into the keep. Everybody ready? Off you go now."

I pull the rope, and the peg pops out. The counterweight swings with a satisfying creak and the first load of squealing, excited, undead monsters sails high into the air. Thomlinson watches them go critically. My aim is not very good. It overshoots and most of them fall into the moat on the opposite side of the castle. A few bounce and bump down the distant turret roof. I can't see that well because the bulk of the castle is in the way but it sounds like a few have landed on the distant ramparts. The men stationed there are apparently not expecting it to rain animated body parts and the sound of screaming is very satisfying.

Excellent.

I still have the element of surprise.

I will teach them what happens when people come into my forest uninvited.

As Thom and I adjust the trebuchet, the drawbridge comes crashing down with a great thud. A score of knights come riding out. I open my mouth to tell my monsters to attack, and then close it again. There is no need. My monsters have all been so well behaved and now they stampede across the grounds in an ecstasy of murderous excitement. The wight geese lead the charge, and the noise of blood-curdling honks fill the castle grounds.

Battle is joined both above and below.

The first wights hurl themselves onto the armoured knights with a great clash. A small monster is smashed into the ground and churned underfoot, while another knight skewers the slower moving torso-monster through one of its many ribs. It bellows and twists, knocking the man off his horse with the impact from its thrashing tail. He is instantly buried in beautifully sewn undead limbs.

Tearing my eyes away, I move to help Thom crank back the counterweight while the knights are distracted. The draugr witch and my void knight have hung back at my side. They watch as I chase up another batch of monsters and load them into the sling.

Once more I pull the lever and the trebuchet sings. This time my aim is true and the entire payload of creatures falls directly into the centre courtyard. I was a little worried that the monsters' stitching wouldn't hold, or that they would be crushed on impact but from the noises issuing forth from inside it seems enough of them have survived.

I hope I have time for a third shot but things are beginning to heat up.

I am not the only one with ranged attack options.

A light flares from the ramparts and a solid, molten glob sails into the sky, briefly illuminating the battlefield. It sails up and over the fight, targeting the trebuchet.

"Watch out!" I scream, and push Thomlinson hard to one side. Burning pitch rains down upon us, and we narrowly avoid being splattered. Several fist sized globs land on the trebuchet and the wood sparks and starts to burn. I beat at them with my skirts, then give up and shovel earth onto it. It does no good and the beam continues to burn. The torso-snake monster undulates past smoking and sizzling. It heads for the moat, falling in with a colossal splash. Good beastie.

"Quickly!" I say to Thom and he runs to help me. We work fast to load up the sling. The trebuchet catches fire in earnest, and the oil of the channel is now burning bright and hot in a fiery line. The heavy scent of burning flesh fills the air, the little monsters waiting in the sling are alight and starting to burn. I pull the lever anyway and they streak, screaming and whistling through the air overhead, lighting up the sky like a comet.

I watch with grim satisfaction as they land, still on fire, and the flames spread to the timbers of the parapet. If the Baron's men didn't want the castle to catch on fire they shouldn't have started playing with fire. Sadly, that will be the last batch of flying monsters as the trebuchet is now burning fast.

Thomlinson leaps back with a cry as the ropes snap, sparks flying.

"Go home," I growl at him, swatting the flames out of my skirt. "I'll finish up here. See you later."

With a startled nod the engineer jogs out of the gate and disappears into the darkness, casting longing looks over his shoulder at the burning siege engine.

The castle drawbridge crashes down once more, and a troupe of shielded archers with crossbows marches out, and strikes a formation, shield wall at the front. Burning arrows spit through the air, pinning several of the smaller monsters to the ground. About half the knights are down, but they are still fighting.

I draw my war-axe with a hiss and run into the fray.

Chapter Twenty-Four

BLACKHOLE SUN

I lock eyes with the nearest knight.

"Foul creature!" he cries, urging his gore splattered charger towards me. I lift my axe and rush to meet him, leaping up at the last minute in a flying kick. The power in my limbs still surprises me sometimes, and I misjudge, landing awkwardly on my side. I do, however, manage to knock the knight from his saddle. He lies on the ground, dazed, a thin trickle of blood leaking from his nose. His charger rears, and gallops away into the night, whinnying.

Jumping to my feet I grab his helmet and tug, fully intending to stomp on his head but the draugr witch is there first. Tearing at his throat with desiccated fingers she lets out a shuddering howl. Her body is such a putrid mass of rotting flesh I'm surprised she is capable of making a noise at all, but there it is. She pushes the stumps of her fingers into the knight's eyes and presses down. He screams and writhes, crimson pouring down his face.

A flaming arrow strikes me on the shoulder, distracting me. I turn with a snarl, searching for the culprit. Across the parade ground an archer blanches and backs away, frantically winding the crank on his crossbow. I sprint the distance and chop off his hands with an overhand blow, before kicking him bodily into the moat. I scoop up his crossbow, aim a bolt at the floundering, screaming archer's head and fire. Huh. It is much easier to fire than my hunting bow. The bolt rips through his neck and he topples over. The water of the moat is quickly turning a darker shade as his body gushes.

A blade whistles past my face, coming perilously close to slashing my skirt. Leaping backwards, I hastily stash the crossbow. I lift my war-axe to brain the offending knight, but before I can a daring little monster latches onto his face. The man screams and falls to the ground trying to dislodge it. This is a mistake. I watch as he is swarmed by a dozen more beautifully embroidered creatures. The little ones seem to be moving in a pack. Fascinating. I spot Mr Philpot's wrinkly visage in the thick of it, his teeth red with blood, and I turn away with a smile.

There are two other knights fighting nearby and I think about playing some more but I find I am growing impatient.

Enough of these games.

I devour the souls of the combatants with a twist of my hand. Their bodies flop to the ground in a succession of thuds and clanks as the light of their souls streams into me. The parade ground quietens, and my monsters still, deprived of their prey. I stand amidst the corpses of the newly fallen dead, and consider. I raise half the knights and archers to swell my ranks, and keep the rest of their soul energy for myself.

The rattle of chains alerts me to the descending drawbridge.

Golden light spills out onto the battlefield, illuminating the churned mud and strewn viscera. The sun paladin has finally come out to play. My lips curve upward. With my void knight on one side and the draugr witch on the other, I advance to meet her challenge.

She stands in the centre of the gate, glittering silver and gold.

For a moment, diaphanous wings flare at her back. I wonder if I imagined it, but no. I am not crazy. Her hair is very annoying. She stands there looking majestic and virtuous, and I wonder if she has ever suffered a hardship in her life. I am probably being unfair but I really want to kill her. Her nose is small and pert and I want to rip it off her face. Slowly.

The sun paladin strides forward, and draws her sword with a metallic rasp. It is a silver monstrosity of a broadsword and she holds it with a casualness that belies its weight. Some of my little monsters take a step backwards but I do not.

"Decided I am worth your time?" I ask, wishing I had an eyebrow to raise.

"We cannot suffer a lich to live," the paladin says, with obnoxious serenity. "You are a scourge upon the earth. If there is any part of you left inside, that is human, you must know this. I beseech you. Call off your foul minions. Too many have died already. Let me return your bones to the earth so that you may rest in peace."

At my side the undead witch gurgles something in her throat. She sounds angry and I don't blame her. The paladin stinks of hypocrisy.

"Who are you to judge the balance of life and death?" I say. "Why do you get to decide that Baron's life is worth more than hers?"

Yes, I am acting out of self-interest. Aggressive self-defence, let's call it, but somewhat surprisingly, I find myself believing my own words. I have never accepted the divine right of kings. The Baron will not be missed by his half-starved, beaten and down trodden subjects. He definitely won't be missed by the witches. Of course, there is no guarantee that whoever I put in charge will do any better, but that is not the point.

The sun paladin looks confused and I gesture to the rotted, foetid form of the undead witch at my side. The paladin shrugs, her eyes slipping off the corpse and back to me.

"Whatever it is," she says, dismissively, "whatever it *was*, it is dead. It should have stayed dead."

"'It' was a woman." I grin, hefting my axe. "I may be an abomination, but at least I do not preach virtue that only extends to those with coin. Now. Get out of my way."

My void knight shifts beside me, and the paladin's eyes snap to him. She seems genuinely appalled as she takes in Timothy's gore-stained surcoat, and his corroding armour. She gazes into the darkness of his pupil-less eyes, her face going paper-white.

"What have you done?" she whispers. "Sir? What has she done to you?" He stares back, his expression blank. "I will avenge you, Sir Arkwright," the paladin cries, and her voice throbs with passion. Ah. They know each other. Figures.

"I will avenge this desecration! On the Bright One's name I swear, though it take my dying breath!"

"I'm waiting," I say.

The paladin snarls and rushes forward, swinging at me two handed. The enormous silver sword cuts through the air and I only just manage to block it, with the length of my war-axe. The blow is unexpectedly strong. It would have driven a human to its knees. Fastening my grip, I dig my heels into the ground and shove the paladin backwards. She staggers, those golden wings flaring again.

This one is more powerful than the paladins I killed on the road.

"Decipula alma," I whisper at the same time she shouts *"Ægisfortissimavirtus!"*

Our magics flare and clash, then fade to nothing.

I grit my teeth. I hate this. I would rather hit things than mutter stupid spells. At least until I know I have the upper hand. She might have more spellcraft at her disposal but I am not alone. My wights and draugr launch themselves at her. The paladin slashes and hacks but they keep coming and a moment later she is buried beneath a twisting pile of undead.

"*Solemfero!*" she shouts, her voice muffled by the bodies.

Light explodes out. Everyone is thrown back. Some of the monsters and wights dissolve in the blast. I land on my coccyx, my own skin starting to sizzle. I pat it out with a hiss and leap up once more.

Muttering spells, I launch myself forward as Timothy rushes her other side.

"*Alis grave nil!*"

The sun paladin springs into the air, going higher than is humanly possible, her magical wings flaring gold once more. She drops, bowling me aside and lands on top of Timothy, with a heavy thud, one knee on his chest. Such is her weight that he is driven into the ground. He grabs for her throat, fastening his undead fingers around her neck. They grapple, but she is stronger, and lifts her sword for a killing blow.

"*Solemfero!*" shouts Timothy.

Void-black globes appear, orbiting the hand gripping her neck. They hum with feral energy, sucking in the light as they rotate. Thick, black liquid starts to leak from the joints of his armour, and she screams, bringing down her sword in a crushing blow. Timothy's head bounces in the muck, the stitching broken.

But the void globes do not vanish. They stick to her like burs. She swats at them desperately, her light flaring but they spread, sinking into the joints of her armour. Where they disappeared, corruption follows. Within seconds she is coated in a growing web of darkness. Spider veins of bituminous black streak across her armour.

"No!" The sun paladin leaps up, scrubbing at herself, desperately trying to cleanse herself. "*Solemfero! Ægisfortissimavirtus!*"

Her light flares, again and again but it is weaker now, like a sputtering candle.

I step back to watch, curious. We all watch her, a silent circle of dead things, and Timothy's severed head. No matter how hard she rubs and scratches the rust grows, the corruption grows, and not just on her armour, but in her body. Veins of darkness are crawling up her face. The silver sword clatters at her side with a dull tinkle. She gropes at her neck, eyes bulging.

"Bright One take me!" she cries, dropping to her knees. "I will not let you take me! I will not-" Her words taper off into a scream. "*Fidem servo!*"

The sun paladin spreads her arms wide, the darkness is crawling towards her eyes now, the corners are black as night, and oozing thick, black teardrops.

"*Fidem servo!*" she screams. "*Fidem servo!*"

Light flares, burning, blinding white.

A plume of fire roars through her body. A raging inferno shoots up and out, as hot as the sun. For a moment everything is incandescent. I fall back, shielding my face from that scorching heat. Fire pours from the paladin's eyes, streaming from her hands, from the crown of her head. Her hair fans out behind her in a radiant flare, her diaphanous wings growing brighter and brighter. She is burning. There is no way she can survive this. I am worried she will take us all with her, and stagger back, dragging the witch and a handful of monsters with me.

An explosion of energy bursts from her, and we are sent tumbling to the ground. The whole world is white and I can see nothing. My head rings like a bell and my skull rattles.

Once my vision clears I sit up.

The sun paladin is gone. No wait! There! A faint shimmer streaks for the stars, a golden ghost set free from its mortal shell. Now she is truly gone. Free, I suppose, and certainly free from me. Her scorched suit of armour topples forward, empty. My head is still ringing.

I frown down at the armour, nudge it aside with my foot. It rolls away, hollow and jingling. A whisper of ash drifts on the wind. Half of my wights and monsters are gone too, disintegrated in the blast. Timothy's head lies to one side, his nose pressed in the muck. I walk over to it and bend to pick it up. As I do so the eyes swivel toward me, and I let out a small shriek.

"She has ascended," the head says. It has to mumble a little because half of its face is in the dirt.

"Oh," I say, recovering myself. "You are still alive."

I'm not sure if I should be surprised or not. Perhaps it has to do with the manner of his first death? Or the magic of my sewing? Or the corrupted energy that flows through him? Whatever it is, I find myself glad. I will miss the monsters who have perished in this fight. They served their purpose but I loved each and every one.

Timothy's head lets out a groan.

I bustle to get my sewing kit, prop his head on my lap and quickly work to reattach it to his body. The stitching is not the best ever but it should hold as long as he stays away from sharp objects. I will figure out what an ascended sun paladin means later. Trouble for later, no doubt. Right now I have a castle to steal.

"There you go," I say, and Timothy clambers to his feet, clanking. He twists his neck, fingers probing at the fresh stitching.

"Thank you," he says, and I nod.

"Thank *you*," I say. But it is time to be getting on.

The parade grounds are eerily quiet. I stare up at the castle battlements. I can't see anyone. The distant sound of muffled fighting echoes up faintly. A plume of smoke is rising into the sky from the central courtyard. No one is watching me, or paying attention to me, and the drawbridge is still up. I feel like I have been left outside of a party I wish to attend.

I glare at the drawbridge for a while but nothing happens. Opening it is probably beyond the ken of my little monsters, and all the surviving wights and draugr are outside here with me. What to do. Hmm. I look up at the rough stone of the castle. Can I climb it?

I wade into the moat, and clamber to the wall, the water closing over my head. Unpleasant but at least I don't need to draw breath. At the wall I grasp the stone with my fingers. There is just enough purchase for me to pull myself up, aided by my undead strength. Hand over hand I scramble my way upwards, like an undignified and rather bony spider.

My little monsters jump and mewl beneath me, some of them attempting to climb themselves. Most of them lack the coordination (and the fingers) to follow. The Mr Philpot-monster, however, scuttles up with ease, his twenty digits making light work of the ascent. I reach the battlements unchallenged, and leap over, my velvet skirts slapping damp as I land, crouched on all fours.

There are only a few defenders left on the wall and they are all focused inwards, firing arrows into the courtyard where, presumably, my remaining monsters are still causing a delightful ruckus. I sneak up behind the closest and kick him over the ramparts with a giggle. He screams as he falls, and lands with a sick, wet thump.

This alerts the others to my presence. With a curse they turn their weapons on me. Mr Philpot goes for the nearest one's ankles, and I suck in their souls with relish. That taken care of, I lean over the cold stone of the battlements.

The scene below is one of chaos and carnage. Running fights are taking place across the courtyard. One side of the castle is alight, the wooden gallery that overhangs the keep belching orange flames and dirty smoke upwards. I scour the area for the Baron. Where is he? Is he hiding or leading the defence? I suspect the latter. I hope I do not have to check every room of the castle to find him, but no. There he is.

Oh yes. I spy his greasy face, the jowls slack with terror and as pale as defrosting mutton. He is hiding behind a bunch of upturned barrels with a group of noblemen and women, trying to fend off the affections of my monsters with varying degrees of success. Or rather the Baron is cowering at the back while his nobles defend him.

I watch in impressed silence as one of the women manages to fend off an assault by a wight goose. She brandishes a rapier as thin as a needle. It looks ceremonial, but the tip is bloody. She looks familiar. Ah. My loud, feisty friend from the carriage. I see she has acquired some new jewellery and a rather lovely burgundy gown that is decidedly snug on the bust. I try not to stare at the embroidery. Focus.

Locating a flight of stone stairs, I tread down them, as menacingly as possible. The Baron catches sight of me, since he is the only one not currently engaged in battle. He squeals like the dying pig that he is soon to be, and points, pulling on the sleeve of the men next to him. I ignore him for the moment, focussing my attention on the handful of people who are still hostile.

Three peasant boys in kitchen uniforms and a stablemaster with a pole-axe are putting up a good fight next to the drawbridge. Brave souls. I knock them all unconscious. Carefully. I think they all survive?

A single bloodied knight remains, hard pressed. He has acquitted himself well, and is surrounded by crushed body parts and unravelling thread. He advances on me, muttering the usual insults about demons and nonsense. He swings a morning-star, a vicious looking weapon that would look well in my collection. The spikes are devastatingly aggressive.

I duck and the spikes whistle over my head, catching one of my helmet horns a glancing blow, and fastening around it. I straighten, chain still wrapped and jolt the knight forwards, then kick him, hard, in the chest. He flies backwards and lands on his back with a crash. I stomp on his chest until it is a mass of red, oozing out from between the joints of his armour. I suppose I could have just consumed his soul but I am feeling rather nervous. I'm not good at talking to people and I know I will have to talk, at least a little.

I sweep up the flail and examine it with some interest. The spiked ball at the end of the chain gives me some interesting attack options. For starters it should travel around corners and over shields. I look up at the cowering Baron with a grin.

I take a moment to lower the drawbridge.

My small horde enters the castle looking a little worse for wear, but still impressive. With my monsters and minions arranged about me I approach the makeshift barricade with nonchalant grace. The noblemen and women all squeal and scream. As I open my mouth to speak, a piece of wood hits me on the head.

"Leave us alone, you monster!"

It is the lady from the carriage. Really she is wasted on the aristocracy.

"I have no interest in you whatsoever," I say, advancing slowly. I put down my weapons and show them my empty hands. An elderly woman in rich velvets faints at the back.

"Y-you don't?" a man in a blood spotted velvet doublet stammers. Lord Henry, I believe his name was?

"Don't listen to the lich!" cries the Baron. "Its lips exist only to speak evil and twist the words of the faithful!"

"Him," I say, pointing with one bony finger. "He's going to die." The Baron's eyes nearly bulge out of his head. "The rest of you?" I shrug. "Are optional. Really it is up to you."

"Why should we believe you?" cries the feisty lady.

"I have no interest in lying," I say. "At least not today. My aim is to take control of this castle and these lands. Mostly I am interested in maintaining the separation of forest and town. If you try to get in my way you will die. That is all. Your choice."

I wait.

There is a pregnant pause. Some of them are looking at the remains of the knight behind me.

"I want to live," says the feisty lady. No surprises there.

"Good choice," I say. "What about the rest of you?"

There is a stillness. Suddenly, without appearing to move, the nobles have made space around the Baron where before there was none.

"Let's talk," he says, to me desperately. "Didn't you say you wanted to talk? Something about a forest?"

"Too late," I say.

I drive my sharp bony fingers right into his chest and rip. It is harder to gouge his flesh than I thought but I still manage. The nobles and the priest squeal as blood splatters their finery. I scrabble around until I find the right organ, and then draw out the Baron's still beating heart in my hand. I hold it up to show the nobles with my best smile, as the Baron's body topples gently to the ground.

It is melodramatic but I don't want any of them to forget this moment. And I deserve to be a little dramatic after such a long night. Afterall, Greater Downing is now mine.

Chapter Twenty-Five
PUPPET SHOW

The surviving members of the castle stand around awkwardly as I disembowel the Baron. I have always wanted to try my hand at puppetry. When I was a little girl my mother took me to Lowcroft for the day and while she was at market I sat and watched a puppet show. Such a happy memory. The stage was a simple thing, just a bit of old plank stretched between barrels, and covered in a small white and red tent. But I'll never forget that hour of magic, the men and women crouched behind the awning bringing life to those dolls of wood and paint and cloth. Well, now the late Baron of Greater Downing will be my life sized puppet.

I am going to enjoy playing with my dolls immensely.

I slice the Baron's belly open with my dagger and root around for his innards. Perhaps I will change the banners of Greater Downing to white and crimson stripes. My own private joke. I chortle to myself as I pull bits out, my arms stained crimson to the elbow. I must remember to take these organs with me, I wonder if my new ghost garden will enjoy some mulch? What next? Ah yes. I send one of the wights to fetch my work bag which I had left with Dark Star at the castle gate. I had anticipated the need for stuffing.

It does not take long to pull out all the unnecessary things, and to fill the Baron full of sweet scented lavender and rosemary. I, myself, have gotten used to the smell of death. Sometimes I even find it pleasant, but I suspect the humans will be less forgiving. He really won't be needing them anymore. Hopefully if he is stuffed to the gills with herbs he will be more acceptable to the living.

My original plan was to return the Baron to life in a stealthy manner. However, I think my theatrics have put paid to that notion. I wipe my hands clean and carefully thread a needle, keeping an eye on the watching nobles. One of the women is vomiting into a barrel. I think they have definitely noticed that the Baron is dead. Whoops.

Having so many people observe puts me off my sewing, so I send them off to extinguish the fires. Probably the first honest day's work most of them have ever done in their lives. They do as I ask without hesitation, which pleases me. It bodes well for their future. I keep Timothy and a couple of my favourite draugrs by my side, just in case. I do not think I will have any trouble however. The nobility have lost their nerve. My arguments were, ahem, violently persuasive.

My surviving monsters and the geese, I banish home. They have served their purpose and they are making the humans uncomfortable.

"Good job," I tell them, patting Mr Philpot on the head. He is looking a little worse for wear but has come through the battle surprisingly well. One of the wight geese bites me in the shin, and comes away with a sparse chunk of green-tinged flesh. I shoo it away. The poor things are all overexcited. "I will come and stitch you up later, those that need it. Go and rest in the barn at home for now."

The geese take to the sky, and for a moment the castle grounds echoes with their evil honking. The monsters scuttle off in a horde.

I watch them go fondly. I wonder, belatedly, if I should have told them not to kill anyone they find on the roads. I'm not entirely sure how much autonomy they actually have. They don't *seem* to have free will, not exactly, but they definitely have ideas of their own. It is very late however, and it is unlikely anyone honest is abroad on the King's Road. And if they are, well, they probably deserve to be mauled a bit. I put it out of my mind. It is so late it is almost early and the eastern sky is stained rosy pink.

The rest of the wights I send to collect the bodies of those that were slain in the battle. I get them to load them into a couple of carts for easy transportation purposes and send them home as well. Fresh supplies for later! I have consumed so many souls I am feeling quite jolly, and I swear I can feel the gentle fuzz of hair starting on my scalp. I think. I will check in the mirror as soon as I am able.

Once that is all taken care of, I return to my sewing in peace. The puppet Baron is coming along nicely. My stitching is not the best ever, but it is serviceable. He will likely have clothes on most of the time anyway, so I doubt anyone will even see it. Depending how long I decide to keep him I will probably have to change his stuffing anyway, but I'll worry about that later.

Sitting back on my heels I look down at him. Yes, he will do nicely. His rather bulbous eyes stare upwards, reflecting the torchlight and the coming dawn. For a moment I am tempted to bring him back as a wight, but then, if he can't talk he won't be a useful puppet. Either way he is going to need a supervisor.

I bring him back as a draugr. He coughs and sits up, crying out in alarm.

"Welcome back," I say, dryly.

I hear a murmur of surprise. Looking up, I spy the feisty lady from the carriage peering at me from around a corner. A herd of anxious nobility mills behind her like headless chickens. I beckon her over, and she blanches, but picks up her skirts and comes quickly enough, treading her way carefully through the aftermath of the battle field, and around the piles of the Baron's guts. Her eyes dart to the Baron, and then back to me.

"Smile at the lady, there's a dear," I say to him, and he grins at her. Her face is pale and smudged with soot and blood, but her back is as straight as a poker and there is a hint of iron about her. She will do.

"What is your name?" I ask, packing away my needle and thread.

"Lady Marguerite D'Arcy, my er- my lady," she says, bobbing a curtsey. "Of the House Montgomery in Wradshire."

"Yes, yes," I say testily. I have no interest in houses. Or politics, or whatever it is these people spend their lives occupied with. "I have a proposition for you. How would you like to marry the Baron?"

The words hang between us like a bell. She blinks, and then shakes her head. Then her mouth falls open and her eyes dart to the puppet, her lips turning down in a mew of disgust. Then her eyes narrow speculatively. It is like watching a mummery of someone's inner brain workings. But then it has been a long night for all of us.

"Before you answer," I say. "Let me explain the terms of your marriage. The Baron will continue in his position, but as a figurehead only. Won't you, dear?" The puppet Baron nods, enthusiastically. "You will be Baroness in name, and the ruler of the castle in fact."

Lady Marguerite's cheeks flush, and her eyes brighten. Oh dear, I hope she is not *too* ambitious. But humans are like rabbits. I can always replace her.

"You don't want to rule yourself, your...er ladyship?" she asks, carefully.

"I have no interest in the petty details of your lives," I say. Standing up, I brush my skirts off. "I will be keeping an eye on you, of course, and I will have certain... requests that I want you to honour. Other than that, you can do as you wish as long as you keep your people out of my damn forest. Understood?"

She bobs, anxiously, spreading her blood-stained skirts, her cheeks red with excitement. I fix her with a dignified glare and she bows her head with suitable respect. Excellent. This might actually work. Once the castle is settled I can get on with the important things. Like finding out who her seamstress is.

Elding and Tora flutter down to perch on my shoulders, and Lady Marguerite exclaims, taking a step back.

"Ka!" Elding says. "The townspeople come."

"They come," echoes Tora.

"Excellent," I say. I had told the mayor to arrive at dawn, and it seems he is sensible. Perhaps we will get on. Then I pause. "Do they come alone? No hidden clerics, no torches and pitchforks?"

"Just the townspeople," says Tora.

"The people," says Elding.

"Good," I say, and the crows fly away. I turn to the soon-to-be Baroness. "Is there a hall?" I say. "Or a throne room? Where did the Baron conduct his business?"

I have never been in a castle before.

"Through here, your ladyship," says Lady Marguerite, and she sweeps through the courtyard towards a fine set of double doors, which she throws open with a flourish. I peer inside behind her and then straighten. This will do nicely.

The Baron's great hall has a vaulted ceiling, an enormous fireplace and a great iron chandelier hung about with many beeswax candles. I sniff approvingly. Even better, at the end of the hall is a smart wooden throne on a dais. I turn back to the noblewoman.

"Go and change," I say. "And come back down to get married in ten minutes."

"Yes, my lady," she bobs a curtsy, and rushes off with flushed cheeks. She dashes through the courtyard and calls out stridently, before disappearing into the castle through a side door. Several young women detach from the pack of wobbling aristocracy and streak after her.

I turn and smile at the rest of them. They gasp and step back. Oh, honestly.

"Come inside," I say. Not bothering to see if they follow, I turn with a swish of blood-soaked velvet, and stalk through the hall to seat myself on the throne. I cross my gaunt legs demurely at the ankle and arrange my skirts around me. My mother would be proud. I will definitely have to dig her up to tell her about all this.

The nobles trickle into the hall, looking anxious, the townspeople gasping and shuffling behind them. I send Timothy to speed them along. Some of the peasants run screaming back out of the gates but that is fine. For the most part, curiosity is winning over instinct. This will be easy.

"Come in, come in!" I shout. "Gather round. I have tidings. Tell them to come in," I say to the Baron.

"Come in!" he shouts, grinning broad and placid. It does the trick. From a distance he definitely looks alive. I see the mayor in his gold chain looking anxious, and the lovely seamstress hovering at the back. Slowly, slowly the hall fills up, although there is a wide empty space left open in front of the dais. That is fine. I like personal space.

Once the hall is full to bursting, and people are spilling out of the doorways I rise to my feet. The Baron stands next to me, beaming.

"Greetings," I say, and there is absolute silence. "Let me introduce myself. I am the Lady of Downing Forest, and I am here as both your protector and as your conqueror. Let me start by telling you that while I expect absolute obedience and submission from each and every one of you, I wish you no harm."

I pause, letting my words sink in. There is a disbelieving murmur although no one is brave enough to utter any words. The crowd is watching me with avid attention, eyes wide and fearful. Fear will certainly get me cooperation for a while, certainly, but I do not want to rule these people. No. I want them to leave me alone. I don't want them getting any ideas about fires, or rebellion. I want them to feel safe. You catch more flies with honey and I know what it is like to be covered in flies. The big fat ones that like carrion.

"Today is a happy day, isn't that right, Baron?"

"Yes, that's right," the Baron says, and the crowd murmurs again, elbowing each other in the ribs.

"I have invited you all here for a celebration," I say, glibly. "The Baron is about to get married, with my blessing, to the very lovely Lady Marguerite," I gesture dramatically and everyone swivels, taking in the blushing woman who stands at the back of the hall, her cheeks pink with excitement. I can't see what she is wearing as there are too many people in the way, and I resist the urge to yell.

Lady Marguerite walks forward, and the crowd parts to let her through. She is radiant in a dark blue silk kirtle. Her blood-stained shift peaks out beneath voluminous skirts, and her white chemise is puffed out through the openings in her sleeves, in the style of the king's court at Fairhaven. Her overgown in silk brocade is a little askew, and the lacing on her bodice has clearly been done in haste. Her breasts seem a little squished, but she looks the part, if you ignore the blood. And the look in her eye. I think she is enjoying herself and it occurs to me that I might be dealing with a psychopath. Ah well.

I marry my two puppets in front of the slightly confused crowd, and then turn to address them with the Baron and his new Baroness at my side.

"Alright, let's get to the details," I say. I seek out the mayor and beckon him forward. "Please pay close attention," I say. "You might want to jot this down." The portly man is sweating profusely, but he nods and pulls out a piece of parchment. Someone hurries over with an inkpot and a quill. "Ready?" I ask, and he nods. Good, we are getting along very nicely.

"Henceforth," I say, in my fanciest, most booming voice, "trespass in Downing Forest is punishable by death. Witchcraft is no longer a hanging offence, in fact," I warm to my subject, "Witching is now a tax-deductible occupation. Isn't that right Mayor Davies?" The mayor nods, and scribbles, sweat gleaming on his forehead. I look up satisfied. "No clerics in Greater Downing. They are not needed or necessary. Please make that clear to the relevant authorities." I glare at the Baron and his new wife, and they both bow and nod energetically. Good. "I will also be lowering taxes on all material, thread, ribbon and bread. Got it?"

More nodding. "If I can think of anything else I will contact you via crow," I say grandly, staring around at the crowd.

"But why?" said the mayor. "Why are you doing this?"

"I do not want to rule," I say with a shrug. "I want to be left alone. Apparently, that is too much to ask, so I must take steps to ensure my peace. Mark my words, however. This is my territory now. Mine. Stay out of my forest or else." I glare around at the assembled humans. "If you have complaints or suggestions." I pause. "I suggest you keep them to yourselves. However, if you *insist* on disturbing me, speak with Baroness Marguerite. She will know how to contact me."

I look back at the assembly.

"Does anyone have any objections?"

The hall is quiet, although there are some quiet mutterings. The remaining nobles look at one another, the townspeople shuffle, all of them avoiding my gaze. Then one burly peasant raises his hand.

I shoot him through the left eye with my crossbow.

"Does anyone *else* have any objections?"

This time the quiet is absolute. Good. Perhaps they can be taught.

"I will be leaving now." I turn to my puppets. "I will also be watching. Take care."

There is silence.

"That...that's it?" stutters the mayor.

"Did you want something else?" I ask with icy politeness. The fat man blanches, his chains jingling.

"No, no," he says. "That's absolutely fine."

"Good," I say, and sweep down the steps and through the hall, the throng parting before me like a magical tide. I hear whispering and muttering break out as I leave. I do not care. Baroness Marguerite and her new husband can deal with it.

I have things to do at my cottage. Jenkins will be missing me.

EPILOGUE

The Cathedral, the Well, the King

D*owning Forest and the Cathedral City*
  Two Days Earlier

The stallion panicked and ran through the trees, the dead body of the sun paladin slumped across its saddle. Sweat lathered the horse's sides. It galloped as fast as it could, hoping to outrun the frightening sounds, and the foul stench of death. The battle was soon a distant murmur, but the scent of death lingered, clinging to its back, spooking the animal again and again and again.

The stallion ran wildly, fleeing without thought. Instinct drove it gradually home to the familiar roads of the west. He galloped through thick forest, and then dormant orchards and fallow fields. He slowed to a trot, his breath laboured. A lonely peasant cried out and tried to grab his reins. The stallion snorted and ran once more. Hours later, foot-sore and scared, the exhausted animal stumbled his way through the golden gates of the cathedral city of Barrowmere.

The watch let it through, recognising the sunbursts on the paladin's gore splattered armour.

"Sir!" One shouted. "Sir! Do you need aid?"

The dead sun paladin made no answer.

In the chill morning light, the weary stallion plodded through the cobbled streets. People came out of their houses to stare. Some, like the watch, tried to help, but the stallion shied and reared. Seeking home and comfort, the stallion found his way at long last to the cathedral stables, passing through the gates with head bowed, and past the small, anxious crowd gathering in his wake.

A stable boy rushed to see what the noise was about. He shouted in shock when he saw the paladin, lolling fitfully from the desperate charger's saddle. The poor horse snorted, backing away, knocking over some barrels and the stable master rushed to calm him, grabbing its bridle and making shushing noises.

At last, the quivering stallion quieted, its sides heaving as the master smoothed its nose. Three stony-faced stable hands were able to untangle the corpse from the horse's back and the quivering animal was finally led away to rest.

The stable master knew trouble when he saw it.

He could feel the weight of eyes on him, the barely suppressed panic of the crowd at the gate, of the stable boys, so he shook his head and gave instructions hastily, and the body was rushed into the cathedral.

"Nothing to see," he said to the gawking crowd. "Nothing to fear! Go home!"

The stablemaster knew how to sound convincing, and he shut the doors without letting his expression slip. Mumbling, the crowd dispersed, although he knew they would take their gossip with them. This was a problem for his superiors.

Scratching his neck thoughtfully, the stable master went to check on the exhausted stallion. That done, he removed his cap and made his way into the cathedral proper, seeking the Archon.

He crept along the brightly lit corridors feeling like a speck of dust in the Bright One's eye. At the light flooded nave, he stopped briefly to bow to the enormous sunburst that hung suspended from the vaulted ceiling. Catching the subdued light it cast it back in shimmering rays, stronger and brighter than ever. He drew strength from the sight of it. There was nothing to fear. Accidents happened. The Archon would know what to do.

As soon as he had informed her, he could go back to his horses, and put it all out of his mind. This last thought carried his feet to her door. He knocked and it was opened by the Archon's secretary, who looked up at him inquiringly.

He explained himself, in as few words as possible.

"What do you mean a dead sun paladin?" demanded the Archon, from inside, where she was clearly listening. The stablemaster jumped. The secretary opened the door fully to reveal the Archon in her ceremonial robes. She had leapt to her feet, knocking over a glass of wine. The secretary dived for the glass, desperately mopping before the red liquid stained the Archon's papers crimson.

"What happened? Who is it? Where? *How?*"

The stable master twisted his cap in his hands and explained as well as he could. The Archon's lips thinned as she listened.

"Sir Wainscot?" she asked.

"I believe so, your grace, I recognised him, I did. Working in the stables and all, I see the paladins come and go."

"And he is definitely dead? Not unconscious? Not badly wounded?"

"Dead," said the stablemaster. "I am certain. More than a day, at least. Dead as a doornail." He swallowed.

"He rode out with Sir Arkwright and the Blind Queen's Acolyte? To investigate the potential lich sighting in that little village...what was it called... Lowcroft?"

The stablemaster shrugged, his eyes a little wild. He knew horses. His job revolved around hoof management and feed, not such lofty matters. He didn't usually set foot in the cathedral except for mass on Sun Days, and he had never before spoken to the Archon. The fact that she was talking to him at all was more than a little alarming.

The secretary came to the rescue, diving into the paperwork and placing the information in front of the Archon's nose.

"Yes," said the Archon, squinting. "Sir Wainscot. They rode out five days ago. Not usual for a mission to take that long but...yes. I assume there is no sign of Arkwright and the Acolyte? There has been no news from the Blind Queen's Temple?"

"They have not returned," came the reply. "There has been no news."

The Archon's eyes narrowed to a golden glimmer.

"I will inspect the body," she announced.

She swept out of the office in a flurry of gold and cream silk. The white of her train puffed behind her like a sail, and sparks of magic briefly illuminated the air behind her, such was her agitation. The secretary and the stablemaster jogged behind her, surreptitiously slapping out the little embers that threatened to burn their clothing. They followed her down the stone cathedral's echoing, inner passages, down a twisting flight of stairs towards the healers' rooms, and the morgue.

"Where is he?" demanded the Archon, bursting through the door.

"Who?" said the healer, looking up from a cadaver in surprise. "Oh, good morning, your Grace. They are preparing Sir Wainscot for the pyre two rooms over."

The Archon nodded and swept on her way.

They found the sun paladin's corpse, lying in state on a stone slab, his sword clasped over his chest, sunflowers and chrysanthemums heaped around him. His eyes were closed, two sun medallions placed over each, as the healers spoke the Bright One's blessings over his body. Gentle hands washed clean the muck from his face and his armour. He looked peaceful, but not so the healer tending to him.

The healer glared up at them, as if they were personally responsible for the paladin's death, completely unphased by his superior's presence.

"There is no mark on this body," the man said, his mouth turned down at the corners. "I do not know his manner of death. What would do such a thing?"

The Archon looked at him, her eyes gleaming metal bright.

"Many things," she said. "There is much evil in the world, my child. That is why our Order exists after all." Her expression softened, and she rested one palm on Sir Wainscot's forehead. "May the Bright One, guide your passage home," she said, in the formal, solemn voice the stablemaster recognised from Sun Day Mass. "May the sun accept your sacrifice."

Her face paled, cheeks hollowing. She blinked.

"What is it?" demanded the stablemaster, forgetting himself in his alarm.

"His soul," said the Archon. "His soul has been taken." She snatched back her hand. "This is just an empty vessel. This is confirmation. We are dealing with a powerful lich, and a canny one at that if it can survive an encounter with three clerics."

She stared down at the body for a long moment, then turned abruptly and strode through the door.

"Where are we going?" asked the secretary, hurrying along behind her.

"To send a message," said the Archon. "The king's council needs to hear of this."

The Wave-Walker's Shrine
Three Days Later

Friar Julian knelt in front of the well, his blue robes gathered around him. His face was serene, his shaved head smooth as a seashell. He shut his eyes, and breathed in. The air was cool, with a hint of frost and already a tinge of salt. He smiled, and breathed out. His God was among them. His heart thudded in his chest. He listened, calmed, and moved on, breathing in and out.

The tattoos that covered his body swayed and whirled in gentle undulation, keeping rhythm with a distant, unseen tide. Julian couldn't see them, but he could feel them, trickling across his neck, his shoulders, his back, their touch as light and hopeful as spring rain.

He listened.

Peace came and wrapped him in a blanket of serenity. The trance was like being underwater. Sounds slowed, and quieted, other senses sharpened. He was weightless and floating in a warm, empty space. Waiting.

Julian opened himself to the ebb and flow of the world around him, inviting it in. He could hear the whispers, taste its essence on his tongue. He opened his eyes, and then opened them again.

The watching apprentices gasped.

Irises rolled back in his head, his eyes glowed white with the gentle power of the Wavewalker's blessing. Gracefully he rose from the sand, and walked with measured steps to the well at the centre of the shrine. He held out his hand—on the palm, a single silver coin, coated in a drop of his blood. He let it fall.

The coin spun, seeming to take a long time to reach the water, before landing with a melodic splash. Julian heard each individual drop land. Instinctively, he took a gulp of air as the weight of the water swallowed the coin, and smiled gently at his folly. He felt the coin sink into the void below, for the sacred well at the heart of the Wavewalker's Shrine had no bottom, at least none that humans could perceive.

Julian walked with god-touched grace back to the flat expanse of sand that lay beyond the well. He stood, arms outstretched, patient. The gathered apprentices watched in awe as the granules shifted and billowed, reforming themselves to make a three-dimensional map of the Kingdom of Einheath. Little mountains, inches tall, forests with trees like miniscule blades of grass, each detail was perfect, the land recreated in miniature.

Julian stood over it, his arms wide, and embracing.

"Wavewalker!" he cried. "Command me! Where should we go? Where are we needed? Who shall we heal?" He waited for his God, serene, waiting for guidance. "Wavewalker, where will the suffering be?"

Usually, the Wavewalker answered the divination with a voice soft and somnolent, like falling drops of mist, a tempered, musical trickle. But today the God's voice crashed through Julian's skull in a howling tempest of fear and agony that ripped his brain to shreds, leaving him bruised and screaming. Julian fell to the ground panting, clutching at his bleeding ears.

"Wavewalker, where will the pain be?"

"EVERYWHERE!" roared the Wavewalker. The God's voice rippled across the shrine, flattening the sand.

"EVERYWHERE!"

The King's Council Chamber, Castle Rock, Fairhaven
One Week Later

His Royal Highness, King Lewin, Son of Aelfstan, the Consequence, House of Svien, Lord Protector of Einheath, and Defender of the Faith, stood at the castle window and watched the gulls. They wheeled, white-winged and carefree over the capital. The day was dark and gusty. Thunderous clouds blew across the horizon. The king shivered, wondering if there would be a dusting of snow before nightfall. It certainly looked that way.

His ministers and advisors droned on in the background, and the elderly king let his mind wander, milky eyes drifting over the rooftops and streets far below. From his vantage point high on the mount, the king could see all the way to the distant docks. On the horizon grey ships floated on a slate ocean. Then, for a brief moment, the sun broke through the clouds, the rays dancing along the wavetops like scattered diamonds. The king leaned forward, entranced. It was as beautiful as it was brief, and in no time at all the light dimmed.

King Lewin sighed. It had been a long day, and his bones ached. A long day, and a long life, if he was being honest with himself. He was looking forward to a quiet dinner with his wife, and young sons, after the Council wrapped up. As he pondered, he became aware that the room had gone quiet, his advisors must be awaiting his response. He looked up from his window with a bashful smile.

"My apologies," he said. All the Councillors were watching him, their faces grave. The king resumed his seat at the head of the table, trying not to groan as he sat. When had the cushion gotten so thin? "My thoughts wandered. Please forgive me. Do continue."

"We were discussing the reports of undead," said the Lord Chancellor. "And a rather emotive missive from the Friars at Berwick."

"What?" asked the king, sharply. "Where?"

"Lowcroft," said the Lord Chancellor.

"I think it's highly unlikely there are undead in Lowcroft," said Lord Philips. The two men glared at each other across the table. "My nephew is the Baron of Greater Downing, and I corresponded with him only yesterday. He has just got married and he said nothing about undead, and his castle is less than a day's travel from Lowcroft."

"And are these reports verified?" asked the king. "Or merely the chatter of foolish peasants?"

"Superstition to be sure," murmured Lord Philips.

"The Archon of the Bright One is hardly a superstitious peasant, my lord," said the Lord Chancellor, mildly.

"Kara Crag, now," said Lord Philips, leaning back and folding his hands over his paunch. "There have been some rather disturbing reports. I, for one, am very concerned."

"There's not much there, is there?" said the king, frowning and pulling a map towards himself. "In Kara Crag?"

"No, my liege, its mountains, mostly, and forest. It's cut off from most of Einheath for the majority of the winter. Sparsely populated, a few trappers, fewer villages. Mining is the primary occupation. The people are rough, and there are not many of them."

"So, what is the concern?"

"Monsters, Sire," said Lord Philips, blowing out his cheeks.

"Not just monsters," said the Lord Chancellor. "*Undead* monsters. Reports of undead hordes stalking the frost."

"A plague," said Lord Philips, darkly.

"Let us hope not," said the king in alarm.

Lord Philips and the Lord Chancellor started to argue and outside the castle the clouds thickened, enveloping the mount in dense mist. Hail began to rattle against the glass and the wind grew to a roar. The king shivered, and looked meaningfully at the fire. A servant rushed to add more wood.

Despite this the room grew colder still. The king looked down and frowned. Frost was spreading across the table. He cried out in shock, and leapt to his feet.

"What is it, sire?" asked the Lord Chancellor.

King Lewin looked down at the table, which was smooth and frost-free. He sat back down, carefully.

"Nothing," he said, and rubbed his eyes. "I'm just tired. Kara Crag," he said, "we were talking about Kara Crag."

"Yes," said the Lord Chancellor. "I was just about to show you this. I received it, with the Royal Mail, yesterday." He laid a scroll out on the table. It was battered, and stained dark brown in places. A black seal was broken.

"From the Baron of Kara Keep?" asked the King, recognising the seal.

The Lord Chancellor nodded. "Be warned," he said, passing the scroll over. "It is rather...pungent."

King Lewin picked up the scroll and unrolled it. A foul stench of carrion wafted across the chamber and they all coughed. The parchment was thin, and cold to the touch, and in places, rather tacky. The writing was spidery. It looked like it had been scrawled in haste. His lips moved as he read.

"What tidings?" asked Lord Philips, leaning forward.

"Bleak tidings," said the King. "He writes...he writes that Karra Keep is surrounded by undead forces. He writes that he does not think that he will be able to withstand the assault, that they are fighting for their lives and if help does not arrive within a week they will all perish. He writes that they are outnumbered, and that...the undead are commanded by a lich-king of great power."

He looked up, his face pale. "How far away is Karra Crag?"

"At least a week's hard ride," said the Lord Chancellor. "If the passes are clear."

He set the scroll down on the table and stared at it as if it was a live thing. The foul scent hung in the air.

"Do you think the castle has fallen," he said softly.

"Who would send the letter if the castle is overrun?" demanded Lord Philips.

King Lewin and the Lord Chancellor looked at each other.

"We cannot know," said the Lord Chancellor.

The king passed a weary hand in front of his eyes, and then straightened.

"Gentlemen," he said, "summon the full council! The undead have risen. We prepare for war."

THE END

(Maud will return in *Liching Hour*)

Acknowledgements

Thank you to you! For reading this book I wrote. To help others find and enjoy this book, please consider leaving a review or rating! Dark Ritual

A great many people helped me during the time I wrote this book: Marfether, Naomi, Zay, Jiwa, Rhaegar, my readers on Royal Road, and later my patreons. Thank you all so much I could not have done it without you. Thank you, especially to Mattias (Baconstrap) for the gorgeous cover, and to Ella Lynch for bringing Maud to life in the audiobook. I am so lucky to know you both.

This book was written as part of the Inkfort Press Publishing Derby—check out the community and other entries at https://inkfortpress.com/publishing-derby/2021-derby-books/

About the Author

HJ Tolson lives and writes in the beautiful, soggy north of England, where graveyards are plentiful and the skies are decidedly gothic. Her favourite bird is a rook.

My website and mailing list: hjtolson.com
My Patreon (first drafts and news): www.patreon.com/heskethj
You can find me on Royal Road writing under Hesketh or Hesketh II
(www.royalroad.com/profile/230476)

Also by HJ Tolson

Liches Get Stitches
Liching Hour
Lich, Please
Lich Hunt
A Lich In Time

Twilight Kingdom
Twilight Kingdom
Night Nation